HEAVY WATER
and other stories

Martin Amis is the author of nine novels, two collections of stories and three works of non-fiction. He lives in London.

ALSO BY MARTIN AMIS

Fiction

Non-Fiction

Martin Amis

HEAVY WATER

and Other Stories

V

VINTAGE

Published by Vintage 1999

2 4 6 8 10 9 7 5 3 1

First published in Great Britain in 1998
by Jonathan Cape

Vintage
Random House, 20 Vauxhall Bridge Road,
London SW1V 2SA

Random House Australia (Pty) Limited
20 Alfred Street, Milsons Point, Sydney
New South Wales 2061, Australia

Random House New Zealand Limited
18 Poland Road, Glenfield,
Auckland 10, New Zealand

Random House South Africa (Pty) Limited
Endulini, 5A Jubilee Road, Parktown 2193,
South Africa

Random House UK Limited Reg. No. 954009

A CIP catalogue record for this book
is available from the British Library

ISBN 0 09 927266 0

Papers used by Random House UK Ltd are natural,
recyclable products made from wood grown in sustain-
able forests. The manufacturing processes conform to the
environmental regulations of the country of origin

Printed and bound in Germany by
Graphischer Großbetrieb Pößneck GmbH

To Delilah and Fernanda

Contents

Career Move

When Alistair finished his new screenplay, *Offensive from Quasar 13*, he submitted it to the *LM*, and waited. Over the past year, he had had more than a dozen screenplays rejected by the *Little Magazine*. On the other hand, his most recent submission, a batch of five, had been returned not with the standard rejection slip but with a handwritten note from the screenplay editor, Hugh Sixsmith. The note said:

> I was really rather taken with two or three of these, and seriously tempted by *Hotwire*, which I thought close to being fully achieved. Do please go on sending me your stuff.

Hugh Sixsmith was himself a screenplay writer of considerable, though uncertain, reputation. His note of encouragement *was* encouraging. It made Alistair brave.

Boldly he prepared *Offensive from Quasar 13* for submission. He justified the pages of the typescript with fondly lingering fingertips. Alistair did not address the envelope to the Screenplay Editor. No. He addressed it to Mr Hugh Sixsmith. Nor, for once, did he enclose his curriculum vitae, which he now contemplated with some discomfort. It told, in a pitiless staccato, of the screenplays he had published in various laptop broadsheets and comically obscure pamphlets; it even told of screenplays published in his university magazine. The truly disgraceful bit came at the end, where it said 'Rights Offered: First British Serial *only*.'

Alistair spent a long time on the covering note to Sixsmith – almost as long as he had spent on *Offensive from Quasar 13*. The note got shorter and shorter the more he worked on it. At last he was satisfied. There in the dawn he grasped the envelope and ran his tongue across its darkly luminous cuff.

That Friday, on his way to work, and suddenly feeling completely hopeless, Alistair surrendered his parcel to the sub-post office in Calchalk Street, off the Euston Road. Deliberately – very deliberately – he had enclosed no stamped-addressed envelope. The accompanying letter, in its entirety, read as follows: 'Any use? If not – w.p.b.'

'W.p.b.' stood, of course, for 'waste-paper basket' – a receptacle that loomed forbiddingly large in the life of a practising screenplay writer. With a hand on his brow, Alistair sidled his way out of there – past the birthday cards, the tensed pensioners, the envelopes, and the balls of string.

When Luke finished the new poem – entitled, simply, 'Sonnet' – he xeroxed the printout and faxed it to his agent. Ninety minutes later he returned from the gym downstairs and prepared his special fruit juice while the answering machine told him, among many other things, to get back to Mike. Reaching for an extra lime, Luke touched the preselect for Talent International.

'Ah. Luke,' said Mike. 'It's moving. We've already had a response.'

'Yeah, how come? It's four in the morning where he is.'

'No, it's eight in the evening where he is. He's in Australia. Developing a poem with Peter Barry.'

Luke didn't want to hear about Peter Barry. He bent, and tugged off his tank top. Walls and windows maintained a respectful distance – the room was a broad seam of sun haze and river light. Luke sipped his juice: its extreme astringency caused him to lift both elbows and give a single, embittered nod. He said, 'What did he think?'

'Joe? He did backflips. It's "Tell Luke I'm blown away by the new poem. I just know that 'Sonnet' is really going to happen." '

Luke took this coolly. He wasn't at all old but he had been in poetry long enough to take these things coolly. He turned. Suki, who had been shopping, was now letting herself into the apartment, not without difficulty. She was indeed cruelly encumbered. Luke said, 'You haven't talked numbers yet. I mean like a ballpark figure.'

Mike said, 'We understand each other. Joe knows about Monad's interest. And Tim at TCT.'

'Good,' said Luke. Suki was wandering slenderly towards him, shedding various purchases as she approached – creels and caskets, shining satchels.

'They'll want you to go out there at least twice,' said Mike. 'Initially to discuss . . . They can't get over it that you don't live there.'

Luke could tell that Suki had spent much more than she intended. He could tell by the quality of patience in her sigh as she began to lick the sweat from his shoulderblades. He said, 'Come on, Mike. They know I hate all that L.A. crap.'

On his way to work that Monday Alistair sat slumped in his bus seat, limp with ambition and neglect. One fantasy was proving especially obdurate: as he entered his office, the telephone on his desk would actually be *bouncing* on its console – Hugh Sixsmith, from the *Little Magazine*, his voice urgent but grave, with the news that he was going to rush Alistair's screenplay into the very next issue. (To be frank, Alistair had had the same fantasy the previous Friday, at which time, presumably, *Offensive from Quasar 13* was still being booted round the floor of the sub-post office.) His girlfriend, Hazel, had come down from Leeds for the weekend. They were so small, he and Hazel, that they could share his single bed quite comfortably – could sprawl and stretch without constraint. On the Saturday evening, they attended a screenplay reading at a bookshop on Camden High Street. Alistair hoped to impress Hazel with his growing ease in this milieu (and managed to exchange wary leers with a few shambling, half-familiar figures – fellow screenplay writers, seekers, knowers). But these days Hazel seemed sufficiently impressed by him anyway, whatever he did. Alistair lay there the next morning (her turn to make tea), wondering about this business of being impressed. Hazel had impressed him mightily, seven years ago, in bed: by not getting out of it when he got into it. The office telephone rang many times that Monday, but none of the callers had anything to say about *Offensive from Quasar 13*. Alistair sold advertising space for an agricultural newsletter, so his callers wanted to talk about creosote admixes and offal reprocessors.

He heard nothing for four months. This would normally have been a fairly good sign. It meant, or it might mean, that your screenplay was receiving serious, even agonized, consideration. It was better than having your screenplay flopping back on the mat by return post. On the other hand, Hugh Sixsmith might have responded to the spirit and the letter of Alistair's accompanying note and dropped *Offensive from Quasar 13* into his waste-paper basket within minutes of its arrival: four months ago. Rereading his fading carbon of the screenplay, Alistair now cursed his own (highly calibrated) insouciance. He shouldn't have said, 'Any use? If not – w.p.b.' He should have said, 'Any use? If not – s.a.e.'! Every morning he went down the three flights of stairs – the mail was there to be shuffled and dealt. And every fourth Friday, or thereabouts, he still wrenched open his *LM*, in case Sixsmith had run the screenplay without letting him know. As a surprise.

'Dear Mr Sixsmith,' thought Alistair as he rode the train to Leeds. 'I am thinking of placing the screenplay I sent you elsewhere. I trust that . . . I thought it only fair to . . .' Alistair retracted his feet to accommodate another passenger. 'My dear Mr Sixsmith: In response to an inquiry from . . . In response to a most generous inquiry, I am putting together a selection of my screenplays for . . .' Alistair tipped his head back and stared at the smeared window. 'For Mudlark Books. It seems that the Ostler Press is also interested. This involves me in some paperwork, which, however tedious . . . For the record . . . Matters would be considerably eased . . . Of course if you . . .'

Luke sat on a Bauhaus love seat in Club World at Heathrow, drinking Evian and availing himself of the complimentary fax machine – clearing up the initial paperwork on the poem with Mike.

Everyone in Club World looked hushed and grateful to be there, but not Luke, who looked exhaustively displeased. He was flying first class to LAX, where he would be met by a uniformed chauffeur who would convey him by limousine or courtesy car to the Pinnacle Trumont on the Avenue of the Stars. First class was no big thing. In poetry, first class was something you didn't need to think about. It wasn't discussed. It was statutory. First class was just business as usual.

Luke was tense: under pressure. A lot – maybe too much – was riding on 'Sonnet'. If 'Sonnet' didn't happen, he would soon be able to afford neither his apartment nor his girlfriend. He would recover from Suki before very long. But he would never recover from not being able to afford her, or his apartment. If you wanted the truth, his deal on 'Sonnet' was not that great. Luke was furious with Mike except about the new merchandizing clause (potential accessories on the poem – like toys or T-shirts) and the improved cut he got on tertiaries and sequels. Then there was Joe.

Joe calls, and he's like, 'We really think "Sonnet"'s going to work, Luke. Jeff thinks so too. Jeff's just come in. Jeff? It's Luke. Do you want to say something to him? Luke. Luke, Jeff's coming over. He wants to say something about "Sonnet".'

'Luke?' said Jeff. 'Jeff. Luke? You're a very talented writer. It's great to be working on "Sonnet" with you. Here's Joe.'

'That was Jeff,' said Joe. 'He's crazy about "Sonnet".'

'So what are we going to be talking about?' said Luke. 'Roughly.'

'On "Sonnet"? Well, the only thing we have a problem on "Sonnet" with, Luke, so far as I can see, anyway, and I know Jeff agrees with me on this – right, Jeff? – and so does Jim, incidentally, Luke,' said Joe, 'is the form.'

Luke hesitated. Then he said, 'You mean the form "Sonnet"'s written in.'

'Yes, that's right, Luke. The sonnet form.'

Luke waited for the last last call and was then guided, with much unreturned civility, into the plane's nose.

'Dear Mr Sixsmith,' wrote Alistair,

Going through my files the other day, I vaguely remembered sending you a little effort called *Offensive from Quasar 13* – just over seven months ago, it must have been. Am I right in assuming that you have no use for it? I might bother you with another one (or two!) that I have completed since then. I hope you are well. Thank you so much for your encouragement in the past.

Need I say how much I admire your own work? The austerity, the depth. When, may I ask, can we expect another 'slim vol.'?

He sadly posted this letter on a wet Sunday afternoon in Leeds. He hoped that the postmark might testify to his mobility and grit.

Yet, really, he felt much steadier now. There had been a recent period of about five weeks during which, Alistair came to realize, he had gone clinically insane. That letter to Sixsmith was but one of the many dozens he had penned. He had also taken to haunting the Holborn offices of the *Little Magazine*: for hours he sat crouched in the coffee bars and sandwich nooks opposite, with the unsettled intention of springing out at Sixsmith – if he ever saw him, which he never did. Alistair began to wonder whether Sixsmith actually existed. Was he, perhaps, an actor, a ghost, a shrewd fiction? Alistair telephoned the *LM* from selected phone booths. Various people answered, and no one knew where anyone was, and only three or four times was Alistair

successfully connected to the apparently permanent coughing fit that crackled away at the other end of Sixsmith's
extension. Then he hung up. He couldn't sleep, or he
thought he couldn't, for Hazel said that all night long he
whimpered and gnashed.

Alistair waited for nearly two months. Then he sent in
three more screenplays. One was about a Machine hitman
who emerges from early retirement when his wife is slain by
a serial murderer. Another dealt with the infiltration by the
three Gorgons of an escort agency in present-day New York.
The third was a heavy-metal musical set on the Isle of Skye.
He enclosed a stamped-addressed envelope the size of a
small knapsack.

Winter was unusually mild.

'May I get you something to drink before your meal? A
cappuccino? A mineral water? A glass of sauvignon blanc?'

'Double decaf espresso,' said Luke. 'Thanks.'

'You're more than welcome.'

'Hey,' said Luke when everyone had ordered. 'I'm not
just welcome any more. I'm more than welcome.'

The others smiled patiently. Such remarks were the
downside of the classy fact that Luke, despite his appearance
and his accent, was English. There they all sat on the terrace
at Bubo's: Joe, Jeff, Jim.

Luke said, 'How did "Eclogue by a Five-Barred Gate"
do?'

Joe said, 'Domestically?' He looked at Jim, at Jeff. 'Like –
fifteen?'

Luke said, 'And worldwide?'

'It isn't *going* worldwide.'

'How about "Black Rook in Rainy Weather"?' asked Luke.

Joe shook his head. 'It didn't even do what "Sheep in Fog" did.'

'It's all remakes,' said Jim. 'Period shit.'

'How about "Bog Oak"?'

'"Bog Oak"? Ooh, maybe twenty-five?'

Luke said sourly, 'I hear nice things about "The Old Botanical Gardens".'

They talked about other Christmas flops and bombs, delaying for as long as they could any mention of TCTs ''Tis he whose yester-evening's high disdain', which had cost practically nothing to make and had already done a hundred and twenty million in its first three weeks.

'What happened?' Luke eventually asked. 'Jesus, what was the publicity budget?'

'On "'Tis"?' said Joe. 'Nothing. Two, three.'

They all shook their heads. Jim was philosophical. 'That's poetry,' he said.

'There aren't any other sonnets being made, are there?' said Luke.

Jeff said, 'Binary is in post-production with a sonnet. "Composed at – Castle". *More* period shit.'

Their soups and salads arrived. Luke thought that it was probably a mistake, at this stage, to go on about sonnets. After a while he said, 'How did "For Sophonisba Anguisciola" do?'

Joe said, '"For Sophonisba Anguisciola"? Don't talk to me about "For Sophonisba Anguisciola".'

It was late at night and Alistair was in his room working on a screenplay about a high-IQ homeless black man who is transformed into a white female junk-bond dealer by a South Moluccan terrorist witchdoctor. Suddenly he shoved this aside with a groan, snatched up a clean sheet of paper, and wrote:

Dear Mr Sixsmith,
It is now well over a year since I sent you *Offensive from Quasar 13*. Not content with that dereliction, you have allowed five months to pass without responding to three more recent submissions. A prompt reply I would have deemed common decency, you being a fellow-screenplay writer, though I must say I have never cared for your work, finding it, at once, both florid and superficial. (I read Matthew Sura's piece last month and I thought he got you *bang to rights*.) Please return the more recent screenplays, namely *Decimator*, *Medusa Takes Manhattan* and *Valley of the Stratocasters*, immediately.

He signed it and sealed it. He stalked out and posted it. On his return he haughtily threw off his drenched clothes. The single bed felt enormous, like an orgiast's four-poster. He curled up tight and slept better than he had done all year.

So it was a quietly defiant Alistair who the next morning came plodding down the stairs and glanced at the splayed mail on the shelf as he headed for the door. He recognized the envelope as a lover would. He bent low as he opened it.

Do please forgive this very tardy reply. Profound apologies. But allow me to move straight on to a verdict on your work. I won't bore you with all my personal and professional distractions.

10

Bore me? thought Alistair, as his hand sought his heart.

I think I can at once give the assurance that your screenplays are unusually promising. No: that promise has already been honoured. They have both feeling and burnish.

I will content myself, for now, by taking *Offensive from Quasar 13*. (Allow me to muse a little longer on *Decimator*.) I have one or two very minor emendations to suggest. Why not telephone me here to arrange a chat?

Thank you for your generous remarks about my own work. Increasingly I find that this kind of exchange – this candour, this reciprocity – is one of the things that keep me trundling along. Your words helped sustain my defences in the aftermath of Matthew Sura's vicious and slovenly attack, from which, I fear, I am still rather reeling. Take excellent care.

'Go with the lyric,' said Jim.

'Or how about a ballad?' said Jeff.

Jack was swayable. 'Ballads are big,' he allowed.

It seemed to Luke, towards the end of the second day, that he was winning the sonnet battle. The clue lay in the flavour of Joe's taciturnity: torpid but unmorose.

'Let's face it,' said Jeff. 'Sonnets are essentially hieratic. They're strictly period. They answer to a formalized consciousness. Today, we're talking consciousnesses that are in *search* of form.'

'Plus,' said Jack, 'the lyric has always been the natural medium for the untrammelled expression of feeling.'

'Yeah,' said Jeff. 'With the sonnet you're stuck in this thesis-antithesis-synthesis routine.'

Joan said, 'I mean what are we doing here? Reflecting the world or illuminating it?'

It was time for Joe to speak. 'Please,' he said. 'Are we forgetting that "'Tis" was a sonnet, before the rewrites? Were we on coke when we said, in the summer, that we were going to go for the *sonnet*?'

The answer to Joe's last question, incidentally, was yes; but Luke looked carefully round the room. The Chinese lunch they'd had the secretary phone out for lay on the coffee table like a child's experiments with putty and paint and designer ooze. It was four o'clock and Luke wanted to get away soon. To swim and lie in the sun. To make himself especially lean and bronzed for his meeting with the young actress Henna Mickiewicz. He faked a yawn.

'Luke's lagged,' said Joe. 'Tomorrow we'll talk some more, but I'm pretty sure I'm recommitted to the sonnet.'

'Sorry,' said Alistair. 'Me yet again. Sorry.'

'Oh yes,' said the woman's voice. 'He *was* here a minute ago . . . No, he's there. He's there. Just a second.'

Alistair jerked the receiver away from his ear and stared at it. He started listening again. It seemed as if the phone itself were in paroxysm, all squawk and splat like a cabby's radio. Then the fit passed, or paused, and a voice said tightly but proudly, 'Hugh Sixsmith?'

It took Alistair a little while to explain who he was. Sixsmith sounded surprised but, on the whole, rather intrigued to hear from him. They moved on smoothly enough to arrange a meeting (after work, the following Monday), before Alistair contrived to put in: 'Mr Sixsmith, there's just one thing. This is very embarrassing, but last night I got into a bit of a state about not hearing from you for so long and I'm afraid I sent you a completely mad letter which I . . .' Alistair waited. 'Oh, you know how it is. For these screenplays, you know, you reach into yourself, and then time goes by and . . .'

'My dear boy, don't say another word. I'll ignore it. I'll throw it away. After a line or two I shall simply avert my unpained eye,' said Sixsmith, and started coughing again.

Hazel did not come down to London for the weekend. Alistair did not go up to Leeds for the weekend. He spent the time thinking about that place in Earls Court Square where screenplay writers read from their screenplays and drank biting Spanish red wine and got stared at by tousled girls who wore thick overcoats and no make-up and blinked incessantly or not at all.

Luke parked his Chevrolet Celebrity on the fifth floor of the studio car park and rode down in the elevator with two minor executives in tracksuits who were discussing the latest records broken by ''Tis he whose yester-evening's high disdain'. He put on his dark glasses as he crossed the other car park, the one reserved for major executives. Each bay had a name on it. It reassured Luke to see Joe's name there, partly obscured by his Range Rover. Poets, of course, seldom had that kind of clout. Or any clout at all. He was glad that Henna Mickiewicz didn't seem to realize this.

Joe's office: Jim, Jack, Joan, but no Jeff. Two new guys were there. Luke was introduced to the two new guys. Ron said he spoke for Don when he told Luke that he was a great admirer of his material. Huddled over the coffee percolator with Joe, Luke asked after Jeff, and Joe said, 'Jeff's off the poem,' and Luke just nodded.

They settled in their low armchairs.

Luke said, 'What's "A Welshman to Any Tourist" doing?'
Don said, 'It's doing good but not great.'
Ron said, 'It won't do what "The Gap in the Hedge" did.'
Jim said, 'What did "Hedge" do?'
They talked about what 'Hedge' did. Then Joe said, 'Okay. We're going with the sonnet. Now. Don has a problem with the octet's first quatrain, Ron has a problem with the second quatrain, Jack and Jim have a problem with the first quatrain of the sestet, and I think we *all* have a problem with the final couplet.'

Alistair presented himself at the offices of the *LM* in an unblinking trance of punctuality. He had been in the area for hours, and had spent about fifteen quid on teas and coffees. There wasn't much welcome to overstay in the various snack bars where he lingered (and where he moreover imagined himself unfavourably recollected from his previous *LM* vigils), holding with both hands the creaky foam container, and watching the light pour past the office windows.

As Big Ben struck two, Alistair mounted the stairs. He took a breath so deep that he almost fell over backwards – and then knocked. An elderly office boy wordlessly showed him into a narrow, rubbish-heaped office that contained, with difficulty, seven people. At first Alistair took them for other screenplay writers and wedged himself behind the door, at the back of the queue. But they didn't look like screenplay writers. Not much was said over the next four hours, and the identities of Sixsmith's supplicants emerged only partially and piecemeal. One or two, like his solicitor and his second wife's psychiatrist, took their leave after no more than ninety minutes. Others, like the VAT man and the probation officer, stayed almost as long as Alistair. But by six forty-five he was alone.

He approached the impossible haystack of Sixsmith's desk. Very hurriedly he started searching through the unopened mail. It was in Alistair's mind that he might locate and intercept his own letter. But all the envelopes, of which there were a great many, proved to be brown, windowed, and registered. Turning to leave, he saw a Jiffy bag of formidable bulk addressed to himself in Sixsmith's tremulous hand. There seemed no reason not to take it. The old office boy, Alistair soon saw, was curled up in a sleeping-bag under a worktable in the outer room.

On the street he unseamed his package in a ferment of grey fluff. It contained two of his screenplays, *Valley of the Stratocasters* and, confusingly, *Decimator*. There was also a note:

I have been called away, as they say. Personal ups and downs. I shall ring you this week and we'll have – what? Lunch?

Enclosed, too, was Alistair's aggrieved letter – unopened. He moved on. The traffic, human and mechanical, lurched past his quickened face. He felt his eyes widen to an obvious and solving truth: Hugh Sixsmith was a screenplay writer. He understood.

After an inconclusive day spent discussing the caesura of 'Sonnet''s opening line, Luke and his colleagues went for cocktails at Strabismus. They were given the big round table near the piano.

Jane said, 'TCT is doing a sequel to "'Tis".'

Joan said, 'Actually it's a prequel.'

'Title?' said Joe.

'Undecided. At TCT they're calling it "'Twas".'

'My son,' said Joe thoughtfully, after the waiter had delivered their drinks, 'called me an asshole this morning. For the first time.'

'That's incredible,' said Bo. '*My* son called me an asshole this morning. For the first time.'

'So?' said Mo.

Joe said, 'He's six years old, for Christ's sake.'

Phil said, 'My son called me an asshole when he was five.'

'My son hasn't called me an asshole yet,' said Jim. 'And he's nine.'

Luke sipped his Bloody Mary. Its hue and texture made him wonder whether he could risk blowing his nose without making yet another visit to the bathroom. He hadn't called Suki for three days. Things were getting compellingly out of hand with Henna Mickiewicz. He hadn't actually promised her a part in the poem, not on paper. Henna was great, except you kept thinking she was going to suddenly sue you anyway.

Mo was saying that each child progresses at its own rate, and that later lulls regularly offset the apparent advances of the early years.

Jim said, 'Still, it's a cause of concern.'

Mo said, 'My son's three. And he calls me an asshole all the time.'

Everybody looked suitably impressed.

The trees were in leaf, and the rumps of the tourist buses were thick and fat in the traffic, and all the farmers wanted fertilizer admixes rather than storehouse insulation when

Sixsmith finally made his call. In the interim, Alistair had convinced himself of the following: before returning his aggrieved letter, Sixsmith had *steamed it open and then resealed it*. During this period, also, Alistair had grimly got engaged to Hazel. But the call came.

He was pretty sure he had come to the right restaurant. Except that it wasn't a restaurant, not quite. The place took no bookings, and knew of no Mr Sixsmith, and was serving many midday breakfasts to swearing persons whose eyes bulged over mugs of flesh-coloured tea. On the other hand, there was alcohol. All kinds of people were drinking it. Fine, thought Alistair. Fine. What better place, really, for a couple of screenplay writers to . . .

'Alistair?'

Confidently Sixsmith bent his long body into the booth. As he settled, he looked well pleased with the manoeuvre. He contemplated Alistair with peculiar neutrality, but there was then something boyish, something consciously remiss, in the face he turned to the waiter. As Sixsmith ordered a gin and tonic, and as he amusingly expatiated on his weakness for prawn cocktails, Alistair found himself wryly but powerfully drawn to this man, to this rumpled screenplay writer with his dreamy gaze, the curious elisions of his somewhat slurred voice, and the great dents and bone shadows of his face, all the faulty fontanelles of vocational care. He knew how old Sixsmith was. But maybe time moved strangely for screenplay writers, whose flames burnt so bright . . .

'And as for my fellow artisan in the scrivener's trade: Alistair. What will *you* have?'

At once Sixsmith showed himself to be a person of some candour. Or it might have been that he saw in the younger screenplay writer someone before whom all false reticence could be cast aside. Sixsmith's estranged second wife, it emerged, herself the daughter of two alcoholics, was an alcoholic. Her current lover (ah, how these lovers came and went!) was an alcoholic. To complicate matters, Sixsmith explained as he rattled his glass at the waiter, his daughter, the product of his first marriage, was an alcoholic. How did Sixsmith keep going? Despite his years, he had, thank God, found love, in the arms of a woman young enough (and, by the sound of it, alcoholic enough) to be his daughter. Their prawn cocktails arrived, together with a carafe of hearty red wine. Sixsmith lit a cigarette and held up his palm towards Alistair for the duration of a coughing fit that turned every head in the room. Then, for a moment, understandably disorientated, he stared at Alistair as if uncertain of his intentions, or even his identity. But their bond quickly re-established itself. Soon they were talking away like hardened equals – of Trumbo, of Chayevsky, of Towne, of Eszterhas.

Around two thirty, when, after several attempts, the waiter succeeded in removing Sixsmith's untouched prawn cocktail, and now prepared to serve them their braised chops with a third carafe, the two men were arguing loudly about early Puzo.

Joe yawned and shrugged and said languidly, 'You know something? I was never that crazy about the Petrarchan rhyme scheme anyway.'

Jan said, '"Composed at – Castle" is ABBA ABBA.'

Jen said, 'So was "'Tis". Right up until the final polish.'

Jon said, 'Here's some news. They say "Composed at – Castle" is in turnaround.'

'You're not serious,' said Bo. 'It's released this month. I heard they were getting great preview reaction.'

Joe looked doubtful. '"'Tis" has made the suits kind of antsy about sonnets. They figure lightning can't strike twice.'

'ABBA ABBA,' said Bo with distaste.

'Or,' said Joe. '*Or* . . . *or* we go unrhymed.'

'*Un*rhymed?' said Phil.

'We go blank,' said Joe.

There was a silence. Bill looked at Gil, who looked at Will.

'What do you think, Luke?' said Jim. 'You're the poet.'

Luke had never felt very protective about 'Sonnet'. Even its original version he had regarded as little more than a bargaining chip. Nowadays he rewrote 'Sonnet' every night at the Pinnacle Trumont before Henna arrived and they started torturing room service. 'Blank,' said Luke. 'Blank. I don't know, Joe. I could go ABAB ABAB or even ABAB CDCD. Christ, I'd go AABB if I didn't think it'd tank the final couplet. But blank. I never thought I'd go *blank*.'

'Well, it needs something,' said Joe.

'Maybe it's the pentameter,' said Luke. 'Maybe it's the iamb. Hey, here's one from left field. How about syllabics?'

At five forty-five Hugh Sixsmith ordered a gin and tonic and said, 'We've talked. We've broken bread. Wine. Truth. Screenplay-writing. I want to talk about your work, Alistair. Yes, I do. I want to talk about *Offensive from Quasar 13*.'

Alistair blushed.

'It's not often that . . . But one always knows. That sense of pregnant arrest. Of felt life in its full . . . Thank yoú, Alistair. Thank you. I have to say that it rather reminded me of my own early work.'

Alistair nodded.

Having talked for quite some time about his own

maturation as a screenplay writer, Sixsmith said, 'Now. Just tell me to shut up any time you like. And I'm going to print it anyway. But I want to make one *tiny* suggestion about *Offensive from Quasar 13*.'

Alistair waved a hand in the air.

'Now,' said Sixsmith. He broke off and ordered a prawn cocktail. The waiter looked at him defeatedly. 'Now,' said Sixsmith. 'When Brad escapes from the Nebulan experiment lab and sets off with Cord and Tara to immobilize the directed-energy scythe on the Xerxian attack ship – where's Chelsi?'

Alistair frowned.

'Where's Chelsi? She's still in the lab with the Nebulans. On the point of being injected with a Phobian viper venom, moreover. What of the happy ending? What of Brad's heroic centrality? What of his avowed love for Chelsi? Or am I just being a bore?'

The secretary, Victoria, stuck her head into the room and said, 'He's coming down.'

Luke listened to the sound of twenty-three pairs of legs uncrossing and recrossing. Meanwhile he readied himself for a sixteen-tooth smile. He glanced at Joe, who said, 'He's fine. He's just coming down to say hi.'

And down he came: Jake Endo, exquisitely Westernized and gorgeously tricked out and perhaps thirty-five. Of the luxury items that pargeted his slender form, none was as breathtaking as his hair, with its layers of pampered light.

Jake Endo shook Luke's hand and said, 'It's a great pleasure to meet you. I haven't read the basic material on the poem, but I'm familiar with the background.'

Luke surmised that Jake Endo had had his voice fixed. He

could do the bits of the words that Japanese people were supposed to find difficult.

'I understand it's a love poem,' he continued. 'Addressed to your girlfriend. Is she here with you in L.A.?'

'No. She's in London.' Luke found he was staring at Jake Endo's sandals, wondering how much they could possibly have cost.

A silence began its crescendo. This silence had long been intolerable when Jim broke it, saying to Jake Endo, 'Oh, how did "Lines Left Upon a Seat in a Yew-Tree, Which Stands Near the Lake of Easthwaite, on a Desolate Part of the Shore, Commanding a Beautiful Prospect" do?'

'"Lines"?' said Jake Endo. 'Rather well.'

'I was thinking about "Composed at – Castle",' said Jim weakly.

The silence began again. As it neared its climax Joe was suddenly reminded of all this energy he was supposed to have. He got to his feet saying, 'Jake? I guess we're nearing our tiredness peak. You've caught us at kind of a low point. We can't agree on the first line. First line? We can't see our way to the end of the first *foot*.'

Jake Endo was undismayed. 'There always are these low points. I'm sure you'll get there, with so much talent in the room. Upstairs we're very confident. We think it's going to be a big summer poem.'

'No, we're very confident too,' said Joe. 'There's a lot of belief here. A lot of belief. We're behind "Sonnet" all the way.'

'Sonnet?' said Jake Endo.

'Yeah, sonnet. "Sonnet".'

'"Sonnet"?' said Jake Endo.

'It's a sonnet. It's called "Sonnet".'

In waves the West fell away from Jake Endo's face. After

a few seconds he looked like a dark-age warlord in mid-campaign, taking a glazed breather before moving on to the women and the children.

'Nobody told me,' he said as he went towards the telephone, 'about any *sonnet*.'

The place was closing. Its tea trade and its after-office trade had come and gone. Outside, the streets glimmered morbidly. Members of the staff were donning macs and overcoats. An important light went out. A fridge door slammed.

'Hardly the most resounding felicity, is it?' said Sixsmith.

Absent or unavailable for over an hour, the gift of speech had been restored to Alistair – speech, that prince of all the faculties. 'Or what if . . .' he said. 'What if Chelsi just leaves the experiment lab earlier?'

'Not hugely dramatic,' said Sixsmith. He ordered a carafe of wine and enquired as to the whereabouts of his braised chop.

'Or what if she just gets wounded? During the escape. In the leg.'

'So long as one could avoid the wretched cliché: girl impeded, hero dangerously tarrying. Also, she's supernumerary to the raid on the Xerxian attack ship. We really want her out of the way for that.'

Alistair said, 'Then let's kill her.'

'Very well. Slight pall over the happy ending. No, no.'

A waiter stood over them, sadly staring at the bill in its saucer.

'All right,' said Sixsmith. 'Chelsi gets wounded. Quite badly. In the arm. *Now* what does Brad do with her?'

'Drops her off at the hospital.'

22

'Mm. Rather hollow modulation.'

The waiter was joined by another waiter, equally stoic; their faces were grained by evening shadow. Now Sixsmith was gently frisking himself with a deepening frown.

'What if,' said Alistair, 'what if there's somebody passing who can *take* her to the hospital?'

'Possibly,' said Sixsmith, who was half standing, with one hand awkwardly dipped into his inside pocket.

'Or what if,' said Alistair, 'or what if Brad just gives her *directions* to the hospital?'

Back in London the next day, Luke met with Mike to straighten this shit out. Actually it looked okay. Mike called Mal at Monad, who had a thing about Tim at TCT. As a potential finesse on Mal, Mike also called Bob at Binary with a view to repossessing the option on 'Sonnet', plus development money at rolling compound, and redeveloping it somewhere else entirely – say, at Red Giant, where Rodge was known to be very interested. 'They'll want you to go out there,' said Mike. 'To kick it around.'

'I can't believe Joe,' said Luke. 'I can't believe I knocked myself out for that flake.'

'Happens. Joe forgot about Jake Endo and sonnets. Endo's first big poem was a sonnet. Before your time. "Bright star, would I were steadfast as thou art." It opened for like one day. It practically bankrupted Japan.'

'I feel used, Mike. My sense of trust. I've got to get wised up around here.'

'A lot will depend on how "Composed at – Castle" does and what the feeling is on the "'Tis" prequel.'

'I'm going to go away with Suki for a while. Do you know anywhere where there aren't any shops? Jesus, I need a holiday. Mike, this is all bullshit. You know what I *really* want to do, don't you?'

'Of course I do.'

Luke looked at Mike until he said, 'You want to direct.'

When Alistair had convalesced from the lunch, he revised *Offensive from Quasar 13* in rough accordance with Sixsmith's suggestions. He solved the Chelsi problem by having her noisily eaten by a Stygian panther in the lab menagerie. The charge of gratuitousness was, in Alistair's view, safely anticipated by Brad's valediction to her remains, in which sanguinary revenge on the Nebulans was both prefigured and legitimized. He also took out the bit where Brad declared his love for Chelsi, and put in a bit where Brad declared his love for Tara.

He sent in the new pages, which three months later Sixsmith acknowledged and applauded in a hand quite incompatible with that of his earlier communications. Nor did he reimburse Alistair for the lunch. His wallet, he had explained, had been emptied that morning – by which alcoholic, Sixsmith never established. Alistair kept the bill as a memento. This startling document showed that during the course of the meal Sixsmith had smoked, or at any rate bought, nearly a carton of cigarettes.

Three months later he was sent a proof of *Offensive from Quasar 13*. Three months after that, the screenplay appeared in the *Little Magazine*. Three months after that, Alistair received a cheque for £12.50, which bounced.

Curiously, although the proof had incorporated Alistair's corrections, the published version reverted to the typescript, in which Brad escaped from the Nebulan lab seemingly without concern for a Chelsi last glimpsed on an operating table with a syringe full of Phobian viper venom being eased into her neck. Later that month, Alistair went along to a reading at the Screenplay Society in Earls Court. There he got talking to a gaunt girl in an ash-stained black smock who claimed to have read his screenplay and who, over glasses of red wine and, later, in the terrible pub, told him he was a weakling and a hypocrite with no notion of the ways of men and women. Alistair had not been a published screenplay writer long enough to respond to, or even recognize, this graphic proposition (though he did keep the telephone number she threw at his feet). It is anyway doubtful whether he would have dared to take things further. He was marrying Hazel the following weekend.

In the new year he sent Sixsmith a series – one might almost say a sequence – of screenplays on group-jeopardy themes. His follow-up letter in the summer was answered by a brief note stating that Sixsmith was no longer employed by the *LM*. Alistair telephoned. He then discussed the matter with Hazel and decided to take the next day off work.

It was a September morning. The hospice in Cricklewood was of recent design and construction; from the road it resembled a clutch of igloos against the sheenless tundra of the sky. When he asked for Hugh Sixsmith at the desk, two men in suits climbed quickly from their chairs. One was a writ-server. One was a cost-adjuster. Alistair waved away their complex requests.

The warm room contained clogged, regretful murmurs, and defiance in the form of bottles and paper cups and cigarette smoke, and the many peeping eyes of female grief. A young woman faced him proudly. Alistair started explaining who he was, a young screenplay writer come to . . . On the bed in the corner the spavined figure of Sixsmith was gawkily arranged. Alistair moved towards it. At first he was sure the eyes were gone, like holes cut out of pumpkin or blood orange. But then the faint brows began to lift, and Alistair thought he saw the light of recognition.

As the tears began, he felt the shiver of approval, of consensus, on his back. He took the old screenplay writer's hand and said, 'Goodbye. And thank you. Thank you. Thank you.'

Opening in four hundred and thirty-seven theatres, the Binary sonnet 'Composed at – Castle' did seventeen million in its first weekend. At this time Luke was living in a two-bedroom apartment on Yokum Drive. Suki was with him. He hoped it wouldn't take her too long to find out about Henna Mickiewicz. When the smoke cleared he would switch to the more mature Anita, who produced.

He had taken his sonnet to Rodge at Red Giant and turned it into an ode. When that didn't work out he went to Mal at Monad, where they'd gone for the villanelle. The villanelle had become a triolet, briefly, with Tim at TCT, before Bob at Binary had him rethink it as a rondeau. When the rondeau didn't take, Luke lyricized it and got Mike to send it to Joe. Everyone, including Jake Endo, thought that now was surely the time to turn it back into a sonnet.

Luke had dinner at Rales with Joe and Mike.

'I always thought of "Sonnet" as an art poem,' said Joe. 'But sonnets are so hot now I've started thinking more commercially.'

Mike said, 'TCT is doing a sequel *and* a prequel to "'Tis" and bringing them out at the same time.'

'A sequel?' said Joe.

'Yeah. They're calling it "'Twill".'

Mike was a little fucked up. So was Joe. Luke was a little

fucked up too. They'd done some lines at the office. Then drinks here at the bar. They'd meant to get a little fucked up. It was okay. It was good, once in a while, to get a little fucked up. The thing was not to get fucked up too often. The thing was not to get fucked up to excess.

'I mean it, Luke,' said Joe. He glittered potently. 'I think "Sonnet" could be as big as "–".'

'You think?' said Luke.

'I mean it. I think "Sonnet" could be another "–".'

' "–"?'

' "–".'

Luke thought for a moment, taking this in. ' "–" . . .' he repeated wonderingly.

New Yorker, 1992

Denton's Death

Suddenly Denton realized that there would be three of them, that they would come after dark, that their leader would have his own key, and that they would be calm and deliberate, confident that they had all the time they needed to do what had to be done. He knew that they would be courtly, deferential, urbane – whatever state he happened to be in when they arrived – and that he would be allowed to make himself comfortable; perhaps he would even be offered a last cigarette. He never seriously doubted that he would warm to and admire all three immediately, and wish only that he could have been their friend. He knew that they used a machine. As if prompted by some special hindsight, Denton thought often and poignantly about the moment when the leader would consent to take his hand as the machine began to work. He knew that they were out there already, seeing people, making telephone calls; and he knew that they must be very expensive.

At first, he took a lively, even rather self-important interest in the question of who had hired the men and their machine. Who would bother to do this to him? There was his brother, a huge exhausted man whom Denton had never liked or disliked or felt close to or threatened by in any way: they had quarrelled recently over the allotment of their dead mother's goods, and Denton had in fact managed to secure a few worthless extras at his brother's expense; but this was just one more reason why his brother could never afford to do this to him. There was a man at the office whose life Denton had probably ruined: having bullied his friend into assisting him with a routine office theft, Denton told all to his superiors, claiming that he had used duplicity merely to test his colleague (Denton's firm not only dismissed the man – they also, to Denton's mild alarm, successfully prosecuted him for fraud); but someone whose life you could ruin so easily wouldn't have the determination to do this to him. And there were a few women still out on the edges of his life, women he had mistreated as thoroughly as he dared, all of whom had seemed to revel in his frustrations, thrill to his regrets, laugh at his losses: he had heard that one of them was about to marry somebody very rich, or at any rate somebody sufficiently rich to hire the three men; but she had never cared about him enough to want to do this to him.

Within a few days, however, the question of who had hired them abruptly ceased to concern Denton. He could muster no strong views on the subject; it was all done now, anyway. Denton moved slowly through the two rooms of his half-converted flatlet, becalmed, listless, his mind as vacant as the dust-filmed window panes and the shrilly pictureless walls. Nothing bored him any more. All day he wandered silently through the flat, not paying for it (no payment seemed to be seriously expected), not going to his office more than once or twice a week and then not at all (and no one there seemed to mind; they were tactful and remote like understanding relatives), and not thinking about who had hired the three men and their machine. He had a little money, enough for milk and certain elementary foods. Denton had been an anorexic in his youth because he hated the idea of becoming old and big. Now his stomach had rediscovered that ripe, sentimental tenseness, and he usually vomited briskly after taking solids.

He sat all day in his empty living-room, thinking about his childhood. It seemed to him that all his life he had been tumbling away from his happiness as a young boy, tumbling away to the insecurity and disappointment of his later years, when gradually, as if through some smug consensus, people stopped liking him and he stopped liking them. Whatever happened to me? thought Denton. Sometimes he would get a repeated image of himself at the age of six or seven, running for the school bus, a satchel clutched to his side, his face fresh and unanxious – and suddenly Denton would lean forward and sob huskily into his hands, and stand up after a while, and make tea perhaps, and gaze out at the complicated goings-on in the square, feeling drunk and wise. Denton thanked whoever had hired the three men to do this to him; never before had he felt so alive.

Later still, his mind gave itself up entirely to the coming of the men and their machine, and his childhood vanished along with all the other bits of his life. Facelessly, Denton 'rationalized' his kitchen supplies, importing a variety of canned milks and wide-spectrum baby foods, so that, if necessary, he should never have to leave the flat again. With the unsmiling dourness of an adolescent Denton decided to stop washing his clothes and to stop washing his body. Every morning subtracted clearness from the window panes; he left the dry, belching heaters on day and night; his two rooms became soupy and affectless, like derelict conservatories in summer thunder. Once, on an impulse, Denton jerked open the stiff living-room window. The outdoors tingled hatefully, as if the air were full of steel. He shut the window and returned to his chair by the fire, where he sat with no expression on his face until it was time to go to bed.

At night, exultant and wounding dreams thrilled and tormented him. He wept on scarlet beaches, the waves climbing in front of him until they hid the sun. He saw cities crumble, mountains slide away, continents crack. He steered a dying world out into the friendly heat of space. He held planets in his hands. Denton staggered down terminal arcades, watched by familiar, hooded figures in dark doorways. Little flying girls with jagged predatory teeth swung through the air towards him at impossible, meandering speed. He came across his younger self in distress and brought him food but an eagle stole it. Often Denton awoke stretched diagonally across the bed, his cheeks wet with exhausted tears.

When would they come? What would their machine be like? Denton thought about the arrival of the three men with the gentle hopelessness of a long-separated lover: the knock at his door, the peaceful and reassuring smiles, the bed, the request for a cigarette, the offer of the leader's hand, the machine. Denton imagined the moment as a painless mood-swing, a simple transference from one state to another, like waking up or going to sleep or suddenly realizing something. Above all he relished the thought of that soothing handclasp as the machine started to work, a ladder-rung, a final handhold as life poured away and death began.

What would his death be like? Denton's mind saw emblem books, bestiaries. Nothing and a purple hum. Deceit. An abandoned playground. Hurtful dreams. Failure. The feeling that people want to get rid of you. The process of dying repeated for ever, 'What will my death be like?' he thought – and knew at once, with abrupt certainty, that it would be just like his life: different in form, perhaps, but nothing new, the same balance of bearables, the same.

Late that night Denton opened his eyes and they were there. Two of them stood in the backlit doorway of his bedroom, their postures heavy with the task they had come to do. Behind them, next door, he could hear the third man preparing the machine; shadows filled the yellow ceiling. Denton sat up quickly, half-attempting to straighten his hair and clothes. 'Is it you?' he asked.

'Yes,' said the leader, 'we're here again.' He looked round the room. 'And *aren't* you a dirty boy.'

'Oh don't tell me that,' said Denton, '– not now.' He felt an onrush of shame and self-pity, saw himself as they saw him, an old tramp in a dirty room, afraid to die. Denton lapsed into tears as they moved forward – it seemed the only way left to express his defencelessness. 'Nearly there,' one of them called fruitily through the door. Then all three were upon him. They hauled him from his bed and pushed him into the living-room. They began to strap him with leather belts to an upright chair, handling him throughout like army doctors with a patient they knew to be difficult. It was all very fast. 'A cigarette – please,' said Denton. 'We haven't got all night, you know,' the leader whispered. 'You do know that.'

The machine was ready. It was a black box with a red light and two chromium switches; it made a faraway rumble; from the near side came a glistening, flesh-coloured tube, ending in what looked like a small pink gas-mask or a boxer's mouthpiece. 'Open wide,' said the leader. Denton struggled weakly. They held his nose. 'Tomorrow it'll be a thing of the past,' said the leader, 'finished ... in just ... a couple of minutes.' He parted Denton's clenched lips with his fingers. The soft mouthpiece slithered in over his front teeth — it seemed *alive*, searching out its own grip with knowing fleshy surfaces. A plunging, nauseous, inside-out suction began to gather within his chest, as if each corpuscle were being marshalled for abrupt and concerted movement. The hand! Denton stiffened. With hopeless anger he fought for the leader's attention, tumescing his eyes and squeezing thin final noises up from deep in his throat. As the pressure massed hugely inside his chest, he bent and flexed his wrists, straining hard against the leather bands. Something was tickling his heart with thick strong fingers. He was grappling with unconsciousness in dark water. He was dying alone. 'All right,' one of them said as his body slackened, 'he's ready.' Denton opened his eyes for the last time. The leader was staring closely at his face. Denton had no strength; he frowned sadly. The leader understood almost at once, smiling like the father of a nervous child. 'Oh yes,' he said. 'About now Denton always likes a hand.' Denton heard the second switch click and he felt a long rope being tugged out through his mouth.

The leader held his hand firmly as life poured away, and Denton's death began.

Suddenly Denton realized that there would be three of them, that they would come after dark, that their leader would have his own key, and that they would be calm and deliberate, confident that they had all the time they needed to do what had to be done. At first, he took a lively, even rather self-important interest in the question of who had hired the men and their machine. Within a few days, however, the question of who had hired them abruptly ceased to concern Denton. He sat all day in his empty living-room, thinking about his childhood. Later still, his mind gave itself up entirely to the coming of the men and their machine, and his childhood vanished along with all the other bits of his life. At night, exultant and wounding dreams thrilled and tormented him. When would they come? What would his death be like? Late that night Denton opened his eyes and they were there, 'Yes,' said the leader, 'we're here again.' 'Oh don't tell me that,' said Denton, '– not now.' The machine was ready. The leader held his hand firmly as life poured away, and Denton's death began.

Encounter, 1976

State of England

1. Mobile Phones

Big Mal stood there on the running track in his crinkly linen suit, with a cigarette in one mitt and a mobile phone in the other. He also bore a wound, did the big man: a shocking laceration on the side of his face, earlobe to cheekbone. The worst thing about his wound was how *recent* it looked. It wasn't bleeding. But it might have been seeping. He'd got his suit from Contemporary Male in Culver City, Los Angeles – five years ago. He'd got his wound from a medium-rise carpark off Leicester Square, London – last night. Under high flat-bottomed clouds and a shrill blue sky Big Mal stood there on the running track. Not tall but built like a brick khazi: five feet nine in all directions . . . Mal felt he was in a classic situation: wife, child, other woman. It was mid-September. It was Sports Day. The running track he was strolling along would soon be pounded in earnest by his nine-year-old son, little Jet. Jet's mother, Sheilagh, was on the clubhouse steps, fifty yards away, with the other mums. Mal could see her. She too wielded a cigarette and a mobile phone. They weren't talking except on their mobile phones.

He put the cigarette in his mouth and with big, white, cold, agitated fingers prodded out her number.

'*A!*' he said. A tight sound, sharp-pitched – the short 'a', as in 'Mal'. It was a sound Mal made a lot: his general response to pain, to inadvertency, to terrestrial imperfection. He went '*A!*' this time because he had jammed his mobile into the wrong ear. The sore one: so swollen, so richly traumatized by the events of the night before. Then he said, 'It's me.'

'Yeah, I can see you.'

Sheilagh was moving away from the clump of mums, down the steps, towards him. He turned his back on her and said, 'Where's Jet?'

'They come up on the bus. Christ, Mal, whatever have you done to yourself? The state of your face.'

Well that was nice to know: that his wound was visible from fifty yards. 'Load of ballocks,' he said, by way of explanation. And it was true in a sense. Mal was forty-eight years old, and you could say he'd made a pretty good living from his fists: his fists, his toe caps, his veering, butting brow. Last night's spanking was by no means the worst he'd ever taken. But it was definitely the weirdest. 'Hang about,' he said, while he lit another cigarette. '*A!*' he added. Wrong ear again. 'When's the bus due?'

'Have you had that looked at? You want to get that sorted.'

'It was dressed,' said Mal carefully, 'by a trained nurse.'

'Who's that then? Miss India? What she call herself? *Linzi* . . .'

'Oi. Not Linzi. Yvonne.'

The mention of this name (wearily yet powerfully stressed on the first syllable) would tell Sheilagh its own story.

'Don't tell me. You were out rucking with Fat Lol. Yeah. Well. If you've been with Fat Lol for thirty years . . .'

Mal followed her line of reasoning. Been with Fat Lol for thirty years and you knew your first aid. You were a trained nurse whether you liked it or not. 'Yvonne sorted it,' he went on. 'She cleaned it out and bunged some stuff on it.' This was no less than the truth. That morning, over tea and toast, Yvonne had scalded his cheek with Fat Lol's aftershave and then dressed it with a section of kitchen roll. But the section of kitchen roll had long since disappeared into the wound's gurgling depths. It was like that film with the young Steve McQueen. Oh, yeah: *The Blob*.

'Does it throb?'

'Yeah,' said Mal resignedly, 'it throbs. Look. Let's try and be civilized in front of the kid. Okay? Come on now, She. We owe it to Jet. Right?'

'Right.'

'Right. Now give me my fucking money.

'*Whoff* fucking money?'

'Whoff fucking money? *My* fucking money.'

She hung up and so, unsuccessfully (and murmuring, 'Where are you mate?'), he tried Fat Lol – tried Fat Lol on *his* mobile.

Moving in a broad arc, maintaining a fixed distance from his wife, Mal trudged along the track and then closed in on the far end of the clubhouse. The clubhouse with its black Tudor wood: maybe they had a bar in there. Mal hesitated, and even staggered; the coil, the spring in the person was winding down awful low. And here were all the other dads, on the steps round the side, with *their* mobiles.

Delaying his approach, Mal tarried on the verge and tried Linzi on *her* mobile.

Jet's school, St Anthony's, was a smart one, or at least an

expensive one. Mal it was who somehow met the startling fees. And showed up on days like today, as you had to do. He also wanted and expected his boy to perform well.

During his earliest visits to the parent-teacher interface, Mal had been largely speechless with peer-group hypochondria: he kept thinking there was something terribly wrong with him. He wanted out of that peer group and into a different peer group with weaker opposition. Mal made She do all the talking, with her greater confidence and higher self-esteem – deriving, as their marriage counsellor had once phrased it, from her 'more advanced literacy skills'. In truth, Mal's writing left much to be desired, to put it mildly. Not what you'd call overly clever on the reading neither. Either. Confronted, say, by a billboard or the instructions on a Band-Aid tin, his lips moved, tremulously, miming his difficulty. He spoke bad too – he knew it. But all that prejudice against people such as himself was gone now. Or so they said. And maybe they were partly right. Mal could go to virtually any restaurant he liked, and sit there surrounded by all these types squawking and honking away, and pick up a tab as dear as an air ticket. He could go to this or that place. And yet nobody could guarantee that he would *feel okay* in this or that place. Nobody could guarantee that, ever. Big Mal, who grunted with a kind of assent when he saw a swung fist coming for his mouth, could nonetheless be laid out by the sight of a cocked pinkie. *A!* Always it was with him, every hour, like an illness, like a haunting. Go on then – stare. Go on then: laugh. Why else d'you think he'd loved the States so much? L.A., mate: working for Joseph Andrews . . .

Mal felt he was a man in a classic situation. He had run away from home (five months ago) and moved in with a younger woman (Linzi), abandoning his wife (Sheilagh) and his child (little Jet). A classic situation is, by definition, a second-hand situation – third-hand, eleventh-hand. And more and more obviously so, as the aggregate climbed. Late at night, Mal sometimes found himself thinking, If Adam had left Eve, and run off with a younger woman – supposing he could find one – he'd have been stepping into the entirely unknown. Call Adam a cunt, but you couldn't call him corny. Now all that was just routine: stock, stale, dead. And nowadays too there was this other level of known ground. You'd picked up some information from all the studies and the stats: and there you were on TV every night, in the soaps and the sitcoms, generally being played for laughs. One out of two did it: left home. Of course, *not* leaving home was corny, too, but nobody ever went on about that. And Adam, by sticking around, remained in the entirely unknown.

He sensed he was a cliché – and sensed further that he'd even fucked *that* up. Let's think. *He ran away from home and moved in with a younger woman.* Ran away? Linzi only lived across the street. Moved in? He was at a bed-and-breakfast in King's Cross. A younger woman? Mal was getting surer and surer that Linzi was, in fact, an *older* woman. One afternoon, while she was enjoying a drugged nap, Mal had come across her passport. Linzi's date of birth was given as '25 Aug 19 . . .' The last two digits had been scratched out, with a fingernail. Under the angle lamp you could still see a dot of nail polish – the same vampiric crimson she often used. Opposite, staring at him, was Linzi's face: delusions of grandeur in a Woolworth's photobooth. All he knew for certain was that Linzi had been born this century.

A! Wrong ear again. But he *wanted* the wrong ear, this time. For now he was about to join the dads – the peer group; and Mal's mobile would help conceal his wound.

Mobiles meant social mobility. With a mobile riding on your jaw you could enter the arena enclosed in your own concerns, your own preoccupation, your own business. 'Cheers, lads,' he said, with a wave, and then frowned into his phone. He'd called Linzi, and was therefore saying things like 'Did you, babes? . . . Have a cup of tea and a Nurofen . . . Go back to bed. With them brochures . . . They the Curvilinear or the Crescent? . . . Are you, darling?' Hunched over his mobile, his knees bent, Mal looked like a man awaiting his moment in the shot put. He was doing what all the other dads were doing, which was putting in an appearance. Presenting an appearance to one another and to the world. And what did Mal's appearance say? With fights and fighting, this was ancient knowledge. When you received a wound, you didn't just have to take it, sustain it. You didn't just have to bear it. You also had to wear it, for all to see, until it healed.

Nodding, winking, grasping an arm or patting a shoulder here and there, he moved among them. Blazers, shell suits, jeans and open shirts, even the odd dhoti or kaftan or whatever you like to call them. The dads: half of them weren't even English – thus falling at the first hurdle, socially. Or so Mal might once have thought. 'Manjeet, mate,' he was saying. 'Mikio. Nusrat!' Socially, these days, even the Pakkis could put the wind up him. Paratosh, for instance, who was some kind of Sikh or Pathan and wore a cravat and acted in radio plays and had beautiful manners. And if I can tell he's got beautiful manners, thought Mal, then they must be really ace. 'Paratosh, mate!' he now cried . . . But Paratosh just gave him a flat smile and minutely re-angled his stately gaze. It seemed to Mal that they were all doing that. Adrian. Fardous. Why? Was it the wound? He thought not. See, these were the nuclear dads, the ones who'd stuck with their families, so far, anyway. And everybody knew that Mal had broken out, had reneged on the treaty and gone non-nuclear. These men, some of them, were the husbands of Sheilagh's friends. Clumping and stamping around among them (and trying Fat Lol again now), Mal felt ancient censures ranged against him in these faces of ochre and hazel, of mocha and java. He was pariah, caste-polluter; and he thought they thought he had failed, as a man. Awkward, massively cuboid, flinching under a thin swipe of dark hair, his fingers quaking over the contours of his damaged cheek, Mal was untouchable, like his wound.

Other dads talked on mobiles, their conversations disembodied, one-way. For a moment they sounded insane, like all the monologuists and soliloquizers of the city streets.

2. Asian Babes

Linzi's real name was Shinsala, and her family came from Bombay, once upon a time. You wouldn't guess any of this, talking to her on the phone. Most of the foreign dads – the Nusrats, the Fardouses, the Paratoshes – spoke better English than Mal. Much better English. While presumably also being pretty good at Farsi, Urdu, Hindi, or whatever. And he had to wonder: how could that be? How come there was so little *left over* for Mal? Linzi, on the other hand, prompted no such reproaches. She spoke worse than Sheilagh, worse than Mal. She spoke as bad as Fat Lol. She spoke straight East End, with only this one little exoticism, in the way she handled her pronouns. Linzi said *he* where an English person would say *him* or *his*. Like 'compared to he'.

41

Or 'driving he car'. Same with *she*. Like 'the way she wears
she skirts'. Or 'I hate she'. It sometimes gave Mal a fright,
because he thought she was talking about She. Sheilagh.
And Linzi was always threatening a confrontation with She:
like today, for instance. Mal didn't want to think about those
two getting together. *A!*

But now the big man was shouldering his way indoors.
He passed a Coke machine, bulletin boards, the entrance to
the changing rooms, a snack hatch and its hamburger
breath. Jesus. Mal wasn't a big boozer, like some. But last
night, after the smacking they'd taken, he and Fat Lol had
got through a bottle of Scotch. A bottle of Scotch *each*. So he
now had the notion that after a couple of pints he'd feel
twice the price. He peered round a corner, paused, and then
strode forward, jangling his change. Everything in him
responded to what he saw: the fruit machine, the charity jar
full of brown coins, the damp grey rags beneath the wok-
sized ashtrays, the upended liquor bottles with their optics
on the nozzles, guaranteeing fair trading, guaranteeing fair
play. And here was the ornately affable barman, plodding
up through the floor.

'Mal!'

He turned. 'Bern, mate!'

'All right?'

'All right? How's little Clint?'

'He's a terror. How's . . . ?'

'Jet? He's handsome.'

'Here, Mal. Say hi to Toshiko.'

Toshiko smiled with her Japanese teeth.

'Nice to meet you,' said Mal, and added, uncertainly,
helplessly, 'I'm sure.'

Bern was the dad that Mal knew best. They'd rigged up
an acquaintanceship on the touchline of yet another sports

field: watching their sons represent St Anthony's at football. Clint and Jet, paired strikers for the Under Nines. The dads looked on, two terrible scouts or stringers, shouting things like 'Zonal marking!' and 'Sweeper system!' and '4–4–2!' – while their sons, and all the others, ran around the place like so many dogs chasing a ball. Afterwards Mal and Bern sloped off down the drinker. They agreed it was small fucking wonder their boys had taken a caning: nine-nil. The defence was crap and midfield created fuck-all. Where was the *service* to the lads up front?

'I heard an interesting thing the other night,' Bern was suddenly saying. Bern was a photographer, originally fashion but now glamour and social. He spoke worse than Mal. 'A very interesting thing. I was covering the mayor's do. Got talking to these uh, detectives. Scotland Yard. Remember that bloke who broke into Buckingham Palace? Caused all that fuss?'

Mal nodded. He remembered.

'Well guess what.' And here Bern's face went all solemn and priestly. 'They reckon he fucked her. Reckon he gave her one.'

'Who?'

'The Queen. Remember he was found in her bedroom, right?'

'Right.'

'Well these blokes reckon he fucked her.'

'Phew, that's a bit steep innit mate?'

'Yeah well that's what they reckon. Reckon he fucked her. So you uh – you moved out.'

'Yeah, mate. Couldn't hack it.'

'Because every man has a . . .'

'His limit.'

'Right. I mean, how much shit can you take, right?'

'Right.'

It was good, talking to Bern like this. Get it off your chest. Bern had left home while his wife was *pregnant* with little Clint. Not for this Toshiko, who was presumably Japanese, but for somebody else. Every time Mal bumped into him, Bern had some new sort on his arm: foreign, thirtyish. As if doing it country by country. To keep himself young.

'Look at this one,' said Bern. 'Twenty-eight. You know something? She's me first Nip. Ain't you, Tosh! Where they been all my life?' Without lowering his voice or changing his tone, he said, 'You know, I always thought they're built sideways. Down there. But they ain't. Same as all the others the world over. God bless 'em.

'She don't speak English, do you, Tosh?' continued Bern, putting Mal's mind at rest.

Toshiko quacked something back at him.

'Can speak French.'

Mal lowered his gaze. The thing was ... The big thing with Mal was that his sexuality, like his sociality, was essentially sombre. As if everything had gone wrong forty years ago, some rainy Saturday, when he stared in through department-store windows at fawn, dun, taut, waxy, plastic women, their arms raised in postures of gift-bearing or patient explication ... In bed together, he and Linzi – Big Mal and Shinsala – watched *Asian Babes*. By now their whole sex life was based on it. *Asian Babes*, the magazine, the video, the laser CD, or whatever: *Asian Babes*, Mal had a hunch, represented a milestone in race relations on this island. White men and dark women were coming together in electronic miscegenation. Every video wanker in England had now had his Fatima, his Fetnab. When *Asian Babes* was taking a rest, or when they were button-punching their way through it, and Linzi's set was in neutral, the channel of choice was Zee TV – Indian musicals. And such a chaste culture! When a couple went to kiss, the camera would whip away to twirling, twittering lovebirds or great seas attacking a cliff face. Women of darkly heavenly beauty, laughing, singing, dancing, pouting, but above all weeping, weeping, weeping: milked of huge, glutinous, opalescent tears, on mountaintops, on street corners, under stage moons. Then Linzi would press the 'Play' button and you'd be back with some Arab bint, smiling, chortling, and taking her clothes off to slinky music in some Arab flat at once modern and mosquelike and contorting herself on a polythene-covered settee or an ankle-deep white carpet . . . The other video they kept watching was the one Linzi had procured from Kosmetique. Breast enhancement: Before and After. You could tell that plastic surgery sought to reverse natural prescript, because After was always better than Before, instead of a poor second, as in life. Although Mal liked Linzi as she was, he was nonetheless dead keen on Kosmetique, and this troubled him. But he too wanted to switch his skin. One time, at Speakers' Corner, where men on milk crates had one-way conversations with no visible audience, he had stood with a hand on Linzi's shoulder, staring at the fantastic shoeshine of her hair, and he had felt wonderfully evolved, like a racial rainbow, ready to encompass a new world. He wanted a change. This thing, he thought, this whole thing happened because he wanted a change. He wanted a change, and England wasn't going to give him one.

'Who you with now then?' Bern asked him.

'Linzi. Nuts about her.'

'Ah. Sweet. How old?'

He thought of saying, 'Fortyish.' Yeah: forty-*nine*. Or why not just say, 'Sixteen'? Mal was feeling particularly grateful to Bern – for not saying anything about the state of his face. Well, that was Bern for you: a man of the world. Still, Mal felt unable to answer, and Bern soon started talking about the mysterious disappearance of the man who fucked the Queen (or so they reckoned). Toshiko stood there, smiling, her teeth strangely stacked. Mal had been in her company for half an hour and she still looked wholly terrifying to him, like something out of an old war comic. The extra cladding of the facial flesh, as if she was wearing a mask made out of skin; the brow, and then those orbits, those sockets, those faceted lids . . . He had gained the vague impression, over the years, that Nip skirt ran itself ragged for you in the sack. As they'd need to do, in his opinion. Mal's mind shrugged. Christ. Maybe they let you fuck them in the *eye*.

Sheilagh called him on his mobile to say that the boys' buses had finally arrived.

3. Mortal Kombat

He felt he was a man in a classic situation. Its oddities were just oddities: happenstance, not originality. As he moved outside into the air, exchanging the Irish colorations of the saloon (best expressed, perhaps, in the seething browns of Bern's bourbons) for the polar clarity of a mid-September noon, that was all he saw: his situation. The sun was neither hot nor high, just incredibly intense, as if you could *hear* it, the frying roar of its winds. Every year the sun did this, subjecting the kingdom to the fiercest and most critical scrutiny. It was checking up on the state of England. Sheilagh in her lime boiler suit came and stood beside him.

He turned away. He said, 'We've got to talk, She. Face to face.'

'When?'

'Later,' he said. Because now the boys were filing in through the gateway from the car park. Mal stood there, watching: a lesson in bad posture. In his peripheral vision Sheilagh breathed and swelled. How light the boys looked: how amazingly light.

For a younger woman. Abandoning his wife and his child . . . How true was that? Mal considered it possible to argue that Sheilagh wasn't really his wife. Okay, he'd married her. But only a year ago. As a nice surprise – like a birthday treat. Honestly, it didn't mean a thing. Mal had thought at the time that She overreacted. For months she went around with that greedy look on her face. And it wasn't just a look. She gained ten pounds over Christmas. *Abandoning his child.* Well, that was true enough. They had him bang to rights on that one. On the day he broke the news: the idea was, Mal'd tell him, and then She'd take him off to *Mortal Kombat.* Which Jet had been yearning to see for months – aching, pining. And Jet didn't want to go to it. Mal watched Sheilagh trying to drag him down the street, his gym shoes, his grey tracksuit bottoms, his stubborn bum. Mal took him to *Mortal Kombat* the following week. Fucking stupid. Booting each other in the face for twenty minutes without so much as a fat lip.

Here came the kid now, with his mother already bending over him to straighten the collar of his polo shirt and pat his styled hair. Styled hair? Since when was that? Jesus: an earring. That was Sheilagh playing the fun young mum. You know: take him down Camden Market and buy him a leather jacket. Keeping his counsel, for now, Mal crouched down (*A!*) to kiss Jet's cheek and tousle his – wait. No, he wouldn't want that tousled. Jet wiped his cheek and said, 'Dad? Who beat you up?'

'We was outnumbered. Heavily outnumbered.' He did a calculation. There'd been about thirty of them. 'Fifteen to one. Me and Fat Lol.' He didn't tell Jet that fifteen of them had been women.

'Dad?'

'Yeah?'

'Are you running in the Fathers' Race?'

'No way.'

Jet looked at his mother, who said, 'Mal, you got to.'

'No way, no day. It'll do me back in.'

'Mal.'

'No shape, no form.'

'But Dad.'

'No way José.'

Mal looked down. The boy was staring with great narrowness of attention, almost cross-eyed, and with his mouth dropped open – staring into the hills and valleys of his father's wound.

'You just concentrate on your own performance,' Mal told him.

'But Dad. You're meant to be a *bouncer*,' said Jet.

Bouncing, being a bouncer – as a trade, as a calling – had the wrong reputation. Bouncing, Mal believed, was misunderstood.

Throughout the Seventies, he had served all night long at many an exclusive doorway, had manned many a prestigious portal, more often than not with Fat Lol at his side. The team: Big Mal and Fat Lol. They started together at the Hammersmith Palais. Soon they worked their way up to

West End places like Ponsonby's and Fauntleroy's. He did it for fifteen years, but it only took about a week to get the hang of it.

Bouncing wasn't really about bouncing – about chucking people out. Bouncing was about not letting people in. That was pretty much all there was to it – to bouncing. Oh, yeah. And saying 'Sir', and 'Gentlemen'.

See a heavy drunk or one of those white-lipped weasel-weights, and it's 'Sorry, sir, you can't come in. Why? Cos you're not a member, sir. If you can't find a taxi at this hour, sir, we'd be happy to call you a minicab here from the door.'

See a load of obvious steamers coming down the mews in their suits, and it's 'Good evening to you, gentlemen. No I'm sorry, gentlemen. Gentlemen, this club is members only. Oi! Look, hold up, lads. Gentlemen! Lol! Okay. Okay. If you're still wide awake, gentlemen, may I recommend Jimmy's, at 32 Noel Street, bottom bell. Left and left again.'

About once a week, usually at weekends, Mr Carburton would come down to the door, stare you in the eye, and say, with dreadful weariness, 'Who fucking let *them* in?'

You'd go, 'Who?'

'Who? Them two fucking nutcases who're six foot six with blue chins.'

'Seemed all right.' And you might have added, in your earlier days, 'They was with a bird.'

'They're *always* with a bird.'

But the bird's disappeared and the blokes are hurling soda siphons around and you head up the stairs and you . . . So the only time you did any actual bouncing was when you had failed: as a bouncer. Bouncing was a mop-up operation made necessary by faulty bouncing. The best bouncers never did any bouncing. Only bad bouncers bounced. It might have sounded complicated, but it wasn't.

. . . In their frilly shirts, their reeking tuxes, Mal and Fat Lol, on staircases, by fire exits, or standing bent over the till at five in the morning when the lights came on full, and at the flick of a switch you went from opulence to poverty – all the lacquer, glamour, sex, privilege, empire, wiped out, in a rush of electricity.

That was also the time of genuine danger. Astonishing, sometimes, the staying power of those you'd excluded and turned away – turned away, pushed away, shoved, shouldered, clipped, slapped, smacked, tripped, kicked, kneed, nutted, loafed. Or just told, 'Sorry, sir.' They'd wait all night – or come back, weeks or months later. You'd escort the palely breakfastless hat-check girl to her Mini and then head on down the mews to your own vehicle through the mist of the Ripper dawn. And he'd be waiting, leaning against the wall by the car, finishing a bottle of milk and weighing it in his hands.

Because some people will not be excluded. Some people will not be turned away . . . Mal bounced here, Mal bounced there; he bounced away for year after year, without serious injury. Until one night. He was leaving early, and there on the steps was the usual shower of chauffeurs and minicabbies, hookers, hustlers, ponces, tricks, twanks, mugs and marks, and, as Mal jovially shouldered his way through, a small shape came close, saying breathily, dry-mouthed, *Hold that, mate* . . . Suddenly Mal was backing off fast in an attempt to get a good look at himself: at the blade in his gut and the blood following the pleats of his soiled white shirt. He thought, What's all this you hear about getting stabbed not hurting? Comes later, doesn't it – the pain? No, mate: it comes now. Like a great papercut to the heart. Mal's belly, his proud, placid belly, was abruptly the scene of hysterical

rearrangements. And he felt the need to speak, before he
fell.

The moment was familiar to him. He'd seen them go
down, his comrades, the tuxed custodians of the bronze
door-knocker and the coach-house lantern. The big schwart-
zer Darius, sliding down a lamppost after he'd stopped a
tyre iron outside Ponsonby's. Or Fat Lol himself, in
Fauntleroy's, crashing from table to table with half a beer
bottle in his crown. They wanted to say something, before
they went. It made you think of Fifties war films. What was
it? 'I've copped it in the back, sir.' Not that the falling
bouncer ever managed to blurt much out: an oath, a vow. It
was the look on their faces, wanting acknowledgement or
respect, because here they were, in a kind of uniform – the
big black bow tie, the little black shoes – and going down in
the line of service. Going down, they wanted it recognized
that they'd earned their salt. Did they want to say – or hear
– the word 'Sir'?

He walked backward until his shoulders crashed into the
windowsill. He landed heavily on his arse: *A!* Fat Lol knelt to
cradle him.

'Here, Lol, I'm holding one,' said Mal. 'Jesus, I'm gone,
mate. I'm gone!'

Fat Lol wanted the name of the man who'd done him.
And so did the police. Mal couldn't help them with their
inquiries. 'Don't know him from Adam,' he insisted,
reckoning he'd never before set eyes on the bloke. But he
had. It came to him eventually, his memory stirred by
hospital food.

Hospital food. Mal would never own up to it, but he loved
hospital food. Not a good sign, that, when you start fancying
your hospital food. You hear the creak of the trolley,
instantaneously suffusing the whole ward with that smell of

warm damp newspaper, and suddenly your mauled gut rips into life like an outboard motor and you're gulping down half a pint of drool. It shows you're getting institutionalized in the worst way. He had no use for the pies and quiches that Sheilagh brought in for him. Either he'd bin them or give the grub to the stiffs on his ward. The old guys – in the furnace of the night they whinnied like pub dogs having nightmares under the low tables . . .

It was as he was kissing his bunched fingertips and congratulating the dinner lady on her most recent triumph that Mal suddenly remembered: remembered the man who'd done him. 'Jesus Christ,' he said to the dinner lady in her plastic pinafore. 'Ridiculous, innit. I mean I never even . . .' Warily, the old dear moved on, leaving Mal frowning and shaking his head (and digging into his meal). It was the fried skin of the fish fingers: in this surface Mal recognized the dark ginger of his assailant's hair. On the night of the stabbing, and on another night, months earlier, *months* . . . It was late, it was cold: Mal on the steps of Fauntleroy's, sealing off the lit doorway like a boulder with his bulk, and the little ginge going, 'Am I hearing you saying that I'm not good enough?'

'I don't know what you're hearing, mate, but what I'm saying is it's members only.'

Calling him 'mate' and not 'sir': this meant that Mal's patience was being sorely tried.

'It's as I'm a working man like.'

'No, mate. I'm a working man too. But I won't be if I let you in. Regulations. This is a clipjoint, mate. What you want to do, come in here and buy some tart a glass of Lucozade for eighty-five quid? Go off home.'

'So you don't like my kind.'

'Yeah, it's your ginger hair, mate. Ginger-haired blokes ain't admitted. Here. It's late. It's cold. Walk away.'

'Am I hearing you saying I'm not good enough?'

'Look fuck off out of it.'

And that was that. Something of the sort happened ten times a night. But this little ginge waits until spring and then comes back and leaves a blade in Mal's gut: 'Hold that, mate.' And now *Mal* was on the Lucozade, and eating fish-fingers off a tray that slid up the bed.

I've copped it in the back, sir . . . From *The Dam Busters*, the film that, as a child, he had so pined to see. Like Jet with *Mortal Kombat*. He thought of another of its lines: 'Nigger's dead, sir.' Delivered awkwardly, tenderly, the man breaking it to the senior officer. Meaning the dog. They had a dog called Nigger. Their little black dog, their unofficial mascot, who dies, was called Nigger. You couldn't do that now. No way. In a film. Call a *dog* Nigger? No way, no day. Times change. Call a *black* dog Nigger? No shape, no form. Be down on you like a . . . Call a dead black dog Nigger in a film? No way José.

4. Burger King

So class and race and gender were supposedly gone (and other things were supposedly going, like age and beauty and even education): all the really automatic ways people had of telling who was better or worse – they were gone. Right-thinkers everywhere were claiming that they were clean of prejudice, that in them the inherited formulations had at last been purged. This they had decided. But for those on the pointed end of the operation – the ignorant, say, or the ugly – it wasn't just a decision. Some of them had no new clothes. Some were still dressed in the uniform of their deficiencies. Some were still wearing the same old shit.

Some would never be admitted.

Mal looked on, and stiffened. The gym master went by, with his bullhorn like a prototype mobile phone, calling the names for the first event. The parents faced the track, and the fantastic interrogation of the low sun, with binoculars, cameras, camcorders, and all their *other* children – little sisters, big brothers, and babies (crying, yawning, dangling a pouched foot). Mal looked on, careful to maintain a distance of at least two parents between himself and Sheilagh, her green boiler suit, her fine, light, russety hair. Between them bobbed other heads of hair work – grey streaks, pageboy, urchin, dyed caramel; and, among the men, various tragedies of disappearance, variously borne, and always the guy with a single strand pasted across his dome, as if one sideburn had thrown a line to the other. Maybe the sun wasn't staring but turning the lights on full, like at Fauntleroy's when dawn came (and you wondered at the value of what you'd been guarding), so everybody could just see for themselves.

Runners in regulation off-white shorts and T-shirts were gathering on the starting line. Mal consulted his programme: a single cyclostyled sheet. Lost in concentration (lips working), he felt a pull on his arm.

'Oi,' he said. For it was Jet. 'Better get out there, mate.'

'This is the fourth form.'

'What are you in then?'

'Seventy metres and two-twenty.'

'. . . So you ain't on for a while. Right. Let's work on your preparation.'

Jet turned away. The styled hair, the gold earring. For a second the backs of his ears gleamed orange and transparent. Now Jet turned again and looked at him with that shy leer in the raised upper lip. Jesus: his teeth were blue. But that was okay. It was just the trace of a lolly he'd managed to get down him, not some new way of deliberately looking horrible. The law of fashion said that every child had to offend its parents aesthetically. Mal had offended his parents aesthetically: the drainpipes and brothelcreepers, the hair like a riptide of black grease. Jet had contrived to offend Mal aesthetically. And Jet's kids, when they came, would face the arduous task of aesthetically offending Jet.

'Okay, let's get your head right. Go through the prep drill. Point One.'

And again the boy turned away. Stood his ground, but turned away. For two academic years running, Jet had come nineteenth in his class of twenty. Mal liked to think that Jet made up for this with his dad-tweaked excellence on the sports field. The gym, the squash court, the pool, the park: training became the whole relationship. Of late, naturally, their sessions had been much reduced. But they still went to the rec on Saturday afternoons, with the stopwatch, the football, the discus, the talc. And Jet seemed less keen these days. And Mal, too, felt differently. Now, seeing Jet bottling a header or tanking a sprint, Mal would draw in breath to scold or embolden him and then silently exhale. And feel nothing but nausea. He no longer had the authority or the will. And then came the blackest hour: Jet dropped from the school football team . . . A distance was opening up between father and son, and how do you close it? How do you do that? Every Saturday lunchtime they sat in the tot-party toy-town of McDonald's, Jet with his Happy Meal (burger, fries, and a plastic doodad worth ten pee), Mal with his Chicken

McNuggets or his Fish McCod. They didn't eat. Like lovers over their last supper in a restaurant – the food not even looked at, let alone touched. Besides, for some time now the very sight of a burger was enough to give Mal's stomach a jolt. It was like firing a car when it was in first gear and the hand brake was on: a forward lurch that took you nowhere. Mal had had an extreme experience with burgers. Burger hell: he'd been there.

'Dad?'

'Yeah?'

'Are you running in the dads' race?'

'Told you. Can't do it, mate. Me back.'

'And your face.'

'Yeah. And me face.'

They watched the races. And, well, how clear do you want it to be, that a boy's life is all races? School is an exam and a competition and a popularity contest: it's racing demon. And you saw how the kids were equipped for it by nature – never mind the interminable trials in the rec (never mind the great bent thumb on the stopwatch): lummoxy lollopers, terrifying achievers, sloths, hares, and everything in between. They began as one body, the racers, one pack; and then as if by natural process they moved apart, some forging ahead, others (while still going forward) dropping back. The longer the race, the bigger the differences. Mal tried to imagine the runners staying in line all the way, and finishing as they had begun. And it wasn't human somehow. It couldn't be imagined, not on this planet.

Jet's first event was called.

'Now remember,' said Mal, all hunkered down. 'Accelerate into the lengthened stride. Back straight, knees high. Cut the air with the stiff palms. Shallow breathing till you breast that tape.'

In the short time it took Jet to reach the starting blocks – and despite the heat and colour of Sheilagh's boiler suit as it established itself at his side – Mal had fully transformed himself into the kind of sports-circuit horrorparent you read about in the magazines. Why? Simple: because he wanted to live his life again, through the boy. His white-knuckled dukes were held at shoulder height; his brow was scrunched up over the bridge of his nose; and his bloodless lips, in a desperate whisper, were saying, 'Ventilate! Work the flow! Loosen up! Loosen up!'

But Jet was not loosening up. He wasn't loosening and limbering the way Mal had taught him (the way TV had taught Mal), jogging on the spot and wiggling his arms in the air and gasping like an iron lung. Jet was just standing there. And as Mal stared pleadingly on, he felt that Jet looked – completely exceptional. He couldn't put his finger on it. Not the tallest, not the lithest. But Jet looked completely exceptional. The starting pistol gave its tinny report. After two seconds Mal slapped a hand over his eyes: *A!*

'Last?' he said, when the noise was over.

'Last,' said Sheilagh, steelily. 'Now you leave that boy be.'

Soon Jet was squirming his way through to them and Sheilagh was saying unlucky and never mind, darling, and all this; and his impulse, really, was to do what Mal's dad would have done to Mal at such loss of face, and put Jet in hospital for a couple of weeks. See how he liked that. But such ways were old and gone, and he had no will, and the impulse passed. Besides, the boy was uneasily casting himself about, and wouldn't meet his eye. Mal now felt that he had to offer something, something quixotic, perverse, childish.

'Listen. This Saturday, down the rec, we're going to work on your pace. We'll get a burger down you, for your strength, and then we're going to work on your pace. And guess what. I'll eat a burger. I'll eat two.'

This was a family joke; and family jokes can go either way, when you're no longer a family.

Sheilagh said, 'Hark at Burger King.'

Jet said, '*Return* of Burger King.'

Burger King was a kind of nickname. Jet was smiling at him sinisterly: teeth still blue.

'I will. I swear. For Jet. Blimey. Oop. Jesus. It's happening. I'm for it now. Here, She. Whoop.'

Eat burgers? He couldn't even *say* burgers.

California. When Joseph Andrews's final face-lift went so badly wrong, and he had to cancel the Vegas thing and shut down his whole West Coast operation, Big Mal decided to stay out in L.A. and give it a go on his own. He shifted his real money to London but kept back a few grand, as his stake. There were offers, schemes, projects. He had made many good friends in the business and entertainment communities. Time to call in a few favours.

And this was how it went: after twenty-three days he was, he believed, on the brink of clinical starvation. People had let him down. He had given up eating, drinking and smoking, in that order. He was seeing things, and hearing them, too. In the motel, at night, strangers who weren't really there moved round him, solicitously. He'd be sitting on a patch of grass somewhere and a bird in the tree would start singing a song. Not a bird's song. A Beatles song. Like 'Try and See It My Way', with all the words. By this stage he was rootling through supermarket dumpsters and discovering that food, so various in its colours and textures, could lose identity and become just one thing. Everywhere he went he was turned away. Even the supermarket Dumpsters were often guarded, in case the trash was tainted, and you ate it, and then sued.

Dawn on the final morning: it was Mal's forty-fifth birthday. He awoke in the driver's seat of the old Subaru – in a cinema parking lot out by the airport somewhere. Sheilagh had sorted a ticket for him from the London end: fourteen hours to go. He regarded the flight home not as a journey, not as a return, not as a defeat, but as a free meal. Peanuts first, he thought. Or Bombay Mix.

When he saw the sign he thought it was just another hallucination. 'Maurie's Birthday Burger' . . . All you had to do was show up with your driver's licence. You could expect a free burger, and a hero's welcome. Maurie's had more than seventy outlets in Greater Los Angeles. And once Mal got going, there didn't seem any good reason to stop. After the thirtieth or thirty-fifth burger, you couldn't really say he was in it for the grub. But he kept going. It was because Maurie was doing what nobody else was doing: Maurie was letting Mal in.

Gastrically things were already not looking too bright when he arrived at LAX and checked in his luggage: a ripped ten-gallon bag containing all he owned. He made it to the gate more or less okay. It was on the plane that everything started getting out of hand. It appeared that Maurie, that week, had been sold a dodgy batch of meat. Whatever the facts of the matter, Mal felt, as he reached for his seat belt, that he was buckling in twenty pounds of mad cow.

Five hours later, over the Baffin Bay: serious flight-deck discussion of an emergency landing in Disko, Greenland, as Mal continued to reel around the aircraft patiently devastating one toilet after another. They even let him loose on

Business. Then, finally, as they cruised in over County Cork, and the passengers were being poked awake, and some of them, stretching and scratching, were slipping away with their wash-bags ... well, it seemed to Mal (shrunken, mythically pale, and growing into his seat like a toadstool) that the only possibility was mass ejection. Three hundred parachutes, like three hundred burger buns, streaming down over the Welsh valleys, and the plane heading on, grand and blind.

At the airport he asked She to marry him. He was trembling. Winter was coming and he was afraid of it. He wanted to be safe.

'Jet!' cried Mal. He could hear the kid fumbling around outside.

'Dad!'

'In here!'

Mal was in the clubhouse toilet, alone, cooling his brow against the mirror and leaning on the smudged sink.

'You all right?'

'Yeah, mate. It passed.'

'Does it hurt?' said Jet, meaning his wound.

'Nah, mate. Bit of discomfort.'

'How'd you get it? Who did it?'

He straightened up. 'Son?' he began – for he felt he owed Jet an explanation, a testament, a valediction. The fall rays were staring through the thick wrinkled glass. 'Son? Listen to me.' His voice echoed, godlike, in the Lucozade light. 'Every now and again you're going to get into one. You go into one and it's not going to go your way. Sometimes you can see one coming and sometimes you can't. And some you can *never* see coming. So you just take what comes. Okay?'

'You and Fat Lol.'

'Me and Fat Lol. Should see the state of *him*.'

The boy wagged his haircut towards the door.

Mal said, 'Now what?'

'Two-twenty.'

'Oi. Listen. Jet. I'll run if you will. Okay? I'll run the dads' race. And give it me all. If you will. Deal?'

Jet nodded. Mal looked down at his hair: seemed like they'd gone round the edge of it with a clipper or whatever, leaving a shaved track two or three inches wide . . . As Mal followed him outside he realized something. Jet on the starting line with all the others: he had looked completely exceptional. Not the tallest. Not the lithest. What, then? He was the whitest. He was just the whitest.

Now that prejudice was gone everyone could relax and concentrate on money.

Which was fine if you had some.

5. *Rhyming Slang*

To be frank, Fat Lol couldn't believe that Mal was still interested.

'You?' he said. 'You? Big Mal: minder to the superstars?'

Yeah, that was it. Big Mal: megaminder. Mal said, 'How *you* doing then?'

'Me? I'm onna dole, mate. I'm onna street. So I put meself about. But you?'

'That's all kind of dried up. Joseph Andrews and that. I'm basically short. Temporarily. Hopefully. So with all the changes going down I need any extra I can get.'

Mal could not speak altogether freely. With the two men, round the table, sat Fat Lol's wife, Yvonne, and their six-year-old son, little Vic. They were having lunch in Del's Caff on Paradise Street in the East End – and it was like another world. Mal and Fat Lol were born in the same house in the same week; but Mal had come on, and Fat Lol hadn't. Mal had evolved. There he sat, in his shell suit, with his dark glasses – a modern person. *His* son had a modern name: Jet. Mal could call his Asian babe on his mobile phone. And he had left home. Which you didn't do. And there was Fat Lol in his Sloppy Joe, his sloppy jeans, and his old suedes, with his wife looking like a bank robber and his son flinching when either parent made a move for the vinegar or the brown sauce. Fat Lol was still in the muscle business (this and that). He had felt the tug of no other calling. He had stayed with it, like a brand loyalty.

'So,' said Fat Lol, 'what you're saying, if there's something going – this and that – you'd be on for a bit of it.'

'Exactly.'

'On a part-time basis. Nights.'

'Yeah.'

Fat Lol: he provided dramatic proof of the proposition that you are what you eat. Fat Lol was what he ate. More than this, Fat Lol was what he was eating. And he was eating, for his lunch, an English breakfast – Del's All Day Special at £3.25. His mouth was a strip of undercooked bacon, his eyes a mush of egg yolk and tinned tomatoes. His nose was like the end of a lightly grilled pork sausage – then the baked beans of his complexion, the furry mushrooms of his ears. Paradise Street right down to his bum crack – that was Fat Lol. A loaf of fried bread on legs. Mal considered the boy: silent, cautious, eyeing the fruit machine with cunning and patience.

Yvonne said, 'So you're having a bit of bother making ends meet. Since you went off with that Lucozade.'

'No unpleasantness, please, Yv,' said Mal, aghast. They didn't see each other so often now, but for many years Yv and She had been best mates. And Yv was always sharp, like her name, like her face. 'She ain't a Lucozade anyway. Come on, Yv. In this day and age?'

Yvonne went on eating, busily, with her head down. Last mouthful. There.

'She ain't a Lucozade anyway.' People thought that Lucozade was rhyming slang for *spade*. But Mal knew that spades weren't called Lucozades because spade rhymed with Lucozade. Spades were called Lucozades because spades *drank* Lucozade. Anyway, Linzi was from Bombay and she drank gin. 'She's of Indian extraction but she was born right here on Paradise Street.'

'Same difference,' said Yvonne.

'Shut it,' said Fat Lol.

When closed, as now, *it* – Yv's mouth – looked like a copper coin stuck in a slot. No, there wasn't any slot: just the nicked rim of the penny jamming it. Dear oh dear, thought Mal: the state of her boat. Boat was rhyming slang for face (via *boat race*). It had never struck him as appropriate or evocative until now. Her whole head like a prow, a tight corner, a hairpin bend.

'Linzi – when she signs her name,' said Yvonne. 'Does she do a little circle over the last "i"?'

Mal considered. 'Yeah,' he said.

'Thought so. Just like any other little English slag. Does she do the same with "Pakki"?'

'Shut it,' said Fat Lol.

Later, in the Queen Mum, Fat Lol said, 'What you doing tonight?'

'Not a lot.'

'There's some work on if you fancy it.'

'Yeah?'

'Clamping.'

'Clamping?'

'Yeah,' said Fat Lol. 'Onna clamps.'

Yv had a been-around face, and so did She. She's boat, as he remembered it, because he couldn't look at it, was trusting, gentle, yokelish, under its duster of shallow red hair. Soon Mal would be obliged to look at that face, and look into it, and face that face with his.

But first Jet in the two-twenty!

'Stick to the game plan,' Mal was telling him. 'Remember. Run it like it's three seventy-metre sprints. One after the other.'

Jet leered up at him. What Mal's game plan came down to, plainly enough, was that Jet should run flat out every step of the way.

'Go for it, son. Just do it.'

The raised starting pistol, the ragged lunge from the blocks . . . By the halfway point Jet had pelted himself into a narrow lead. 'Now you dig deep,' Mal murmured, on the terrace, with She's shape at his side. 'Now it's down to your desire. Dig, mate, *dig*. Dig! Dig! Dig!' As Jet came flailing on to the home straight – and as, one by one, all the other runners shot past him – Mal's cold right hand was slowly seeking his brow. But then Jet seemed to topple forward. It was as if the level track had suddenly been tipped at an angle, and Jet wasn't running but falling. He passed one runner, and another . . .

When Mal went over Jet was still lying face down in the

rusty cinders. Mal knelt, saying, 'Fourth. Talk about a recovery. Great effort, mate. It was your character got you through that. It was your heart. I saw your heart out there. I saw your heart.'

Sheilagh was beyond them, waiting. Mal helped Jet to his feet and slipped him a quid for a tin of drink. The running track was bounded by a low fence; further off lay a field or whatever, with a mob of trees and bushes in the middle of it. There She was heading, Mal coming up behind her, head bent. As he stepped over the fence he almost blacked out with culture shock: the running track was a running track but this was *the country* . . .

He came up to her wiggling a finger in the air. 'Look. Sounds stupid,' he said. 'But you go behind that bush and I'll call you.'

'Call me?'

'On your mobile.'

'Mal!'

Turning and bending, he poked out her number. And he began.

'Sheilagh? Mal. Right. You know that woman we went to said I had a problem communicating? Well okay. Maybe she was on to something. But here goes. Since I left you and little Jet I . . . It's like I got gangrene or something. It's all right for about ten minutes if I'm reading the paper or watching the golf. You know. Distracted. Or knocking a ball about with Val and Rodge.' Val and Rodge were, by some distance, the most elderly couple that Mal and Sheilagh played mixed doubles with at Kentish Town Sports. 'Then it ain't so bad. For ten minutes.' By now Mal had both his arms round his head, like a mouth-organist. Because he was talking into his phone and crying into his sleeve. 'I lost something and I never knew I had it. Me peace of mind. It's like I know how you . . . how women feel. When you're upset, you're not just pissed off. You feel ill. Sick. It goes inside. I feel like a woman. Take me back, She. Do it. I swear I –'

He heard static and felt her hand on his shoulder. They hugged: *A!*

'Christ, Mal, who messed with your face?'

'Ridiculous, innit. I mean some people you just wouldn't believe.'

And she breathed out, frowning, and started straightening his collar and brushing away its scurf with the back of her hand.

6. Motor Show

'Park inna Inn onna Park,' said Fat Lol.

'We ain't doing it in there, are we?'

'Don't talk fucking stupid. Pick up me van.'

Access to the innards of the Inn on the Park having been eased by Fat Lol's acquaintance with – and remuneration of – one of the hotel's garage attendants, the two men drove boldly down the ramp in Mal's C-reg. BM. They then hoisted themselves into Fat Lol's Vauxhall Rascal and proceeded east through Mayfair and Soho. Mal kept peering in the back. The clamps lay there, heavily jumbled, like land mines from an old war.

'They don't look like normal clamps. Too big.'

'Early model. Before they introduced the more compact one.'

'Bet they weigh.'

'They ain't light,' conceded Fat Lol.

'How's it go again?'

Mal had to say that the scheme made pretty good sense to him. Because it relied on turnover. Mass clamping: that was the order of the day. Clearly (or so Fat Lol argued), there wasn't a lot of sense in tooling round the West End doing the odd Cortina on a double yellow line. Clamp a car, and you got seventy quid for declamping it. What you needed was cars in bulk. And where did you find cars in bulk? In a National Car Park.

But hang about: 'How can you clamp a car in a National Car Park?'

'If they not in they bay. The marked area.'

'Bit harsh innit mate?'

'It's legal,' said Fat Lol indignantly. 'You can clamp them even in an N.C.P. If they park bad.'

'Bet they ain't too pleased about it.'

'No, they ain't overly chuffed.'

Fat Lol handed Mal a sample windscreen sticker. 'Warning This Vehicle Is Illegally Parked. Do Not Attempt to Move It. For Prompt Assistance . . .' On the side window of his Rascal additional stickers indicated that Fat Lol welcomed all major credit cards.

'Give them a while and they cool off by the time you get there. Just want to get home. What's it going to be anyway? Some little slag from Luton bring his wife in for a night onna town.'

They decided to kick off with a medium-rise just north of Leicester Square. No gatekeeper, no bouncer to deny them entry. The automatic arm of the barrier rose like a salute. On the second floor: 'Bingo,' said Fat Lol. Twenty prime vehicles packed tight at one end, crouching, waiting, gleaming in the dangerous light of car parks.

Out they dropped. 'Fucking *Motor* Show,' said Fat Lol. And it was true: the chrome heraldry, the galvannealed paintwork. They hesitated as a family saloon swung down from Level 3.

'Let's do it.'

Disappointingly, only four vehicles were adjudged by Fat Lol to have outstepped their prescribed boundaries. But he soon saw another way.

'Okay. Let's do them if they're *touching* the white lines.'

'In tennis,' said Mal moderately, 'the white lines count in.'

'Well in clamping,' said Fat Lol, in a tight voice, bending low, 'the white lines count *out*.'

It was warm and heavy work. These ancient gadgets, the clamps – they were like fucking steamrollers. You had to free them from the van and from each other and hump them into position. Next you got down there – *A!* – and worked the pipe wrench on the snap ratchet. Then: *thwock*. There was the clamp with its jaw fast on the car's wheel. One bit was quite satisfying: spreading the gummy white sticker all over the windscreen.

Fat Lol was down there doing a K-reg. Jag when Mal said, 'Oi. I can see you bum crack.'

'Bend down.' Fat Lol stood up. 'I can see yourn.'

'You said dress casual.'

'With a car like this,' Fat Lol announced huskily, '– it tears you apart. I mean, with a car like this, you don't want to clamp it.'

'You want to nick it.'

'Nah. To clamp a motor such as this, it's . . .'

'Sacrilege.'

'Yeah. It's fucking *sacrilege* to mess with a motor such as this.'

Mal heard it first. Like something detaching itself from

the siren song of Leicester Square, where the old sounds of
various thrashed and envassalled machines contended with
the sound of the new, its pings, pips, peeps, beeps, bleeps,
tweets and squawks and yawps ... Big Mal heard it first,
and paused there, down on one knee with his pipe wrench.
A concentrated body of purposeful human conversation was
moving towards them, the sopranos and contraltos of the
women, the sterling trebles and barrelly baritones of the
men, coming up round the corner now, like a ballroom, like
civilization, uniforms of tuxedo and then streaks and plumes
of turquoise, emerald, taffeta, dimity.

'Lol mate,' said Mal.

Fat Lol was a couple of cars further in, doing a Range
Rover and tightly swearing to himself.

'Lol!'

You know what it was like? A revolution in reverse –
that's what it was like. Two bum-crack cowboys scragged
and cudgelled by the quality. Jesus: strung up by the upper
classes. What seemed most amazing, looking back, was how
totally they folded, the two big lads, how their bottom, their
legitimacy, just evaporated on them there and then. Fat Lol
managed to get to his feet and splutter something about
these vehicles being parked illegally. Or parked improperly.
Or plain parked bad. And that was the extent of their
resistance. Big Mal and Fat Lol, those bottle-ripped veterans
of ruck and maul, dispensing the leather in cross alleys and
on walkways, on dance-hall staircases, elbowing their way
out of bowling alleys and snooker-hall toilets, crouching and
panting by dully shining exit doors – they just rolled over.
We didn't want to know ... Mal tried to wriggle in under the
Lotus he was doing but they were on him like the SAS. The
first blow he took from the pipe wrench knocked him spark-
out. Soon afterwards he awoke and, leaning on an elbow in

a pool of blood and oil, watched Fat Lol being slowly hauled by the hair from car to car, with the ladies queuing and jockeying to give him another kick up the arse, as best they could, in their gowns. The ladies! The language! Then they were on Mal again, and he stopped another one from the pipe wrench. I've copped it in the back, sir. Nigger's dead, sir ... No rest for the wicked. And ain't that the fucking truth. They hoisted Mal upright, giving his mouth a nice smack on the headlight frame, and had him slewing from bonnet to bonnet, prising at the windscreen stickers with his cold white fingers. This vehicle is illegally. For prompt assistance. All major ... And after a last round of kicks and taunts their cars were chirruping and wincing and whirring into life; they were gone, leaving Fat Lol and Big Mal groping towards each other through the fumes and echoes and the heap of cheap clamps, gasping, dripping, jetsam of the machine age.

7. Sad Sprinter

'Operagoers.'

Sheilagh said, 'Operagoers?'

'Operagoers. Okay, it was a bit of a liberty, me and Fat Lol. You could argue we was out of order ...'

'You sure it was operagoers?'

'Yeah. I thought it might have been a première crowd. Been to a Royal Première or something.' Mal and Linzi had recently attended a Royal Première, at considerable expense. And he thought it must have been decades since he had been with a rougher crew: fifteen hundred trogs in dinner jackets, plus their molls. 'No, they left programmes. The Coliseum. They ain't nice, you know, She,' he cautioned her. Sheilagh had a weakness for films in which the aristocracy played cute. 'The contempt. They were like *vicious*.'

'I've been to the Coliseum. They do it in English. It's better because you can tell what's going on.'

Mal nodded longsufferingly.

'You can follow the story.'

He nodded a second time.

'You doing the dads' race?'

'Well I got to now.'

'With your face in that state? You're no good on your own, Mal. You're no good on your own.'

Mal turned away. The shrubs, the falling leaves – the trees: what *kind* were they? Even in California . . . Even in California all he knew of nature was the mild reek of rest stops when he pulled over, in his chauffeur's cap, for leaks between cities (a can made of nature and butts and book-matches), or lagoon-style restaurants where mobsters ate lobsters; one year She came out with little Jet for a whole term (not a success) and Mal learned that American schools regarded tomato ketchup as a vegetable. And throughout his life there had been symbols, like fruit machines and hospital fruit salads and the plastic fruit on his mother's hat, forty years ago, at *his* Sports Day. And his dad's curt haircut and Sunday best. Say what you like about forty years ago. Say what you like about his parents, and everyone else's, then, but the main thing about them was that they were married, and looked it, and dressed it, and meant it.

She said, 'If you come back – don't do it if you don't mean it.'

'No way,' he said. 'No way, no day. No shape, no form . . .'

With a nod she started off, and Mal followed. Mal followed, watching the rhythmic but asymmetrical re-arrangements of her big womanly backside, where all her strength and virtue seemed to live, her character, her fathom. And he could see it all. Coming through the door for the bear hug with Jet, and then the hug of Momma Bear and Poppa Bear. The deep-breathing assessment of all he had left behind. And the smile coagulating on his face. Knowing that in ten minutes, twenty, two hours, twenty-four, he would be back out the door with Jet's arms round his knees, his ankles, like a sliding tackle, and She behind him somewhere, flushed, tousled, in a light sweat of readiness to continue with the next fuck or fight, to continue, to continue. And Mal'd be out the door, across the street at Linzi's, watching *Asian Babes* and freeing his mind of all thoughts about the future . . . As he stepped over the fence he looked towards the car park and – whoops – there she was, Linzi, his Asian babe, perched on the low boot of her MG Midget. Sheilagh paused. Linzi on her car boot, She in her boiler suit. Boots and boilers. Where was transformation? If Linzi wanted new breasts, a new bum – if she wanted to climb into a catsuit made out of a teenager – then it was absolutely A-okay with Mal.

'Dad?'

'Jet mate.'

'They're ready.'

Mal kicked off his tasselled loafers and started limbering up: *A!* He was giving Jet his jacket to hold when his mobile rang.

'Lol! Been trying you all day, mate. Some Arab answered.'

Fat Lol said he'd had to flog it: his mobile.
'How come?'
His van got clamped!
'Tell me about it. They did me BM!'
You and all!
'Yeah. Look, can't talk, boy. Got a race to run.'
Fat Lol said he was going to do something tonight.
'Yeah?'
Onna car alarms.
'Yeah?'
'Dad? They're waiting. Boost it.'
'I'm on it, mate. Bye, son.'
'And don't fuck up,' said Jet.
'When do I ever?'
'You're a crap sprinter, Dad.'
'You what?'
'You're a *sad* sprinter.'
'Oh yeah? Watch this.'

The dads were in a rank on the starting line: Bern, Nusrat, Fardous, Someth, Adrian, Mikio, Paratosh and the rest of them, no great differences in age but all at various stages along the track, waistlines, hairlines, worldlines, with various c.v.'s of separation, contentment, estrangement, some of *their* dads dead, some of their mums still living. Mal joined them. This was the dads' race. But dads are always racing, against each other, against themselves. That's what dads do.

It was the gunshot that made the herd stampede. Instantly Mal felt about nineteen things go at once. All the links and joins – hip, knee, ankle, spine – plus an urgent liquefaction on the side of his face. After five stumbling bounds the pain barrier was on him and wouldn't get out of the way. But the big man raced on, as you've got to do. The dads raced on, with heavy ardour, and thundering, their feet stockinged or gym-shoed but all in the wooden clogs of their years. Their heads bent back, their chests outthrust, they gasped and slavered for the turn in the track and the post at the end of the straight.

New Yorker, 1996

Let Me Count the Times

Vernon made love to his wife three and a half times a week, and this was all right.

For some reason, making love always averaged out that way. Normally – though by no means invariably – they made love every second night. On the other hand Vernon had been known to make love to his wife seven nights running; for the next seven nights they would not make love – or perhaps they would once, in which case they would make love the following week only twice but four times the week after that – or perhaps only three times, in which case they would make love four times the next week but only twice the week after that – or perhaps only once. And so on. Vernon didn't know why, but making love always averaged out that way; it seemed invariable. Occasionally – and was it any wonder? – Vernon found himself wishing that the week contained only six days, or as many as eight, to render these calculations (which were always blandly corroborative in spirit) easier to deal with.

It was, without exception, Vernon himself who initiated their conjugal acts. His wife responded every time with the same bashful alacrity. Oral foreplay was by no means unknown between them. On average – and again it always averaged out like this, and again Vernon was always the unsmiling ringmaster – fellatio was performed by Vernon's wife every third coupling, or 60.8333 times a year, or 1.1698717 times a week. Vernon performed cunnilingus rather less often: every fourth coupling, on average, or 45.625 times a year, or .8774038 times a week. It would also be a mistake to think that this was the extent of their variations. Vernon sodomized his wife twice a year, for instance – on his birthday, which seemed fair enough, but also, ironically (or so *he* thought), on hers. He put it down to the expensive nights out they always had on these occasions, and more particularly to the effects of champagne. Vernon always felt desperately ashamed afterwards, and would be a limp spectre of embarrassment and remorse at breakfast the following day. Vernon's wife never said anything about it, which was something. If she ever did, Vernon would probably have stopped doing it. But she never did. The same sort of thing happened when Vernon ejaculated in his wife's mouth, which on average he did 1.2 times a year. At this point they had been married for ten years. That was convenient. What would it be like when they had been married for eleven years – or thirteen! Once, and only once, Vernon had been about to ejaculate in his wife's mouth when suddenly he had got a better idea: he ejaculated all over her face instead. She didn't say anything about that either, thank God. Why he had thought it a better idea he would never know. He didn't think it was a better idea *now*. It distressed him greatly to reflect that his rare acts of abandonment should expose a desire to humble and degrade the loved one. And she *was* the loved one. Still, he had only done it once. Vernon ejaculated all over his wife's face .001923 times a week. That wasn't very often to ejaculate all over your wife's face, now was it?

Vernon was a businessman. His office contained several

electronic calculators. Vernon would often run his marital frequencies through these swift, efficient, and impeccably discreet machines. They always responded brightly with the same answer, as if to say, 'Yes, Vernon, that's how often you do it,' or 'No, Vernon, you don't do it any more often than that.' Vernon would spend whole lunch-hours crooked over the calculator. And yet he knew that all these figures were in a sense approximate. Oh, Vernon knew, Vernon knew. Then one day a powerful white computer was delivered to the accounts department. Vernon saw at once that a long-nursed dream might now take flesh: leap years. 'Ah, Alice. I don't want to be disturbed, do you hear?' he told the cleaning lady sternly when he let himself into the office that night. 'I've got some very important calculations to do in the accounts department.' Just after midnight Vernon's hot red eyes stared up wildly from the display screen, where his entire sex life lay tabulated in recurring prisms of threes and sixes, in endless series, like mirrors placed face to face.

Vernon's wife was the only woman Vernon had ever known. He loved her and he liked making love to her quite a lot; certainly he had never craved any other outlet. When Vernon made love to his wife he thought only of her pleasure and her beauty: the infrequent but highly flattering noises she made through her evenly parted teeth, the divine plasticity of her limbs, the fever, the delirium, and the safety of the moment. The sense of peace that followed had only a little to do with the high probability that tomorrow would be a night off. Even Vernon's dreams were monogamous: the women who strode those slipped but essentially quotidian landscapes were mere icons of the self-sufficient female kingdom, nurses, nuns, bus-conductresses, parking wardens, policewomen. Only every now and then, once a week, say, or less, or not calculably, he saw things that made him suspect that life might have room for more inside – a luminous ribbon dappling the undercurve of a bridge, certain cloudscapes, intent figures hurrying through changing light.

All this, of course, was before Vernon's business trip.

It was not a particularly important business trip: Vernon's firm was not a particularly important firm. His wife packed his smallest suitcase and drove him to the station. On the way she observed that they had not spent a night apart for over four years – when she had gone to stay with her mother after that operation of hers. Vernon nodded in surprised agreement, making a few brisk calculations in his head. He kissed her goodbye with some passion. In the restaurant car he had a gin and tonic. He had another gin and tonic. As the train approached the thickening city Vernon felt a curious lightness play through his body. He thought of himself as a young man, alone. The city would be full of cabs, stray people, shadows, women, things happening.

Vernon got to his hotel at eight o'clock. The receptionist confirmed his reservation and gave him his key. Vernon rode the elevator to his room. He washed and changed, selecting, after some deliberation, the more sober of the two ties his wife had packed. He went to the bar and ordered a gin and tonic. The cocktail waitress brought it to him at a table. The bar was scattered with city people: men, women who probably did things with men fairly often, young couples secretively chuckling. Directly opposite Vernon sat a formidable lady with a fur, a hat, and a cigarette holder. She glanced at Vernon twice or perhaps three times. Vernon couldn't be sure.

He dined in the hotel restaurant. With his meal he

enjoyed half a bottle of good red wine. Over coffee Vernon toyed with the idea of going back to the bar for a crème de menthe – or a champagne cocktail. He felt hot; his scalp hummed; two hysterical flies looped round his head. He rode back to his room, with a view to freshening up. Slowly, before the mirror, he removed all his clothes. His pale body was inflamed with the tranquil glow of fever. He felt deliciously raw, tingling to his touch. What's happening to me? he wondered. Then, with relief, with shame, with rapture, he keeled backwards on to the bed and did something he hadn't done for over ten years.

Vernon did it three more times that night and twice again in the morning.

Four appointments spaced out the following day. Vernon's mission was to pick the right pocket calculator for daily use by all members of his firm. Between each demonstration – the Moebius strip of figures, the repeated wink of the decimal point – Vernon took cabs back to the hotel and did it again each time. 'As fast as you can, driver,' he found himself saying. That night he had a light supper sent up to his room. He did it five more times – or was it six? He could no longer be absolutely sure. But he was sure he did it three more times the next morning, once before breakfast and twice after. He took the train back at noon, having done it an incredible 18 times in 36 hours: that was – what? – 84 times a week, or 4,368 times a year. Or perhaps he had done it 19 times. Vernon was exhausted, yet in a sense he had never felt stronger. And here was the train giving him an erection all the same, whether he liked it or not.

'How was it?' asked his wife at the station.

'Tiring. But successful,' admitted Vernon.

'Yes, you do look a bit whacked. We'd better get you home and tuck you up in bed for a while.'

Vernon's red eyes blinked. He could hardly believe his luck.

Shortly afterwards Vernon was to look back with amused disbelief at his own faintheartedness during those trailblazing few days. Only in bed, for instance! Now, in his total recklessness and elation, Vernon did it everywhere. He hauled himself roughly on to the bedroom floor and did it there. He did it under the impassive gaze of the bathroom's porcelain and steel. With scandalized laughter he dragged himself out protesting to the garden toolshed and did it there. He did it lying on the kitchen table. For a while he took to doing it in the open air, in windy parks, behind hoardings in the town, on churned fields; it made his knees tremble. He did it in corridorless trains. He would rent rooms in cheap hotels for an hour, for half an hour, for ten minutes (how the receptionists stared). He thought of renting a little love-nest somewhere. Confusedly and very briefly he considered running away with himself. He started doing it at work, cautiously at first, then with nihilistic abandon, as if discovery was the very thing he secretly craved. Once, giggling coquettishly before and afterwards (the danger, the danger), he did it while dictating a long and tremulous letter to the secretary he shared with two other senior managers. After this he came to his senses somewhat and resolved to confine his activities to the home.

'How long will you be, dear?' he would call over his shoulder as his wife opened the front door with her shopping-bags in her hands. An hour? Fine. Just a couple of minutes? Even better! He took to lingering sinuously in bed

while his wife made their morning tea, deliciously sand-
wiched by the moist uxoriousness of the sheets. On his
nights off from love-making (and these were invariable now:
every other night, every other night) Vernon nearly always
managed one while his wife, in the bathroom next door,
calmly readied herself for sleep. She nearly caught him at it
on several occasions. He found that especially exciting. At
this point Vernon was still trying hectically to keep count; it
was all there somewhere, gurgling away in the memory
banks of the computer in the accounts department. He was
averaging 3.4 times a day, or 23.8 times a week, or an
insane 1,241 times a year. And his wife never suspected a
thing.

Until now, Vernon's 'sessions' (as he thought of them) had
always been mentally structured round his wife, the only
woman he had ever known – her beauty, the flattering
noises she made, the fever, the safety. His mind came up
with various elaborations, naturally. A typical 'session'
would start with her undressing at night. She would lean out
of her heavy brassière and submissively debark the tender
checks of her panties. She would give a little gasp, half
pleasure, half fear (how do you figure a woman?), as naked
Vernon, obviously in sparkling form, emerged impressively
from the shadows. He would mount her swiftly, perhaps
even rather brutally. Her hands mimed their defencelessness
as the great muscles rippled and plunged along Vernon's
powerful back. 'You're too big for me,' he would have her
say to him sometimes, or 'That hurts, but I like it.' Climax
would usually be synchronized with his wife's howled
request for the sort of thing Vernon seldom did to her in real
life. But Vernon never did the things for which she yearned,

oh no. He usually just ejaculated all over her face. She loved that as well of course (the bitch), to Vernon's transient disgust.

And then the strangers came.

One summer evening Vernon returned early from the office. The car was gone: as Vernon had shrewdly anticipated, his wife was off on her weekly run to the supermarket. Hurrying into the house, he made straight for the bedroom. He lay down and lowered his trousers – and then with a sensuous moan tugged them off altogether. Things started well, with a compelling preamble that had become increasingly popular in recent weeks. Naked, primed, Vernon stood on the bedroom landing. Already he could hear his wife's preparatory murmurs of shy arousal. Vernon stepped forward to swing open the door, intending to stand there menacingly for a few seconds, his restless legs planted well apart. He swung open the door and stared. At what? At his wife sweatily grappling with a huge bronzed gypsy, who turned incuriously towards Vernon and then back again to the hysteria of volition splayed out on the bed before him. Vernon ejaculated immediately. His wife returned home within a few minutes. She kissed him on the forehead. He felt very strange.

The next time he tried, he swung open the door to find his wife upside down over the headboard, doing scarcely credible things to a hairy-shouldered Turk. The time after that, she had her elbows hooked round the back of her kneecaps as a fifteen-stone Chinaman feasted at his leisure on her sobs. The time after that, two silent, glistening negroes were doing what the hell they liked with her. The two negroes, in particular, wouldn't go away; they were quite frequently joined by the Turk, moreover. Sometimes they would even let Vernon and his wife get started before they all came thundering in on them. And did Vernon's wife mind any of this? Mind? She liked it. Like it? She *loved* it! And so did Vernon, apparently. At the office Vernon coldly searched his brain for a single neutrino of genuine desire that his wife should do these things with these people. The very idea made him shout with revulsion. Yet, one way or another, he didn't mind it really, did he? One way or another, he liked it. He loved it. But he was determined to put an end to it.

His whole approach changed. 'Right, my girl,' he muttered to himself, 'two can play at that game.' To begin with, Vernon had 'affairs' with all his wife's friends. The longest and perhaps the most detailed was with Vera, his wife's old school chum. He sported with her bridge-partners, her co-workers in the Charity. He fooled around with all her eligible relatives – her younger sister, that nice little niece of hers. One mad morning Vernon even mounted her hated mother. 'No, Vernon, what about . . . ?' they would all whisper fearfully. But Vernon just shoved them on to the bed, twisting off his belt with an imperious snap. All the women out there on the edges of his wife's world – one by one, Vernon had the lot.

Meanwhile, Vernon's erotic dealings with his wife herself had continued much as before. Perhaps they had even profited in poignancy and gentleness from the pounding rumours of Vernon's nether life. With this latest development, however, Vernon was not slow to mark a new dimension, a disfavoured presence, in their bed. Oh, they still made love all right; but now there were two vital differences. Their acts of sex were no longer hermetic; the safety and the peace had gone: no longer did Vernon attempt to apply any brake to the chariot of his thoughts. Secondly – and perhaps even more crucially – their love-making was, without a doubt, *less frequent*. Six and a half

times a fortnight, three times a week, five times a fortnight
. . . : they were definitely losing ground. At first Vernon's
mind was a chaos of backlogs, shortfalls, restructured
schedules, recuperation schemes. Later he grew far more
detached about the whole business. Who said he had to do it
three and a half times a week? Who said that this was all
right? After ten nights of chaste sleep (his record up till now)
Vernon watched his wife turn sadly on her side after her
diffident goodnight. He waited several minutes, propped up
on an elbow, glazedly eternalized in the potent moment.
Then he leaned forward and coldly kissed her neck, and
smiled as he felt her body's axis turn. He went on smiling.
He knew where the real action was.

For Vernon was now perfectly well aware that any woman
was his for the taking, any woman at all, at a nod, at a
shrug, at a single convulsive snap of his peremptory fingers.
He systematically serviced every woman who caught his eye
in the street, had his way with them, and tossed them aside
without a second thought. All the models in his wife's
fashion magazines – they all trooped through his bedroom,
too, in their turn. Over the course of several months he
worked his way through all the established television
actresses. An equivalent period took care of the major stars
of the Hollywood screen. (Vernon bought a big glossy book
to help him with this project. For his money, the girls of the
Golden Age were the most daring and athletic lovers:
Monroe, Russell, West, Dietrich, Dors, Ekberg. Frankly, you
could keep your Welches, your Dunaways, your Fondas,
your Keatons.) By now the roll-call of names was astounding, Vernon's prowess with them epic, unsurpassable. All the

girls were saying that he was easily the best lover they had ever had.

One afternoon he gingerly peered into the pornographic magazines that blazed from the shelves of a remote newsagent. He made a mental note of the faces and figures, and the girls were duly accorded brief membership of Vernon's thronging harem. But he was shocked; he didn't mind admitting it: why should pretty young girls take their clothes off for money like that – like *that*? Why should men want to buy pictures of them doing it? Distressed and not a little confused, Vernon conducted the first great purge of his clamorous rumpus rooms. That night he paced through the shimmering corridors and becalmed anterooms dusting his palms and looking sternly this way and that. Some girls wept openly at the loss of their friends; others smiled up at him with furtive triumph. But he stalked on, slamming the heavy doors behind him.

Vernon now looked for solace in the pages of great literature. Quality, he told himself, was what he was after – quality, quality. Here was where the high-class girls hung out. Using the fiction and poetry shelves in the depleted local library, Vernon got down to work. After quick flings with Emily, Griselda, and Criseyde, and a strapping weekend with the Good Wife of Bath, Vernon cruised straight on to Shakespeare and the delightfully wide-eyed starlets of the romantic comedies. He romped giggling with Viola over the Illyrian hills, slept in a glade in Arden with the willowy Rosalind, bathed nude with Miranda in a turquoise lagoon. In a single disdainful morning he splashed his way through all four of the tragic heroines: cold Cordelia (this was a bit of a frost, actually), bitter-sweet Ophelia (again rather constricted, though he quite liked her dirty talk), the snake-eyed Lady M. (Vernon had had to watch

85

himself there) and, best of all, that sizzling sorceress Desdemona (Othello had *her* number all right. She *stank* of sex). Following some arduous, unhygienic yet relatively brief dalliance with Restoration drama, Vernon soldiered on through the prudent matrons of the Great Tradition. As a rule, the more sedate and respectable the girls, the nastier and more complicated were the things Vernon found himself wanting to do to them (with lapsed hussies like Maria Bertram, Becky Sharp, or Lady Dedlock, Vernon was in, out, and away, darting half-dressed over the rooftops). Pamela had her points, but Clarissa was the one who turned out to be the true cot-artist of the oeuvre; Sophia Western was good fun all right, but the pious Amelia it was who yodelled for the humbling high points in Vernon's sweltering repertoire. Again he had no very serious complaints about his one-night stands with the likes of Elizabeth Bennett and Dorothea Brooke; it was adult, sanitary stuff, based on a clear understanding of his desires and his needs; they knew that such men will take what they want; they knew that they would wake the next morning and Vernon would be gone. Give him a Fanny Price, though, or better, much better, a Little Nell, and Vernon would march into the bedroom rolling up his sleeves; and Nell and Fan would soon be ruing the day they'd ever been born. Did they mind the horrible things he did to them? Mind? When he prepared to leave the next morning, solemnly buckling his belt before the tall window – how they howled!

The possibilities seemed endless. Other literatures dozed expectantly in their dormitories. The sleeping lion of Tolstoy – Anna, Natasha, Masha, and the rest. American fiction – those girls would show even Vernon a trick or two. The sneaky Gauls – Vernon had a hunch that he and Madame Bovary, for instance, were going to get along just fine . . .

One puzzled weekend, however, Vernon encountered the writings of D. H. Lawrence. Snapping *The Rainbow* shut on Sunday night, Vernon realized at once that this particular avenue of possibility – sprawling as it was, with its intricate trees and their beautiful diseases, and that distant prospect where sandy mountains loomed – had come to an abrupt and unanswerable end. He never knew women behaved like *that* ... Vernon felt obscure relief and even a pang of theoretical desire when his wife bustled in last thing, bearing the tea-tray before her.

Vernon was now, on average, sleeping with his wife 1.15 times a week. Less than single-figure love-making was obviously going to be some sort of crunch, and Vernon was making himself vigilant for whatever form the crisis might take. She hadn't, thank God, said anything about it, yet. Brooding one afternoon soon after the Lawrence débâcle, Vernon suddenly thought of something that made his heart jump. He blinked. He couldn't believe it. It was true. Not once since he had started his 'sessions' had Vernon exacted from his wife any of the sly variations with which he had used to space out the weeks, the months, the years. Not once. It had simply never occurred to him. He flipped his pocket calculator on to his lap. Stunned, he tapped out the figures. She now owed him ... Why, if he wanted, he could have an entire week of ... They were behind with *that* to the tune of ... Soon it would be time again for him to ... Vernon's wife passed through the room. She blew him a kiss. Vernon resolved to shelve these figures but also to keep them up to date. They seemed to balance things out. He knew he was denying his wife something she ought to have; yet at the same time he was withholding something he ought not to give. He began to feel better about the whole business.

For it soon became clear that no mere woman could satisfy him – not Vernon. His activities moved into an entirely new sphere of intensity and abstraction. Now, when the velvet curtain shot skywards, Vernon might be astride a black stallion on a marmoreal dune, his narrow eyes fixed on the caravan of defenceless Arab women straggling along beneath him; then he dug in his spurs and thundered down on them, swords twirling in either hand. Or else Vernon climbed from a wriggling human swamp of tangled naked bodies, playfully batting away the hands that clutched at him, until he was tugged down once again into the thudding mass of membrane and heat. He visited strange planets where women were metal, were flowers, were gas. Soon he became a cumulus cloud, a tidal wave, the East Wind, the boiling Earth's core, the air itself, wheeling round a terrified globe as whole tribes, races, ecologies fled and scattered under the continent-wide shadow of his approach.

It was after about a month of this new brand of skylarking that things began to go rather seriously awry.

The first hint of disaster came with sporadic attacks of *ejaculatio praecox*. Vernon would settle down for a leisurely session, would just be casting and scripting the cosmic drama about to be unfolded before him – and would look down to find his thoughts had been messily and pleasurelessly anticipated by the roguish weapon in his hands. It began to happen more frequently, sometimes quite out of the blue: Vernon wouldn't even notice until he saw the boyish, tell-tale stains on his pants last thing at night. (Amazingly, and rather hurtfully too, his wife didn't seem to detect any real difference. But he was making love to her only every ten or eleven days by that time.) Vernon made a creditable attempt to laugh the whole thing off, and, sure enough, after a while the trouble cleared itself up. What followed, however, was far worse.

To begin with, at any rate, Vernon blamed himself. He was so relieved, and so childishly delighted, by his newly recovered prowess that he teased out his 'sessions' to unendurable, unprecedented lengths. Perhaps that wasn't wise . . . What was certain was that he overdid it. Within a week, and quite against his will, Vernon's 'sessions' were taking between thirty and forty-five minutes; within two weeks, up to an hour and a half. It wrecked his schedules: all the lightning strikes, all the silky raids, that used to punctuate his life were reduced to dour campaigns which Vernon could never truly win. 'Vernon, are you ill?' his wife would say outside the bathroom door. 'It's nearly *tea*-time.' Vernon – slumped on the lavatory seat, panting with exhaustion – looked up wildly, his eyes startled, shrunken. He coughed until he found his voice. 'I'll be straight out,' he managed to say, climbing heavily to his feet.

Nothing Vernon could summon would deliver him. Massed, maddened, cart-wheeling women – some of molten pewter and fifty feet tall, others indigo and no bigger than fountain-pens – hollered at him from the four corners of the universe. No help. He gathered all the innocents and subjected them to atrocities of unimaginable proportions, committing a million murders enriched with infamous tortures. He still drew a blank. Vernon, all neutronium, a supernova, a black sun, consumed the Earth and her sisters in his dying fire, bullocking through the cosmos, ejaculating the Milky Way. That didn't work either. He was obliged to fake orgasms with his wife (rather skilfully, it seemed: she didn't say anything about it). His testicles developed a mighty migraine, whose slow throbs all day timed his heartbeat with mounting frequency and power, until at night Vernon's face was a sweating parcel of lard and his hands shimmered deliriously as he juggled the aspirins to his lips.

Then the ultimate catastrophe occurred. Paradoxically, it was heralded by a single, joyous, uncovenanted climax – again out of the blue, on a bus, one lunchtime. Throughout the afternoon at the office Vernon chuckled and gloated, convinced that finally all his troubles were at an end. It wasn't so. After a week of ceaseless experiment and scrutiny Vernon had to face the truth. The thing was dead. He was impotent.

'Oh my God,' he thought, 'I always knew something like this would happen to me some time.' In one sense Vernon accepted the latest reverse with grim stoicism (by now the thought of his old ways filled him with the greatest disgust); in another sense, and with terror, he felt like a man suspended between two states: one is reality, perhaps, the other an unspeakable dream. And then when day comes he awakes with a moan of relief; but reality has gone and the nightmare has replaced it: the nightmare was really there all the time. Vernon looked at the house where they had lived for so long now, the five rooms through which his calm wife moved on her calm tracks, and he saw it all slipping away from him forever, all his peace, all the fever and the safety. And for what, for what?

'Perhaps it would be better if I just told her about the whole thing and made a clean breast of it,' he thought wretchedly. 'It wouldn't be easy, God knows, but in time she might learn to trust me again. And I really *am* finished with all that other nonsense. God, when I . . .' But then he saw his wife's face – capable, straightforward, confident – and the scar of dawning realization as he stammered out his shame. No, he could never tell her, he could never do that to her, no, not to her. She was sure to find out soon enough anyway. How could a man conceal that he had lost what made him a man? He considered suicide, but – 'But I just haven't got the guts,' he told himself. He would have to wait, to wait and melt in his dread.

A month passed without his wife saying anything. This had always been a make-or-break, last-ditch deadline for Vernon, and he now approached the coming confrontation as a matter of nightly crisis. All day long he rehearsed his excuses. To kick off with Vernon complained of a headache, on the next night of a stomach upset. For the following two nights he stayed up virtually until dawn – 'preparing the annual figures,' he said. On the fifth night he simulated a long coughing fit, on the sixth a powerful fever. But on the seventh night he just helplessly lay there, sadly waiting. Thirty minutes passed, side by side. Vernon prayed for her sleep and for his death.

'Vernon?' she asked.

'Mm-hm?' he managed to say – God, what a croak it was.

'Do you want to talk about this?'

Vernon didn't say anything. He lay there, melting, dying. More minutes passed. Then he felt her hand on his thigh.

Quite a long time later, and in the posture of a cowboy on the back of a bucking steer, Vernon ejaculated all over his wife's face. During the course of the preceding two and a half hours he had done to his wife everything he could possibly think of, to such an extent that he was candidly astonished that she was still alive. They subsided, mumbling soundlessly, and slept in each other's arms.

*

Vernon woke up before his wife did. It took him thirty-five minutes to get out of bed, so keen was he to accomplish this feat without waking her. He made breakfast in his dressing-gown, training every cell of his concentration on the small, sacramental tasks. Every time his mind veered back to the night before, he made a low growling sound, or slid his knuckles down the cheese-grater, or caught his tongue between his teeth and pressed hard. He closed his eyes and he could see his wife crammed against the headboard with that one leg sticking up in the air; he could hear the sound her buttocks made as he two-handedly slapped them into a crimson swelter. Vernon steadied himself against the refrigerator. He had an image of his wife coming into the kitchen – on crutches, her face black and blue. She couldn't very well not say anything about *that*, could she? He laid the table. He heard her stir. He sat down, his knees cracking, and ducked his head behind the cereal packet.

When Vernon looked up his wife was sitting opposite him. She looked utterly normal. Her blue eyes searched for his with all their light.

'Toast?' he bluffed.

'Yes please. Oh Vernon, wasn't it lovely?'

For an instant Vernon knew beyond doubt that he would now have to murder his wife and then commit suicide – or kill her and leave the country under an assumed name, start all over again somewhere, Romania, Iceland, the Far East, the New World.

'What, you mean the –?'

'Oh yes. I'm so happy. For a while I thought that we . . . I thought you were –'

'I –'

'– Don't, darling. You needn't say anything. I understand.

92

And now everything's all right again. Ooh,' she added. 'You were naughty, you know.'

Vernon nearly panicked all over again. But he gulped it down and said, quite nonchalantly, 'Yes, I was a bit, wasn't I?'

'Very naughty. So *rude*. Oh Vernon . . .'

She reached for his hand and stood up. Vernon got to his feet too – or became upright by some new hydraulic system especially devised for the occasion. She glanced over her shoulder as she moved up the stairs.

'You mustn't do that too often, you know.'

'Oh really?' drawled Vernon. 'Who says?'

'*I* say. It would take the fun out of it.'

Vernon knew one thing: he was going to stop keeping count. Pretty soon, he reckoned, things would be more or less back to normal. He'd had his kicks: it was only right that the loved one should now have hers. Vernon followed his wife into the bedroom and softly closed the door behind them.

Granta, 1981

The Coincidence of the Arts

'This is a farce, man. Have you read my novel yet?'

'No.'

'Well why's that now?'

'I've been terribly –'

Across the road a fire truck levered itself backwards into its bay with a great stifled sneeze. Round about, a thousand conversations missed a beat, gulped, and then hungrily resumed.

'The thing is I've been terribly busy.'

'Aren't those the exact same words you used last time I asked you?'

'Yes.'

'Then how many more times do I got to hear them?'

The two men stood facing each other on the corner: that mess of streets, of tracks and rinks, where Seventh Avenue collapses into the Village ... He who posed the questions was thirty-five years old, six foot seven, and built like a linebacker in full armour. His name was Pharsin Courier, and he was deeply black. He who tendered the answers was about the same age; but he was five foot eight, and very meagre. Standing there, confronted by his interrogator, he seemed to be lacking a whole dimension. His name was Sir Rodney Peel, and he was deeply white.

They were shouting at each other, but not yet in exasperation or anger. The city was getting louder every day: even the sirens had to throw a tantrum, just to make themselves heard.

'Find time for my novel,' said Pharsin. He continued to urge such a course on Rodney for a further twenty minutes, saying, in conclusion, 'I gave you that typescript in good faith, and I need your critique. You and I, we're both artists. And don't you think that counts for something?'

In this city?

The sign said: Omni's Art Material – For the Artist in Everyone. But everyone was *already* an artist. The coffeeshop waiters and waitresses were, of course, actors and actresses; and the people they served were all librettists and scenarists, harpists, pointillists, ceramicists, caricaturists, contrapuntalists. The little boys were bladers and jugglers, the little girls all ballerinas (bent over the tables in freckly discussions with their mothers or mentors). Even the babies starred in ads and had agents. And it didn't stop there. Outside, sculptors wheelbarrowed chunks of rock over painted pavements past busking flautists, and a troupe of clowns performed mime, watched by kibitzers doing ad lib and impro. And on and on and up and up. Jesters teetered by on ten-foot stilts. Divas practised their scales from tenement windows. The AC installers were all installationists. The construction workers were all constructivists.

And, for once, Sir Rodney Peel happened to be telling the truth: he *was* terribly busy. After many soggy years of artistic and sexual failure, in London, SW3, Rodney was now savouring their opposites, in New York. You could still see this failure in the darkened skin around his eyes (stained, scarred, blinded); you could still nose it in his pyjamas, unlaundered for fifteen years (when he got out of bed in the morning he left them leaning against the wall). But America had reinvented him. He had a title, a ponytail, a flowery accent, and a pliant paintbrush. He was an unattached heterosexual in Manhattan: something had to give. And Rodney now knew the panic of answered prayers. Like a bit-part player in a dream, he looked on as his prices kept doubling: all you needed was an aristocratic wag of the head, and a straight face. Under the floorboards of his studio, in brown envelopes, lurked ninety-five thousand dollars: cash. And every afternoon he was climbing into an aromatic bed, speechless, with his ears whistling like seashells.

Rodney still felt that he had a chance of becoming a serious painter. Not a good chance – but a chance. Even he could tell that his artistic universe, after ten months in New York, had undergone drastic contraction. The journey into his own nervous system, the groping after spatial relationships, the trawl for his own talent – all this, for the time being, he had set aside. And now he specialized. He did wives. Wives of wealthy professionals and executives: wives of the lions of Madison Avenue, wives of the heroes of Wall Street. His brush flattered and rejuvenated them, naturally; but this wasn't especially arduous or even dishonest, because the wives were never first wives: they were second wives, third wives, subsequent wives. They gazed up at him righteously, at slender Sir Rodney in his smudged smock. 'Perfect,' he would murmur. 'No. Yes. That's quite lovely . . .' One thing sometimes led to another thing; but never to the real thing. Meekly, his lovelife imitated his art. This wife, that wife. Rodney flattered, flirted, fumbled, failed.

Then change came. Now, when he worked, his paint coagulated along traditional lines, and conventional curves. In between the sheets, though, Rodney felt the terrible agitation of the innovator.

'There's been a breakthrough,' he told Rock Robville, his agent or middleman, 'on the uh, "carnal knowledge" front.'

'Oh? Do tell.'

'Quite extraordinary actually. Never known anything quite . . .'

'The fragrant Mrs Peterson, mayhap?'

'Good God no.'

'The bodacious Mrs Havilland then, I'll wager.'

Twenty-eight, sleek, rosy, and darkly balding, Rock, too, was English, and of Rodney's class. The Robvilles were not as old and grand as the Peels; but they were much richer. Rock was now accumulating another fortune as an entrepreneur of things British: holiday castles in Scotland, Cumbrian fishing rights, crests, titles, nannies, suits of armour. Oh, and butlers. Rock did much trafficking in butlers.

'No. She's not a wife,' said Rodney. 'I don't want to say too much about it in case it breaks the spell. Early days and all that.'

'Have you two actually slimed?'

Rodney looked at him, frowning, as if in effortful recall. Then his face cleared and he answered in the negative. Rock seemed to enjoy scattering these phrases of the moment – these progeriac novelties – in Rodney's path. There was another one he used: 'playing Hide the Salami'. Hide the Salami sounded more fun than the game Rodney usually played with women. That game was called *Find* the Salami.

'We uh, "retire" together. But we haven't yet done the deed.'

'The act of darkness,' said Rock, causing Rodney to contemplate him strangely. 'How sweet. And how retro. You're getting to know each other first.'

'Well that's just it. She doesn't . . . We don't . . .'

Rock and Rod were leaning backwards on a mahogany bar, drinking Pink Ladies, in some conservatorial gin-palace off Lower Park Avenue. Inspecting his friend's anxious leer, Rock felt a protective pang and said suddenly,

'Have you done anything about your money yet? Talk to Mr Jaguar about it. Soon. Americans are very fierce about tax. You could get locked up.'

They fell silent. Both of them were thinking about the four or five seconds Rodney would last in an American jail. Now Rodney stirred and said,

'I'm in a mood to celebrate. It's all very exciting. Let me get you another one of those.'

'Ah. You're a white man,' said Rock absentmindedly. 'And do let me know,' he added, 'when you've slimed.'

Rodney was one of those Englishmen who had to get out of England. He had to get out of England and grow his hair. Helpless against his mother, his grandmother, helpless against each dawdling, prating, beaming milady they somehow conscripted him to squire. When he tried to break out they always easily reclaimed him, drawing him back to what was theirs. They owned him . . . Rodney had a fat upper lip which, during those soggy years, often wore a deep lateral crease of resignation – of vapid resignation. In the Chinese restaurants of Chelsea you might have glimpsed him, being lunched and lectured by a heavy-smoking aunt, his arms folded in the tightness of his jacket, his upper lip philosophically seamed.

*

'You get to my novel yet?'

'What?'

'Have you read my novel yet?'

'Ah. Pharsin.' Rodney collected himself. 'The thing is, I've been trying to make time for it in the afternoons. But the thing is . . .' He gazed unhappily down Greenwich Avenue. Sunday morning, and everyone was staggering around with their personal burden of prolixity, of fantastic garrulity, of uncontainable communicativeness: the *Sunday Times*. 'The thing is . . .'

The thing was that Rodney worked every morning and drunkenly socialized every evening, and in the afternoons – the only time of day he might conceivably pick up a book, or at any rate a magazine or a catalogue – he went to bed. With humming ears. And perpendicular in his zeal.

'Come on, man. This is getting insane.'

Rodney remembered a good tip about lying: stay as close to the truth as you dare. 'I've been trying to make time for it in the afternoons. But in the afternoons . . . My lady friend, do you see. I uh, "entertain" her in the afternoons.'

Pharsin assumed a judicious air.

'For instance,' Rodney enthused, 'on Friday afternoon I was just settling down to it. And in she came. I had your novel on my lap.'

This was of course untrue. Pharsin's ruffled, slewing typescript had never made it on to Rodney's lap. It was still under the piano, or in whatever corner or closet he had booted it into, months ago.

'She come every day?'

'Except weekends.'

'So what's your solution, Rod?'

'I'm going to clear some evenings. Settle down to it.'

'You say Friday afternoon you had my novel on your lap?'

'Just settling down to it.'

'Okay. What's the title?'

Pharsin stood there, skyscrapering over him. Each of his teeth was about the size of Rodney's head. When he leant over to spit in the gutter, you'd think someone had voided a bucket from the third floor.

'Give it up! What's the fucking title!'

'Um,' said Rodney.

Pharsin he had first encountered in the southwest corner of Washington Square Park, that inverted parliament of chess, where the junkies were all Experts, the winos were all Grand Masters, and the pizza-bespattered babblers and bums were all ex-World Champions. Rodney, who for a year had played second board for the University of Suffolk, approached the marble table over which Pharsin showily presided. In half an hour he lost a hundred dollars.

Never in his dealings with the thirty-two pieces and the sixty-four squares had Rodney been so hilariously out-classed. He was a mere centurion, stupidly waiting, in his metal miniskirt, his short-sword at his side; whereas Pharsin was the career gladiator, hideously experienced with the weighted net and the bronze trident. After half a dozen moves Rodney could already feel the grip of the cords, the bite of the tines. In the third game Pharsin successfully dispensed with the services of his queen: things looked good until Black drove the first of his rooks into the groin of White's defence.

They got talking as they loped together, seranaded by

saxophones and sirens, past the bobbing dopedealers of the northwest corner and out on to Eighth Street.

'Do you uh, "make a living" at it?'

'Used to,' said Pharsin through the backbeat of nineteen different boomboxes and radios turned out on to the road. 'Chess hustling is down with the economy. Forcing me to diversify.'

Rodney asked him what kind of thing.

'It's like this: chess is an art. You can do one art, you can do them all.'

Rodney said how interesting, and toddled on after him. It seemed to Rodney that he could walk through Pharsin's legs and out the other side. No, not enough room: muscles stood like heavies leaning against the tunnel walls. Pharsin's head, perched up there on that body, could only look to be the shape and size of a car neckrest. Rodney experienced respect for Pharsin's head. Whatever chess was (an art, a game, a fight), chess was certainly a mountain. Rodney strolled its foothills. Whereas the forward-leaning cliff face that closed out the sky had Pharsin halfway up it.

'You see this?'

Halting, Pharsin from inside his hoodie produced a fistful of scrolled paper: an essay, a polemic, entitled 'The Co-Incidence of the Arts, Part I: The Indivisibility of Poetry, Photography, and Dance.' Rodney ran his eye down the opening sentence. It was the kind of sentence that spent a lot of time in reverse gear before crunching itself into first.

'Are you sure you mean "coincidence"? Not uh, "correspondence"?'

'No. *Co*-incidence. The arts happen in the same part of the brain. That's how come I hyphenate. Co-incidence.'

Rodney had a lot of time for coincidence. Everything he now had he owed to coincidence. It happened on a country lane half a mile from his grandmother's house: a head-on collision between two Range Rovers, both of them crammed with patrilinear Peels. All else followed from this: title, nerve, Rock, America, sex, and the five thousand twenty-dollar bills underneath his studio floor. And talent too, he thought: maybe.

'You English?'

'Oh, very much so.'

'My wife is English also. The oppressiveness of the class system caused her to leave your shores.'

'I sympathize. It can be very wearing. Is she in the arts too, your wife?'

'Yeah. She does –'

But Pharsin's monosyllable was quite cancelled by city stridor – someone detonating a low-yield nuclear weapon or dropping a dumpster from a helicopter. 'And yourself?' said Rodney.

'Sulptor. Mathematician. Choreographer. Percussionist. Essayist. Plus the art you and I engaged in some while ago.'

'Oh, I remember,' said Rodney humbly. 'I'm a painter. With other interests.' And he said what he usually said to Americans, because it was virtually true, geographically (and what would *they* know?): 'I studied literature at Cambridge.'

Pharsin gave a jolt and said, 'This intrigues me. Because I've recently come to think of myself as primarily a novelist. Now, my friend. There's something I'm going to ask you to do for me.'

He listened, and said yes. Why not? Rodney reckoned that Pharsin, after all, would be incredibly easy to avoid.

Pharsin said, 'I'll be in an excellent position to monitor your progress with it.'

Rodney waited.

'You don't recognize me. I work the door of your building. Weekends.'

'Oh of course you do.' In fact, Rodney had yet to begin the task of differentiating the three or four black faces that scowled and glinted through the gloom of his lobby. 'The coincidence,' he mused, 'of the arts. Tell me, are you all a little family down there?'

'Why would we be? I don't associate with those animals. Now. I'll bring you my novel early tomorrow. Casting all false modesty aside, I don't believe you'll have a problem falling under its spell.'

'Um,' said Rodney.

'Three months you been sitting on it, and you don't even know the fucking *title*?'

'Um,' he repeated. Like the novel itself, the title, Rodney recalled, was very *long*. Pharsin's typescript ran to more than eleven hundred pages: single-spaced. Pharsin said it comprised exactly one million words – a claim (Rodney felt) that few would ever call him on. 'It's very *long*.' He looked up into Pharsin's blood-spoked eyes and said, '"The . . .."'

'*The* what?'

'"The Words of . . ." Wait. "The Noise of the . . .."'

'Sound.'

'"The Noise of the Sound . . ."'

'Bullshit! *The Sound of the Words, the Sound of the Words,* man. *The Sound of the Words, the Sound of the Words.*'

'Exactly. *The Sound of the Words, the Sound of the Words.*'

'Commit the fucking energy, man. I say this because I'm convinced that your effort will be rewarded. The structure you'll particularly relish. And also the theme.'

After another forty column-inches of reproach, dissimulated threat, moral suasion and literary criticism, Pharsin wrapped things up, adding, as an audible afterthought,

'Thirteen weeks. And he doesn't even know its *name*?'

'Forgive me. I'm stupefied by, uh, "amorous excess".'

'That I can believe. You look totally fucked out. Man, take care: you're going to blow away on the wind. My marriage has survived thus far, but woman action and woman trouble I know all about. What's her name?'

Rodney murmured some feminine phoneme: Jan or Jen or June.

But the truth was he didn't know *her* name either.

'We've slimed.'

'Good man. Tell all.'

This time Rod and Rock were to be found in some kind of *Irish* restaurant high up on Lexington Avenue. They occupied two places near the head of a table laid for eighteen. Their practice on such occasions was to meet an hour early, to chat and drink cocktails, before some Americans showed up and paid for it all. This night, in Rock's comfortable company, Rodney belied his eight-and-a-half stone. Pared down to the absolute minimum (carrying just two or three extra grams in that buxom upper lip), he nevertheless seemed to share in his friend's bland rotundity; they both wore the cummerbund of inner fatness conferred by their class. Black Velvet, quaffed from pewter tankards, was their tipple of the hour.

'What's there to say?' said Rodney. 'Frankly, I'm speechless. Words cannot . . .'

'Dear oh dear. Well describe her body at least.'

'Actually I'd rather not. I mean there's nothing to say, is there, when things go so gloriously?'

'. . . It's Mrs Peterson, isn't it?' Rock paused unkindly. 'No. Far too swarthy for you. You like the dairy-product type. Raised on curds and whey. They have to look like English roses. Or you get culture shock.'

'How very wrong you are,' said Rodney in a strained voice. 'It may interest you to know that my inamorata happens to be . . . "bleck".'

'Bleck?'

'Bleck,' said Rodney with emphasis. It sounded more like *blick* than *black*. A year or two ago they might have said *bluhck*. But having largely shed their class signatures, the two men were now recultivating them.

'Bleck?' repeated Rock. 'You mean a proper . . . ? What are they calling themselves these days. A proper American-African?'

'African-American.' As he continued, Rodney's voice grew drowsy, and it was with a haggard sensuality – slow inhalations, feeding some inner fire – that he relished his nightly cigarette. 'Well, African. I sense Africa in her. I taste Africa in her. One of the French bits, probably. Senegal, perhaps. Sierra Leone. Guinea-Bissau.'

Rock was looking at him.

'She moves like an empress. A Dahomey Amazon. Cleopatra was very dark, you know.'

'So she's posh, too, is she? As well as bleck. Where does *she* says she's from?'

Simultaneously ignoring this and rousing himself, Rodney said, 'It's what's so wonderful about America. There *aren't* any good bleck girls in London. All they've got there are those squeaky Cockneys. Magnificent creatures, some of them, but – quite impossible. Simply not on the cards, over there. But over here, in the great uh, "melting pot" . . .'

'The salad bowl.'

'I beg your pardon?' said Rodney, looking around for the salad bowl.

'They call it the salad bowl now. Not the melting pot.'

'Do they indeed.'

'In a way, you could say that English blecks are posher than their American cousins.'

'How so?'

'How *so*?'

Here were two men living in a silent movie: when they were alone together, the millennium seemed about a century away. Rock was now about to speak of the historical past; but his urbanity faltered, and he suddenly sounded sober.

'Oh come on. We know a *little* bit about this, don't we? The English contingent, they were shipped in after the war. To run the tubes and so on. And the buses. Contract labour. But not – but not like American blecks.'

'Same stock, though. One imagines.'

Rod and Rock: their family trees stood tall. Their family trees stood tall and proud. But what kind of trees were they – weeping willow, sallow, mahogany, ash? And something ailed or cankered them, shaping their branches all arthritic and aghast . . . The Peels had been among the beneficiaries when, on a single day in 1661, Charles II created thirteen baronetcies on the plantation island of Barbados. Rock's lot, the Robvilles, rather disappointingly (rather puzzlingly, from Rodney's point of view), didn't go back quite so far. But the Peels and the Robvilles alike had flourished at a time when every English adult with cash or credit owned a piece of it: a piece of slavery. The place where Rock's dad lived had been assembled by massive shipwright profits out of Liverpool, *circa* 1750. Intelligence of these provenanaces could never be openly acknowledged by either of the two men. Lifelong inhibition protected them: in their childhood it was like something terrible hiding under the bed. Still, Rock was a businessman. And he had never expected business to be pretty. He said,

'There's not much in it, I suppose. But the English contingent were freed longer ago.'

'Yes, well,' pondered Rodney, 'I suppose you can't get much less posh than being a slave. But that's to forget what they might have been originally.'

'Posh in Africa.'

'In a way. You know, Africa was quite advanced for a while. I mean, look at African art. Exquisite. Ancient, but immediate. Immediate. They had great civilizations there when England was just a sheepdip. Ages ago.'

'What have you been reading? The *Amsterdam News*?'

'No. *Ebony*. But it's true! We're just upstarts and counterjumpers compared to them. Scum, Rock. Anyway I have a hunch my one came direct from Africa. The Sudan, quite possibly. Timbuktu was apparently an incredible city. Crammed with princes and poets and amazing *houris*. Jezebel was of –'

'Did you say amazing hoorays? Sorry? Oh never *mind*. What sort of accent does she have? Your one.'

'I don't know.'

'What's her name?'

'I don't know.'

Rock paused and said, 'Pray describe this relationship. How did you meet? Or don't you know that either?'

'We met in a bar. But it wasn't like that.'

*

They met in a bar but it wasn't like that.

It was like this.

Rodney had just asked for a Bullshot. Consisting of vodka and consommé, a Bullshot is arguably a bullshit drink; but Rodney, his eyes lurking and cowering behind his dark glasses, badly needed his Bullshot. What he really felt like was a Bloodshot. He wore a pinched seersucker suit and a grimy cravat. He had spent the morning in a sepulchral brownstone on East Sixty-Fifth Street, doing what he could with the long upper lip and ridiculously interproximate eyebrows of a Mrs Sheehan – wife to the chat-show king.

'Worcestershire sauce, if you please, and the juice of at least one lemon.'

'You know something? I could listen to your voice all day.'

It was not the first time Rodney had been paid this compliment. Sequestered in a deceptively mild cocaine hangover, he said, 'How sweet of you to say so.'

'No. Really.'

'So kind.'

This waitress at some point or other might have wanted to be an actress. She might have had the odd prompting towards the stage. But not recently. And anyway Rodney was looking past her, Rodney was flinching past her . . .

So. She was up on a stool at the counter – and up on the turret of her swivelling haunches, rising in her seat whenever they crossed or uncrossed, uncrossed or crossed. Rodney stared. There she sat, drinking milky tea from a braced glass, being bawled at by some ballgame on the perched TV, and exchanging vigorous but inaudible smalltalk with a hidden figure behind the bar. Unquestionably she was a person of colour, and that colour – or so it seemed to Rodney – was *american*. As in black, brown, american; then beige, white, pink . . . Beyond this room lay another room, where some kind of talent contest was being noisily disputed. Poetry readings. Monologues. Stand-up.

Rodney was staring at her with a pang of recognition, although he knew she was a stranger. He thought he had seen her before, in the neighbourhood. But never fully seen her. Because she was the woman on the street whom you never see fully, sent here to elude you, always turning away or veering off, or exactly maintaining parallax with mailbox or tree bole, or vanishing for ever behind the burning glass of a phonebooth or under the black shadow of a truck. Indignant poems have been written about these women – about these *desaparacidas*. Even the douce Bloom grew petulant about them. Men mind, because for once they are demanding so little, no contact, just a free gaze at the moving form. And this was Rodney's initial disposition. He didn't want to date her. He wanted to paint her.

'There you go, sir.'

'Thank you most awfully.'

'That voice!'

Even now, at the bar, she always seemed to be occluded or eclipsed. In particular a pink lady, a Germanic middle-aged blonde with a whole reef of freckles and moles on her bared throat (how Rodney struggled, each day, with such imperfections in his sitters) kept masking her, kept hiding her and then revealing her. Suddenly the view cleared, and he absorbed the lavish power of her thighs – then her face, her glance, her unspecific smile. What she said to him was Talent. Not just *her* talent. His talent, too.

'Waitress! Waitress! Ah. Thank you. I wonder if you would very kindly lend me your pen there. For just a couple of minutes.'

'Certainly!'

'Thank you *so* much.'

He knew what to do. At his agent's prompting, Rodney had had some cards printed up, headed: Sir Rodney Peel (Baronet): Portraitist. The flipside gave an example of the portraitist's art: looking like non-identical twins, the wife and daughter of a burglar-alarm tycoon were pooling their repose on a pair of French armchairs. Rodney started writing. He still wasn't entirely reconciled to that bracketed 'Baronet'. At first he had argued for the more discreet and conventional abbreviation, '(Bt)'. But he had eventually submitted to the arguments of his agent: according to Rock, Americans might think that Bt was short for Bought.

In the great wreaths and plumes of his embarrassing calligraphy Rodney said that he was an English painter, come to America; said how rare it was, even in this city, with its famed diversity, to encounter a face so *paintable* as her own; said he would, of course, remunerate her for her indulgence; said his rates were high. Rodney then used up a second card and most of a third with a fantastic array of apologies and protestations, of microscopic diffidences – and then added a fourth, for her reply.

'Waitress? Excuse me! Excuse me!' Rodney's voice was having to contend with the espresso machine and the robust applause coming from the back room, as well as with the gasps and hiccups of human communion, all around: like a schoolyard. But Rodney's voice was bigger than he was. Trained by centuries of hollering across very large rooms.

'Ah. There you are.'

The waitress stood by as Rodney outlined her mission. And it seemed that her avowed preparedness to listen to Rodney's voice all day came under immediate strain. Her face toughened, and she knocked a fist into her hip as her shoulders gave a single shrug or shudder. But Rodney just tapped his calling-cards into alignment and contentedly added,

'Now, not the orange-haired one, do you see, with all the freckles. Behind her. The dark one.' Rodney had a witty notion. His interlocutor was a cocktail waitress: why not speak her language? 'The Pink Lady: no. By no means. Rather, the Black Velvet. The Black Velvet.'

He tried to watch as the waitress delivered his note. Its recipient, again, seemed to glance and smile his way; but then a wall of new bards or jokesmiths, heading for the back room, interposed itself, and when the room cleared she was gone.

The shadow of the waitress dropped past him. He looked down at the tray she had placed on his table: the check, plus the fourth postcard, which said tersely and in neat small caps: 'You talk too much.'

Triple-lipped, Rodney paid and added fifteen per cent and took his leave.

It was as he crossed Tenth Street that he realized she was following him. Realized, too, in the light of day, that she was as black as night. And twice his size. His first impulse (one not quickly overcome) was to make a run for it. On Eleventh Street the darkened window of Ray's Pizza told Rodney that she was still behind him. He halted and turned, weakly squinting, and she halted, intelligently smiling, and he took a step towards her, and she took a step back, and he moved on, and she followed. Across Twelfth Street. Now with every step his legs were getting heavier and tenderer; it felt like the marrow-ache of adolescent growth. Despairingly he turned left on Thirteenth Street. She stopped following him. She overtook him. And as her pace slowed and slackened, and as he attended to the amazing machine of her thighs and buttocks, the parts accommodating themselves so equably in the close quarters of her skirt, all his fears (and all thoughts of his easel) gave way to a reptile vacuity. For the first time in his life Rodney was ready for anything. No questions asked.

When she reached his building she turned and waited. He summoned breath to speak – but she smoothly raised a vertical forefinger to her lips. And he understood, and felt like a child. He talked too much. He talked too much . . . Mounting the steps, he pushed the inner glass door and held it open behind him; when he felt the transfer of its weight he withstood a rush of intimacy, as intimate as the press of boiling breasts on his spine. Dismissing the elevator as an impossibility, he began the long ascent, afraid to turn but minutely alert to her tread. His door. His keys all jammed and tangled in their ring, which he weepily picked at. Each lock turned a different way, the English way, the American way. He pushed, and felt the air rearrange itself as her shape moved past his back.

Many times, during that first half hour, speech gulped up in Rodney's throat – and just as often her forefinger sought her lips (and there would be a frown of real warning). The finger side-on, always. But then they were standing near the piano, when she had completed her tour of his space; Rodney swallowed his most recent glottal stop, and her finger was once again raised; only now she turned it, rotating her whole hand through ninety degrees, showing him the bruised pink of the nail. After a beat or two Rodney took this as an invitation. He hovered nearer still and strained upwards. He kissed.

'Well what the fuck's the story, Rod? You read my novel yet or what?'

Jesus: the guy was like a neighbour's dog that just kept on hating you. You never gave him an instant's thought until there he was, balanced upright on the tautness of his leash, and barking in your face.

'Not yet,' Rodney conceded, as he stepped out of the elevator.

'Now this is basically some *rude shit* we're looking at here. Why the contempt, Rod? What's your answer?'

Rodney wrongly regarded himself as an expert at excuses. After all, he and excuses had been through a lot together. Gazing upwards, with tubed lips, he softly said,

'You're going to hate me for this.'

'I hate you already.'

Feeling a furry hum in either armpit, Rodney decided to change tack. The occasion called for something more than a negligent simper. 'But there was nothing I could do,' he found himself saying. 'My aunt died, do you see. Suddenly. And I had to compose the uh, "eulogy" for her funeral.'

'Your aunt where? In England?'

'No. She lives in . . .' This was not the verb Rodney wanted. 'She was in uh, Connecticut. It was all very awkward. I took the train to, to Connecticut, do you see. Now normally I'd have put up with Auntie Jean, but her, her son was there, with his family, and I . . .'

When he wasn't talking, which wasn't often, Pharsin had a stunned look. As if he couldn't believe he was listening to a voice other than his own. Rodney's agonizing tale had brought them out on to Thirteenth Street. In the middle distance the Empire State seemed to sway for a moment, and was then restiffened by its stress equations.

'. . . and *that* train was cancelled too. So with one thing and another I've had my hands full all week.'

Pharsin's expression had softened to something more

113

quizzical, even indulgent. He said, 'I see it. I see what you're doing here, Rod. You're digging yourself into a situation. You *want* to read my novel. But it's like you left it so long you can only see it coming back the other way.' Pharsin tapped his temple. 'I understand the mind. I know the mind. Last year I took a lot of —'

He paused as if to listen. Rodney was expecting the next word to be *Prozac*. But Pharsin went on quickly,

'— psychology courses and I know how we do this, how we set these traps for ourselves and walk right into them. I understand. Rod?'

'Yes, Pharsin?'

'You're going to read my book next week. Isn't that right?'

'Pharsin, I will.'

'One more thing. You got to imagine that novel is written in my blood. In my blood, Rod. It's all there. Everything I am is in that —'

Rodney tuned out for a while and listened to Manhattan. Listened to Manhattan, playing its concerto for horn.

'— the trauma and the wounds. Written in my *blood*, Rod. Written in my blood.'

That night (it was Sunday, and Rock was out of town) Rodney faced a void of inactivity. He was so at a loss that for the first time ever he contemplated digging out his typescript of *The Sound of the Words, the Sound of the Words*. But there turned out to be a reasonably diverting documentary about synchronized swimmers on TV. And he managed to kill the rest of the evening by washing his hair and rolling around in twenty-dollar bills.

'I see her in an Abyssinian setting. Or Ancient Ethiopia.

She's a Nefertiti. Or one of the Candaces. Here'll do.
Actually I think it's a gay place but they don't seem to mind
me coming here.'

No irony was intended or understood by this last remark,
and Rock followed Rodney unsmilingly down the steps.

Rock's older brother Inigo had known Rodney at Eton;
and in his schooldays Rodney had apparently been famed
for his lending library of glamour magazines and his prolific
onanism. So Rock sensed no sexual ambiguity in his friend.
But others did. For instance, it had never occurred to any of
his sitters' husbands that Rodney was straight. And Rodney
himself had entertained inevitable doubts on this score, in
the past, in London, lying on his side and apologetically
stroking the back of yet another unslain giantess of the
gentry.

They ordered their Highballs. The clientele was all-male
but also middle-aged (woollen, paunchy), and Rodney
received no more than his usual deal of stares.

He said, 'This'll amuse you. The first time we uh, "hid the
salami" . . . No. The first time I *revealed* the salami – I felt a
real pleb. A real cur. Like an Untouchable.'

'How so?'

'I'm a Cavalier.'

'Me too.'

'Of course. We're English. But over here they're all
Roundheads. It's posh to be a Roundhead here. Only the
hicks and Okies are Cavaliers.' Rodney well remembered
Mrs Vredevoort, wife to the construction grandee: how,
when at last she had found the salami (the salami having
been located and identified), she gave a little mew of
surprised distaste, and immediately came up for air. 'Ours
look like joints. As opposed to cigarettes. Which is what
they're used to. I bet they're all Roundheads in Africa.'

'But there's not much difference, is there, when you've got the horn.'

'Exactly! That's *exactly* it. Exactly. Mine didn't seem to mind. She didn't say anything.'

'She *never* says anything.'

'True,' said Rodney. 'You know, there's just one thing she won't let me do. No, nothing like that. She won't let me *paint* her. Or even photograph her.'

'Superstitious.'

'And I feel if I could just paint her . . .'

'All slime,' said Rock, 'and no paint. A reversal of your usual setup.'

'Balls. I did pretty well with the wives. All slime and no speech. That's what's really weird.'

'Come out to the house this weekend. It's finished now.'

'Ooh. That does sound like a good idea.'

Love without words. A caveman could do it. And it sounded like something that Picasso or Beckett might have pulled off. But Sir Rodney Peel? He had never shown any sign of pretending to such masterful purity. More scavenger than predator, in matters of the heart, Rodney was the first on the scene after the big cats had eaten their fill. He liked his women freshly jilted. His lips knew the sweet tang of liquefying mascara; his eyes knew the webby rivulets it formed on the blotting-paper of a powdered cheek. He was an old hand at the consoling caress. Rhythmically he would smooth the sideswell of the breast, murmuring *there there* . . . It suited him. Sexual expectation, in such circumstances, was generally low. In such circumstances, impotence could almost be taken as a gallantry.

116

Love without voices. Usually she came around half past two. Flushed and blotchy from his shower, wearing his long blue robe, Rodney would be lying on the chaise longue, trying to skim a magazine or else just dumbly waiting. Sometimes he went and stuck his head out of the window and tried to glimpse her as she glided under the ginko trees; once he saw her out there in the middle of the street, sharply questioning the driver of the cab from which she had slid. When he heard her keys in the locks, he felt, beneath his robe, the ceremony of painless circumcision.

A smile was all she wanted by way of greeting. Humbly he looked on as she walked the room, her head dipped over her folded arms. She had arrived at his place; but it took time for her to get around to him in her thoughts. Then she would move towards the two lacquered screens that bowered the bed. She undressed matter-of-factly, laying her clothes on the chair (as if ready for school). Around now a switch would be thrown in Rodney's head, immersing him in greater gravity. His ears were trained inwards only, and he listened to the muscles creaking in the root of his tongue.

There *was* something primitive about it – about what followed. Not least in the startling elevations engineered by his blood. But she was one thing and he was the other. Rodney Peel had come to Africa. Her body seemed preternatural in its alternations of the soft and the hard; and her skin, unlike his own, did not reflect the light but absorbed it, confidently annexing its powers. As for her scent, it seemed to Rodney to be of a higher proof, or just more concentrated. And his thoughts went further – to her volcanic breasts, her zebra-ripping teeth! Sun-helmeted and canvas-shoed (and settling down to his task of tribute), Sir Rodney parts the lianas and the sweating fronds and sees . . .

Actually it reminded him of a barbecue at Rock's place in Quogue, when he pierced the charred surface of the beef and saw that the flesh was still very rare.

Afterwards she rested. She never slept. Quite often, and increasingly cravenly, he would point to his easel or his brushes; but she always swiped a finger through the air and turned away. And once, early on, when he sat on the bed with his cocked sketch pad, she wrenched it from his grasp with an awful severity in her snuff-coloured eyes. With real strength, too – a strength he knew all about. Still, she had created or revealed something in him, and he thought it might be talent. Rodney's loft contained no internal walls, so he was allowed to watch her as she used the bathroom or made the milky tea she liked. She had the overdeveloped upward-surging calf muscles of a dancer. All her movements showed the mechanical security and high definition of intense technique. Rodney thought about it: of course she was an artist. A non-businesswoman under thirty-five living in Manhattan? Of course she was an artist. A dancer. Maybe a *singer*. The performing arts, without question. But which one?

She never slept. She drank her tea, and rested, sighing sometimes and powerfully yawning, but she never slept. Her thoughtfulness seemed centralized and assiduous, as if she were following an argument taking place on the near side of her eyes. Rodney worried about interrupting this argument when he later returned to the bed, but her body always fully admitted him to its heat. He often imagined, as he squirmed and bounced above her, that the first word he would ever hear her say would be the forename of another man ... All the same, what they did and made together had nothing to do with art. No play: sheer earnest. It felt like honest work.

*

'Hey. Hey! Ain't no damn use you sneaking out like that. Have you read my novel yet?'

'*Yes*,' said Rodney.

Rodney said Yes, not because it was true or anything like that, but to make a change from saying No. It was an impulse thing. And Rodney was surprised it worked so well.

Pharsin stepped back. For several seconds he wore a plugged expression. Then with his brow softly working he bent and lowered his head. Rodney almost reached up a hand to stroke the black filings of Pharsin's hair.

'So, man. What did you think?'

It was gently said. What a welcome change this makes, thought Rodney (putting all that unpleasantness behind him): these chaps are exceptionally sweet and reasonable. He laughed, saying,

'Ho no, my friend. With a novel like that . . . with a *writer* like that, I'm not going to stand here in a doorway as if I'm talking about the weather. Oh no.'

'But you saying it measures up?'

'*Oh* no. Pharsin, don't try and do this! You my friend are going to come up to my studio. One day very soon. We're going to take the phone uh, "off the hook", put a log on the fire, and open a bottle of good red wine. A claret, I rather think – a nice sharp Morgon. *Then* we'll talk.'

'When?' said Pharsin, with familiar vigilance.

'Actually there's a good reason why we can't do it this weekend.'

'What's that?'

'I'm *re*reading it.'

'. . . I applaud your rigour. Such works seldom render up their secrets on a first absorption.'

'Exactly so.'

'As I've said, Rod, a great deal hinges on your critique.

It's been suggested to me that I'm not cut out for fiction, and I'm impatient for a second response. I'm at a stage in my life where . . . You got a minute to hear this?'

Half an hour later Rodney said, 'Of course. On second thoughts, perhaps we'd be better off with something thicker – like a Margaux. We'll have some Stilton. And black olives . . .'

On parting, the two men performed an old ritual (now long disused): a series of street-guy handshakes. Rodney, as ever, looked like someone slowly and painfully learning how to play Paper, Scissors, Stone.

It was a gallery opening near Tompkins Square Park – an occasion sponsored by a new brand of vodka, and marked by a nostalgic deluge of Martinis. Rod and Rock had established themselves near the caterers' table. Sexually at peace, and additionally numbed by cocaine, Rodney was temporarily under the impression that everybody loved him. Now he bantered with the barman, affecting interest in the lot of barmen everywhere. Though invariably polite to servants, Rodney never differentiated them. Failing to see, for example, that this waiter was definitely an actor who had waited way too long.

'I have reached a bold conclusion,' he said, swinging round on Rock. 'All my troubles with women come from . . . from words. From speech.'

And there was something in this. Surprisingly, for such a fragile and ingratiating presence, Rodney, over the years, had had his face slapped practically out of alignment, so often had his patter gone awry. He was a flatterer – by profession. He believed in flattery and was always trying to deploy it. But something went wrong with the words: they came out, as his mother would say, just a bit *off*. If conversation was an art, then Rodney was no artist. He created ratty atmospheres around himself. 'Put a sock in it, Rodney,' they would say. 'Oh shut up, Rodney, do.' And the fat beak of his upper lip, after framing its latest unwelcome bauble, would stoically self-transect. Prose wasn't any better. His scented notes routinely caused year-long *froideurs*: 'non-speaks', as in 'She and I are now on non-speaks.' Non-speaks: that's how they should have *started* . . .

'Silence,' he went on, 'was the only reason I got anywhere with the wives. You can't speak while you paint.'

'I thought women liked the kind of rot you talk.'

'Me too. But they don't. I always seem to say the wrong thing.'

A while ago, as an experiment, Rodney had reopened his flirtations with two of the wives: Mrs Globerman, wife to the telecommunications tycoon, and Mrs Overbye, wife to the airline boss. The idea was to see if his new puissance was transferable and could be tried out elsewhere. Both efforts were failures – impossibilities. The things he said and the things they said. The things they all said. It seemed far stranger than silence. With these women Rodney had felt the utter superfluity of human speech. So the rain held off. So tell me about your week. So how have you been? Oh, you know: so-so. So-and-so said this and so-and-so said that. So tired. So soon? And so on and so on.

'You and your bleck girl seem to made for each other.'

'We do. We are. Capital cocktails, these. Blimey, though. Bit strong, aren't they? Feeling rather tight. It's loosening my tongue. Rock, can I ask you something? Why do I *know* it's going to end in tears? Why do I feel all this anxiety? And all this guilt?'

'Because you're getting something for nothing. Yet again.'

Rodney's eyes widened. He thought about the first time: the fraudulent feeling, when he watched her undress. As if he had reached his objective not by normal means (flattery, false promises, lies) but by something worse: black magic, or betrayal. For a moment he had the strange suspicion that she was his cousin, and they were playing doctors.

'Because you've bucked the work ethic. Yet again. Oh. I'm seeing Jaguar tomorrow. Have you done something with that money yet?'

'Yes,' said Rodney. He *had* done something with that money, if you counted counting it and rolling around in it and spending a lot of it on cocaine.

'I'll check with Jagula. I mean Jaguar. Whew, that last one just hit me.' Rock went on in a smudged voice, '*I* sometimes feel like a trader in slaves. A white-slaver. Onna butlers. Anna nannies. Maybe that's what's worrying you. It's just because she's bleck.'

Rodney said suddenly, 'Blick? No.'

Could that be it? No. No, because he had always felt that she was a woman who carried freedom around with her. On her person. Somewhere in the jaws it seemed to lurk.

Soon afterwards he started to find the bruises.

Nothing florid or fulminant. Just a different kind of dark beneath the dark. The hip, the shoulder, the upper arm. On noticing a new one, Rodney would arrest his movements and attempt to meet her eye – but he never achieved this, and, having faltered, went back to what he was doing before; and afterwards he didn't smile at her in praise and gratitude, as he usually did, turning instead to the stain on the wall, oval and the colour of nicotine, where his head had rested these many months.

He thought he knew something about women and silence. There they would sit before him, the wives, engaged in self-conscious smalltalk as he made his preliminary sketches – as he situated the human posture against the jut and rake of the chair, the wall cabinet, the low table. Artists of course crave silence. They wish their sitters dead, stilled: a bowl of apples, a wineglass, a cold fish. But the sitter is alive, and must talk, perhaps sensing that speech is needed to bring colour and indignation to the throat, the cheeks, the eyes. And the painter chats back with his skeleton staff of words until the moment comes when he is incapable of vocalization: when, in short, he is getting the head. Even Rodney knew this moment of deafened concentration (it felt like talent). And the sensitive sitter would come to note such moments, maintaining a pious hush until her next thrice-hourly intermission. Her breather, when it was okay for her to be alive again.

He thought he knew something about women and silence. But this? Rodney slipped from the bed and, in his blue robe, set about the preparation of English Breakfast Tea. He watched her through the gap between the two screens: the pillow clutched to her breast like a baby. And always she was following the argument inside her own head. The bruise on her shoulder, tinged with betel or cinnabar, looked artificially applied – caste mark, war paint. Rodney assessed it with a professional eye. It was no accident that he worked in oil. Oil was absolutely right. His brush, he realized, was not an artist's wand so much as a cosmeticist's tweezer. Oil, in his hands, was the elixir of youth. It would be different with her, he felt. Because everything else was different with her. But he would never dare broach it now.

For an instant she loomed over him and then moved past, to the shower. Rodney had never supposed that he was her single – or even her principal – erotic interest. How could he own *her*? He thought of a scene in a huge American novel he had read, years back, where a young man comes of age, pleasantly, in a Chicago bordello. And it went something like, He had used what others used. So what? That's what cities are.

On the other hand he suddenly knew what he wanted to say to her. Three words: a verb flanked by two personal pronouns.

'Hey. *Hey.*'

No black shape – no roller or mugger, no prison-yard rapist, no Hutu warrior, no incensed Maroon on the blazing cane fields of Saint Domingue – could be as fearful to Rodney, now, as the man who occasionally guarded his building: namely Pharsin. Rodney's weekends were entirely devoted to avoiding him: four of the last five had been spent in Quogue. He had even made a couple of phone calls about the possibility of moving. There was apparently a place in midtown, quite near Rock's offices . . .

'Ah, Pharsin. There you are.'

Rodney turned, physically wincing, but only from the rain. He was afraid of Pharsin, and generally well attuned to threat. But his anguish here was almost wholly social.

'What's the latest, Rod?'

'Yes it's high time we uh, "broke bread". I find myself leaning towards a Chambertin-Clos de Beze. And a swampy Camembert.'

'I keep hearing about these goddamn wines you got. But I'm thinking these are the exact same hoops we were going through before. What do I got to do, Rod? It's not just me who's hurting – it's everyone around me. I never thought a man could do this to me. I never thought a man could reduce me to this.'

It was raining. Raining on the terrible city, with people suffering through it and giving voice to their pain, groaning, swearing, babbling. In New York, if you had no one to talk to or shout at, then there was always yourself: always yourself. As Rodney debarked his umbrella he noticed the way the raindrops fell from the lobes of Pharsin's childishly small ears.

'Friday at five.'

'That's in stone?'

'On my mother's life. Hock and smoked salmon might be more the thing. Or some Gewurtztraumeiner. Or what about some Trockenbeerenauslese, with Turkish Delight?'

'Friday at five.'

'Busy week?' said Rock on Thursday evening.

They were drinking in a bar they usually went to only very late at night: Jimmy's. Although he had been there perhaps a dozen times, it turned out that Rodney had no idea where it was. 'Where *is* Jimmy's?' he asked, as Rock guided him there. The place looked different, in the happy hour.

'Not really,' Rodney answered. 'But you know how it is in New York. You've got nothing on and you think, I know: I'll stay home and read a book. Then the next thing you know ... there's an opening or something. And then you're bawling your head off across some restaurant.'

'Got anything on tonight? There's a freebie at some punk club in Brooklyn. I've got all-you-can-drink coupons. It doesn't start for hours and it'll be a bugger to get to.'

'Oh all right,' said Rodney.

The next day he left for Quogue rather earlier than usual. He rose at noon and, held upright only by the strata of dried come in his pyjamas, made tea. He took a fifty-minute shower. He performed surprisingly creditably during his tryst (she seemed relieved that afternoon, but expeditious) and he practically joined her in the elevator. To the weekday janitoriat he entrusted a long note for Pharsin about his aunt's exhumation and reburial in another plot; by way of a PS he switched their date to the same time on Monday. Only when the Jitney was idling outside that cinema on its stop near the airport did Rodney question the packing choices in his garment bag: the three new magazines, along with his standard weekend kit.

Just gone one on Monday afternoon.

He was sitting at the kitchen table and reading – in preparation for his task – the back of a cereal packet. Lifting his head and blinking, he thought of the corpulent Victorian novels he had gaped his way through at university, the *Middlemarch*es and *Bleak House*s: they had taken him at least a month each. Still, he had never contemplated spending more than about half an hour with *The Sound of the Words, the Sound of the Words*. He was just beginning to reread the back of the cereal packet when he heard the keys in the door.

Her appearance almost shocked him into speech. What had happened was this. The argument which for months had been taking place inside her head, illegibly, was now written on the outside. For all to see. Her eyes steadily invited him to register this change: the nether lip all smudged and split, and the right cheekbone loudly marked, as if swiped with a hot daub of rouge. The thing that was wrong had now been stated, not by her but by the thing that was wrong.

Aghast, he tottered towards her. And found himself leniently received. He kissed her neck, her jaw, and, with circumspection, her mouth – but then all circumspection was lost. Fearfully and ardently, and for the last time, Sir Rodney Peel stoked the tarry blood of Eve.

Afterwards she did something she'd never done before. She didn't speak. No. She slept.

Rodney got to work, and quite noisily.

He dragged his easel across the floor, shifted the screens, and rattled around with his brushes. There was no sense of tiptoe in his body or his mind: her sleep seemed elementally sure, like hibernation. He pulled off the cover. She was lying on her side, the upper knee raised, one hand beneath the pillow and the other placed flat between her thighs. First get the head, he thought. Then get the neck. Then get the body.

'Artists are waiters!' he said. Waiting for the right thing in the right place at the right time. And with that he said goodbye to his discursive mind – until the painting was about done and somebody seemed to be banging on his door.

And Rodney spoke. In a childishly lucid voice he said, 'Oh dear. That will be Pharsin.'

She was looking up at him over her shoulder. And she spoke too. What she said was obliterating; but it wasn't the content. It was the style. Heard by him before only on English high streets, in supermarket checkout bays, in cauldrons of drycleaning. Maybe, too, in the squawk of the minicab switchboard, endured from the back seat, late at night. She said, 'Eez me yusband.'

*

127

'OPEN THIS FUCKING DOOR RIGHT NOW.'

Rodney would later describe the events that followed as 'something of a blur'. But in fact these events were clear. It was good that he was feeling so talented. And enormous chemicals were igniting his brain.

'YOU GOT ONE MINUTE. THEN I RIP THIS DOOR OFF THE FUCKING WALL. SIXTY. FIFTY-NINE. FIFTY-EIGHT.'

In an ideal world Rodney would have liked rather more than a minute to read *The Sound of the Words, the Sound of the Words*. But before he could read it he first had to *find* it.

Mrs Pharsin Courier having been shushed, and sealed off behind the twin screens, Rodney went and thrashed around in the double-doored closet (FIFTY-ONE), then bent himself under the piano (FORTY-FIVE), then wriggled about among the low shelves and shadows of the kitchen (THIRTY-FOUR). On the half-minute mark he paused to take stock – and to hoist a lumpy brown rug over the gap between the screens, noticing, as he did so, a suspicious wedge in the heap of death-grey newspapers silting up the corner beyond the bed. Rodney pounced (THIRTEEN): A Novel by Pharsin J Courier (NINE, EIGHT). Skilfully he flipped it on to the table (SIX, FIVE), read half a phrase from page one ('Around noon Cissy thought she'd') and, as he rose to answer the door (THREE, TWO), half a phrase from page 1, 123 ('seemed that way to Cissy'). And that was all he had time for.

'Ah, Pharsin. You respond to our cries of "Author! Author!" Step forward, sir, and be recognized. Now. If you'll just sit yourself there, I'll just . . .

'Now I'm not a writer,' said Rodney sternly, laying before

Pharsin a glass of flat Pepsi. And a saucer with most of a Graham Cracker on it. Heartier and more various fare could have been plucked from the surface of Rodney's burred blue robe. 'I'm a painter, a visual artist. But as you have written elsewhere there is a certain . . . affinity between the arts. Now. The *first* time I read your book I was quite overwhelmed by this cascade of visual images. These things you describe – I felt I could reach out and touch them, smell them, taste them. Only on a second reading and, may I say, a third uh, "perusal" did I see that these images were, in fact, connected. In very intricate ways.'

Admiringly hefting the typescript in his hands, Rodney gave Pharsin a candid stare. So far so good. Pharsin's wrath, while still manifest, had reached some trancelike register. Rodney knew enough about novels to know that they all *tried* to do something like that – to connect image with theme. Cautiously he continued with his own variations, feeling the spasms of unused muscles: his lits, his crits. Yes, he could still swim in that pool. He could still ride that old bike.

'. . . shaping the whole composition. I could step back from the fretwork, the mouldings, the beadings, the uh, flutings and so on. I could step back from the gargoyles and see the whole cathedral.'

It looked for a moment as if Pharsin was going to ask a question about this cathedral: what it looked like or where it stood. So with a woozy roll of his head Rodney proceeded,

'And where did you find those *characters*? Quite incredible. I mean – take Cissy, for instance. How did you dream *her* up?'

'You like Cissy?'

'Cissy? Oh, Cissy! Cissy . . . By the time I was finished I felt I'd never known *anyone* as intimately as I knew her.' As he talked he started riffling fondly through the pages. 'Her thoughts. Her hopes and dreams. Her doubts. Her fears. I *know* Cissy. Like you'd know a sister. Or a lover.'

Rodney looked up. Pharsin's face was a screen of tears. Thoroughly emboldened, Rodney hunched himself forward and leafed through the text.

'That bit . . . that bit where she . . . when Cissy —'

'When she comes to the States?'

'Yes. When she comes to America.'

'The thing with Immigration?'

'Yes. Now *that scene* . . . Incredible. But so true! And then, after that — I'm trying to find it — the bit when she . . .'

'When she meets the guy?'

'Yes. The guy: now there's another character. And there's that great scene when they . . . Here it is. No. When they . . .'

'At the rent tribunal?'

'Oh now that scene. Can you believe that?'

'The judge?'

'Please,' said Rodney. 'Don't get me started on the judge.'

And so, for forty-five minutes, always a beat late, he somehow sang along with a song he didn't know. It seemed like scurvy work, of course; and it was strangely shaming to see Pharsin's face awaken out of hunger into vivid varieties of animation and delight (as at the chess board, Rodney felt dwarfed by a superior force of life). It was scurvy work, but it was *easy*. He wondered why he hadn't done it months ago. Then Pharsin said,

'Enough. Forget the laughter, the characters, the images. What's *The Sound of the Words, the Sound of the Words* actually *saying*, Rod?'

'*The Sound of the Words, the Sound of the Words*?'

'What's it *saying*?'

130

'What's it saying? Well, it's a love story. It's about love in the modern world. How love gets hard to do.'

'But what's it *saying*?'

Ten seconds passed. And Rodney thought *fuck it* and said, 'It's about race. It's about the agony of the African-American male. It's about the need, the compulsion, to express that agony.'

Pharsin slowly reached out a hand towards him. Once more tears shone in the bloodbaths of his eyes.

'Thanks, Rod.'

'It's been a pleasure, Pharsin. Hello, is that the time? Shouldn't you be uh . . . ?'

Until that moment Pharsin had seemed insensible of his surroundings. But now he jerked himself upright and began to move around the room with purposeful curiosity, one arm folded, the other crooked, a forefinger tapping on his chin, pausing to inspect a nicknack here, a doodad there. Rodney wasn't thinking about his other guest (who, he assumed, would still be wedged behind the bed). He was thinking of her simulacrum: her portrait, arrayed on its stand, in blazing crime. Redigesting a mouthful of vomit, Rodney watched as Pharsin loped up to the easel and paused.

The black shape on the white sheet. The beauty and power of the rump and haunches. The sleeping face, half-averted. Rodney, out of sheer habit, had salved and healed her bruises. That was probably a good idea, he thought.

'This a real person pose for this?' Pharsin turned, artist to artist, and added, 'Or you take it from a book.'

'A book?'

'Yeah, like a magazine?'

'Yes. From a magazine.'

'Know who this kind of reminds me of? Cassie. My wife

Cassie.' Pharsin smiled ticklishly as he followed the resemblance for another second or two. Then he rejected it. 'Maybe ten years ago. And she never had an ass like that in *all* her born days. Well, Rod. I want you to know what this last hour has meant to me. There was a man crying out in the dark here. You my friend have answered that cry. You've given me what I wanted: a hearing. I sent that novel to every registered publisher and agent in the city. All I got was a bunch of printed slips. Know what I think? They didn't read it. They didn't even *read* it, Rod.'

'That's a terrible thing, Pharsin. A terrible thing. Oh, by the way. You once told me that your wife was an artist. What kind is she?'

Then for a second their eyes met: horribly. And in Pharsin's face you could see the ageless and awful eureka of every stooge and sap and cinch. He said,

'You read my book and you're asking me what Cassie *does*?'

But it came to Rodney and he said, 'I know what *Cissie* does. In the book. I was just wondering how close you were sticking to life. I know what Cissie does.'

Pharsin's voice had Rodney by the lapels. It said, 'What?' And he told him: 'Mime.'

With Pharsin caged and dropping in the elevator, and all loaded up with his typescript like a bearer, Rodney's head remained limp and bent, hangdog with relief. Even the strengthening conviction – not yet entire, needing more thought – that he, Rodney, had no talent: this brought relief. He let his head hang there a little longer, before he faced the music of human speech.

She said, 'You fucking done it now.'

He said, 'Oh dear. Have I said the wrong thing?'

*

'All a slight nightmare, really. She couldn't leave, do you see, because Pharsin was on the door. So she rather let me have it.' Rodney was no stranger to the experience of being denounced from dawn to dusk; but he wasn't used to accents such as hers. 'A terrible way for things to end. Our first night together and it was all talk and no sex. And such talk. She was *livid*.'

'What about? I wish those people would go away.'

Cocktails *al fresco* in Rockefeller Plaza: Amber Dreams under a cold blue sky. The square was punctuated by people dressed as mannequins and posing as statues. Just standing there with painted smiles.

'Oh God, don't ask,' said Rodney – for her grievances had been legion. 'She knew someone or something had been driving him nuts. She didn't know it was me. He'd never been violent before. It was me. *I* put those marks on her.'

'Oh come on. It's in their culture.'

Rodney coughed and said, 'Oh yeah. And she said, "He'll write another one now." She'd been moonlighting for two years. As a waitress. To support him. And she could tell I hadn't read it. By my voice.'

Rock looked on, frowning, as Rodney talentlessly imitated her imitating him. It sounded something like: Ooh, ah say, wort simplay dezzling imagereh. Rodney said,

'She thought I was sneering at him. Him being bleck, do you see.'

'Yes, well, they can be quite chippy about that over here. Do you think his novel might have been *good*?'

'No one will ever know. But I do know this. She won't have to support him while he writes the second one.'

'Why not?'

'Because she stole my money.'

'Oh you *tit*. How many times did I tell you? Jesus Christ, what a silly old tart you are.'

'I know. I know. Waitress? If you please? Two Amber Dreams. No. *Four* Amber Dreams.'

'Are you telling me you just left it lying around?'

'In the middle of the night I . . . Wait. When I first met her, in the bar, do you see, I offered her five hundred dollars. No, as a sitter's fee. So I reckoned I owed her that. Went and got it out for her. Thought she was sleeping.'

'Oh you *tit*.'

'She did leave me the five hundred. Ah. Thank you most awfully.'

And on her way to the door she paused in front of the easel and whispered a single word (stressed as a menacing and devastating spondee): 'Wan*ker*.' And that was the end of that, he thought. That was the end of that.

Rock said, 'Were they in it together, do you think?'

'No no. No. It was all pure . . . coincidence.'

'Why aren't you angrier?'

'I don't know.'

Pharsin he never saw again. But he did see Pharsin's wife, once, nearly two years later, in London Town.

Rodney was consuming a tragic tea of crustless sandwiches in a dark café near Victoria Station. He had just left the Pimlico offices of the design magazine he worked part-time for, and was girding himself to catch a train for Sussex, where he would be met at the station by a childless divorcee in a Range Rover. He no longer wore a ponytail. And he no longer used his title. That sort of thing didn't seem to play very well in England any more. Besides, for a while Rodney had become very interested in his family tree; and this was his puny protest. The scars had deepened around his eyes. But not much else had changed.

Weatherless Victoria, and a café in the old style. Coffee served in leaky steel pots, and children eating Banana Splits and Knickerbocker Glories and other confections the colour of traffic lights. In this place the waitresses were waitresses by caste, contemplating no artistic destiny. Outside, the city dedicated itself to the notion of mobility, fleets of buses and taxis, herds of cars, and then the trains.

She was several tables away, facing him, with her slender eyebrows raised and locked in enquiry. Rodney glanced, blinked, smiled. Then it was dumbshow all over again. May I? Well if you. No I'll just . . .

'Well well. It *is* a small world, isn't it.'

'. . . So you're not going to murder me? You're not going to slag me off?'

'What? Oh no. No no. No.'

'. . . So you're back here now.'

'Yes. And you, you're . . .'

'Me mum died.'

'Oh, I'm so sorry. So you're just here for the . . .'

'For the funeral and that, yeah . . .'

She said that her mother had been very old and had had a good life. Rodney's mother was also very old and had had a good life, at least on paper. But she wasn't dead. On the contrary she was, as the saying had it, 'very much alive'. He was back with his mother. There was nothing he could do about that. He had to talk to her a lot but everything he said enraged her. Better to seal up your lips, he thought. Mum's the word. Seal up your lips, and give no words but – mum. She said,

'I can't believe you're being so sweet about the money. Have you got loads more?'

'No. What? Sweet? No no. I was upset at first, of course. But I . . . What did you do with it in the end?'

'I told him I *found* it. In a cab. It's New York, right?' She shrugged and said, 'Went upstate and got a place in the Poconos. We were there twenty-two months. It was handsome. Look. A boy. Julius. Not quite one.'

As he considered the photograph Rodney was visited by a conventional sentiment: the gift of life! And stronger, according to his experience, in the black than in all the other planetary colours. 'Can he talk yet? When do they talk?' And he pressed on, 'Our code of silence. What was that – sort of a game?'

'You were a Sir. And me with my accent.'

The implication being that he wouldn't have wanted her if she'd talked like she talked. And it was true. He looked at Cassie. Her shape and texture sent the same message to his eyes and his mind. But the message stopped there. It no longer travelled down his spine. Sad and baffling, but perfectly true. 'Well I'm not a Sir any more,' he said, and he almost added 'either'. 'Did uh –?'

'It was nice though, wasn't it. Restful. Uncomplicated.'

'Yes, it was very nice.' Rodney felt close to tears. He said, 'Did uh, Pharsin continue with his . . . ?'

'He got it out of his system. Let's put it like that. He's himself again now.'

She spoke with relief, even with pride. It had not escaped Rodney's plodding scrutiny that her face and her long bare arms were quite free of contusion. Violence: it's in their culture, Rock had said. And Rodney now asked himself: Who put it there?

'He's back doing the chess,' she said. 'Doing okay. It's up with the economy.'

Rodney wanted to say, 'Chess is a high calling' – which

he believed. But he was afraid it might be taken amiss. All he could think to offer was the following: 'Well. A fool and his money are soon parted.'

'That's what they say.'

'Take it as . . .' He searched for the right word. Would 'reparations' answer? He said, 'Still doing the mime?'

'Doing well. We tour now. How about you? Still doing the painting?'

'Got fed up with it. Don't know why really.'

Although Rodney was not looking forward to his rendezvous in Sussex, he was looking forward to the drinks he would have on the train to prepare himself for it. He turned to the window. His upper lip did its thing: slowly folding into two. He said,

'So the rain held off.'

'Yeah. It's been nice.'

'Thought it looked like rain earlier.'

'Me too. Thought it was going to piss down.'

'But it held off.'

'Yeah,' she said. 'It held off.'

1997

Heavy Water

John and Mother stood side by side on the stern deck as the white ship back-pedalled out of the harbour. Some people were still waving in friendly agitation from the shore; but the great machines of the dock (impassive guardians of the smaller, less experienced machines) had already begun to turn away from the parting ship, their arms folded in indifference and disdain ... John waved back. Mother looked to starboard. The evening sun was losing blood across the estuary, weakening, weakening; directly below, the slivers of crimson light slipped over the oil-stained water like mercurial rain off fat lilies. John shivered. Mother smiled at her son.

'Tired and thirsty, are you, John?' she asked him (for they had travelled all day). 'Tired and thirsty?'

John nodded grimly.

'Let's go down then. Come on. Let's go down.'

Things started heating up the next day.

'What, so he's not quite all there then,' said the man called Mr Brine.

'You could say that,' said Mother.

'Bit slow on the old uptake.'

'If you like. Yes,' said Mother simply, gazing across the deck to the sea (where the waves were already rolling on to their backs to bask in the sun). 'Are you too hot, John, my pet? Say if you are.'

'Does he always cry then?' asked Mr Brine. 'Or's he just having a good blub?'

Mother turned. Her nicked mouth was like the crimp at the bottom of a toothpaste tube. 'Always,' she consented. 'It's his eyes. It's not that he's *sad*. The doctors say it's his poor eyes.'

'Poor chap,' said Mrs Brine. 'I do feel sorry for him. Poor love.'

Mr Brine took his sopping cigar out of his mouth and said, 'What's his name. "John"? How are you, John? Enjoying your cruise, are you John? Whoop. Look. He's at it again. Cheer up, John! Cheer up!'

Drunk, thought Mother wearily. Half past twelve in the afternoon of the first full day and everyone was drunk . . . The swimming pool slopped and slapped: water upon water. The sea twanged in the heat. The sun came crackling across the ocean towards the big ship. John was six feet tall. He was forty-three.

He sat there oozily in his dark-grey suit. John wore a plain white shirt – but, as always, an eyecatching tie. Some internal heat-source fuelled his bleeding eyes; otherwise his fat face was worryingly colourless, like an internal organ left too long on its tray. His chin toppled into his breasts and his breasts toppled into his belly . . . With some makes of car, the bigger the model then the smaller the mascot on its bonnet; and so, alas, it was with John. A little shy sprig for his manhood from which Mother, at bathtime, would politely avert her gaze. Water seeped and crept and tiptoed from his eyes all day and all night. Mother loved him with all her heart. This was her life's work: that John should feel no pain.

'Yes,' said Mother, leaning forward to thumb his cheeks, 'he's still a child really – aren't you, John? Come with Mother now, darling. Come along.'

Mr and Mrs Brine watched them start to make their way below. The little woman leading her heavy son by the hand.

At eight o'clock every morning they were brought tea and biscuits and the *Cruise News* in their cabin by the adolescent steward: Mother thought he looked like the Artful Dodger with rickets, for all his cream blazer and burgundy slacks. With a candid groan John rolled off the lower bunk and sat rubbing his eyes with his knuckles, very like a child, as Mother nimbly availed herself of the four-runged wooden ladder. She drank two cups of the taupe liquid, and then gave John his bottle – the usual mixture she knew he liked. Next, tenderly grunting, she inserted his partial (John fell down often and heavily, and one such fall had cost him two incisors – years ago). As she withdrew her hand, threads of saliva would cling yearningly to her fingers: please don't take your hand away, please, not yet. In the bright stall of the bathroom she put him through his motions. And at last she clothed his cumbrous body, her tongue giving a cluck of satisfaction as she furled the giant Windsor of his flaming tie.

Dreamily she said, 'Do you want to go down for your breakfast now, John?'

'Gur,' he said. ('Gur' was yes. 'Go' was no.)

'Come along then, John. Come along.'

Out through the door and the smell of ship seized you by

140

the sinuses: the smell of something pressurized, and fero-
ciously synthetic. They entered the zigzagged dining-room,
with its pearl-droplet lighting, its submarine heat, and its
pocket-sized Goanese staff in their rusty tuxedos. In a spirit
of thrift Mother consumed the full buffet grill – omelette,
sausage, bacon, lamb chop – while John did battle with a
soft-boiled egg, watched with enfeebled irony by Mr and
Mrs Brine. There were two other guests at their table: a
young man called Gary, who had thoughts only for his
sunbathing and the inch-thick tan he intended to present to
his co-workers at the ventilation-engineering plant in
Croydon; and a not-so-young woman called Drew, who
came largely for the sea air and the exotic food – the chop
sueys, the Cheltenham curries. Then, too, perhaps, both
Drew and Gary had hopes of romance: the pretty daughters,
the handsome officers . . . There'd been a Singles' Party in
the Robin's Nest, hosted by the Captain himself, on the
night they sailed. An invitation was waiting for John when
he and Mother came staggering into their cabin. She slipped
it out of sight, of course, being always very careful, you
understand, not to let him get upset with anything of that
sort. Taking a turn on deck that evening, they passed the
Robin's Nest and Mother, with maximum caution, peered
in through the wide windows, expecting to witness some
Caligulan debauch. But really: whyever had she bothered?
Such a shower of old bags you'd never seen. Wherever were
the pretty daughters? And wherever were the officers? 'At it
already,' said Mr Brine at dinner that night, in a slurred
undertone. 'The officers nail down all the talent before the
ship weighs anchor. It's well-known.' Mother frowned.
'Going abroad, the girls want looking after,' said Mrs Brine
indulgently. 'It's the *uniform* . . .' Soft, see-through white of
egg bobbled hesitantly down John's long face, pausing on his

chin to look before it leapt on to the expanse of the serviette secured to his throat by Mother.

Up on deck two Irish builders were stirring and swearing beneath the lifeboats, having slept where they dropped. Mother hurried John along. Soon those two would be up in the Kingfisher Bar with their Fernet Brancas and their kegged lagers. The ship was a pub afloat, a bingo hall on ice. This way you went abroad on a lurching chunk of England, your terror numbed by English barmen serving duty-frees.

Mr Brine was a union man. There were many such on board. It was 1977: the National Front, the IMF, Mr Jenkins's Europe; Jim Callaghan meets Jimmy Carter; the Provos, Rhodesia, Windscale. This year, according to Mother's morning news sheet, the cruise operators had finally abandoned the distinction between first and second class. A deck and B deck still cost the same amount more than C deck or D deck. But the actual distinction had finally been abandoned.

At ten o'clock John and Mother attended the Singalong in the Parakeet Lounge. And here they sang along to the sounds of the Dirk Delano Trio. Or Mother did, with her bloodless lips. John's head wallowed on his wide bent back, his liquid eyes bright, expectant. It was a conviction of Mother's that John particularly relished these sessions. Once, halfway through a slow one that always took Mother back (the bus shelter beneath the sodden Palais, larky Bill in the rain with his jacket on inside-out), John went rigid and let forth a baying moo that made the band stall and stutter, earning him a chuckling rebuke from handsome, dirty-minded Dirk at song's end. John grinned furtively. So did everybody else. Mother said nothing, but gave John a good pinch on the sensitive underflab of his upper arm. And he never did it again.

Afterwards they would take a turn on deck before repairing to the Cockatoo Rooms, where Prize Bingo was daily disputed. Again John sat there stolidly enough as Mother fussed over her card – a bird herself, a nest-proud sparrow, with new and important things to think about. He gave signs of animation only at moments of ritual hubbub – when, say, the contestants wolfwhistled in response to the Caller's fruity 'Legs Eleven!', or when they chanted back a triumphant 'Sunset Strip!' in response to his enticing 'Sevenny *Sev*en . . . ?' This morning Mother got six numbers in a row and reflexively yelped out '*House!*' as if making some shameful declaration about her own existence. Now it was *her* turn to be stared at. Rank upon rank of pastel cruisewear. Faces contracted in disappointment and a sense of betrayal . . . The Caller's assistant, a girl in a catsuit who was actually called Bingo, came to validate Mother's card. But what was this? Oh dear: she'd got a number wrong. Mother's head dipped direly. The game resumed. No more numbers came her way.

At about twelve-thirty John was taken down for a quiet time, with his bottle. Much refreshed, he escorted Mother to the Robin's Nest for the convenient buffet lunch. It took John a long time to get there. For him, dry land was as treacherous as a slewing deck; and so, as the ship rolled, John found himself doubly at sea . . . With trays on their laps they watched through a hot glass window the men and women playing quoits and pingpong and deck tennis. Mother appraised her son, slumped over his untouched food. He didn't seem to mind that he couldn't play. For there were others on board, many others, who couldn't play either. You saw crutches, orthopaedic boots, leg calipers;

down on C Deck it was like a ward at Stoke Mandeville. Mother smiled. Her Bill had been a fine sportsman in his way – bowls on the green, snooker, shove-ha'penny, darts . . . Mother's smile, with its empty lips. She *did* have secrets. For instance, she always told strangers that she was a widow. Not true. Bill hadn't died. He'd walked away, one Christmas Eve. John was fourteen years old when that happened, and apparently a normal little boy. But then his panics started; and Mother's life became the kind of tired riddle that wounding dreams set you to unlock. Such a *cruel* year: Bill gone, the letters from the school, the selling of the house, the move, and John all hopeless now and having to be kept at home. Bill sent cheques. She never said he didn't send cheques. From Vancouver. Whatever was he doing in *Vancouver* . . . ? Mother turned. Ah there: now John slept, his chin tripled over his plump tieknot, the four trails of liquid idly mapping his face, two from the corners of his mouth, two from his eyes, eyes that never quite went to sleep. Mother let him be.

Not until five or so did she gently massage him back to life. Waking was always difficult for him: the problem of re-entry. 'Better now?' she asked. 'After your lovely nap?' John nodded sadly. Then, together, hand in hand, they shuffled below to change.

For John the evenings would elongate themselves in interminable loops and tangles. Half an hour with Mother in the Parakeet Lounge, a friendly tweak on the cheek from Kiri, tonight's Parakeet Girl. Parakeet Tombola, while the pianist played 'The Sting'. Dinner in the Flamingo Ballroom. The ladies' evening wear: a fanned cardpack of blazing taffeta. And then all the *food*. Mother went through the motions of encouraging John to eat something (she had his bottle ready but didn't want to shame him, with the Brines there, and Gary, and Drew). John looked at the food. The food looked at John. John gave the food a look. The food gave John a look. John didn't like the look of the food. The food didn't like the look of John. To him, food never looked convincingly dead. And he got into hopeless muddles and messes with his partial (was that alive too?). He ate nothing. On the way to coffee in the Robin's Nest, Mother liked to linger in one of the Fun Alleys, among the swearing children and the smoking grannies. John stood behind Mother as she lost her nightly fiver on the stocky fruit-machines. The barrels thrummed, the symbols twirled: damson, cherry, apple, grape. Exes and zeros, jagged, unaligned. She never won. The other machines constantly and convulsively hawked out silver tokens into their metal bibs, but Mother's was giving nothing away, all smug and beaming, chockful of good things sneeringly denied to her. Maximize Your Pleasure By Playing All Five Lines, said a notice above each machine, referring to the practice of putting in more than one coin at a time. Mother often tried to maximize her pleasure in this way, so she lost quickly, and they were never there for long.

What next? Every evening had its theme, and tonight was Talent Night – Peacock Ballroom, ten o'clock sharp. The sea was high on Talent Night, with the waves steep but orderly, churning out their fetch and carry . . . Couples eddied towards the double doors, the prismatic women with their handbags, the grimly spruced men with their drinks. They staggered, they gagged and heaved, as the ship inhaled mightily, riding its luck. Someone flew out across the floor in a clattering sprint (this was happening every five minutes), hit the wall and fell over; a purple-jacketed waiter knelt down by the body, yelling out orders to a boy in blue. Mother shouldered John forward, keeping him close to the handrail. She got him through the doors and into the spangled shadows, where at length she wedged his seat against a pillar near the back row. 'All right, my love?' she asked. John hoisted his head out of his saturated suit and stared stageward as the lights went down.

Talent Night. There was an elderly gentleman with a sturdy, well-trained voice who sang 'If I Can Help Somebody' and, as a potent encore, 'Bless This House'. There was a lady, nearly Mother's age, who with clockwork vigour performed a high-stepping music-hall number about prostitution, disease, and penury. There was a dear little girl who completed a classical piece on the electric organ without making a single mistake. That was the evening's highpoint. Next, a man got up and said, 'I uh, I lost me wife last year, so this is for Annette' and sang about a third of 'My Way' ('Go on,' he shouted as he stumbled off. 'That's it. Laugh.' Drunk, thought Mother.) Then a tall, sidling young man appeared and, after some confusion with the compère, unceremoniously proposed to drink a pint of brown ale without at any point using his hands: he lowered himself out of sight on the flat stage and, a few seconds later, his large sandalled feet, quivering and very white, craned into view, the tall brimmed glass wobbling and sloshing in their grip; there followed, in succession, an abrupt crack and a fierce shout of anger and pain. Drunk, thought Mother wearily. Now there was a rumpy blonde in a white bikini: acrobatics. Mother readied herself to leave. She poked John and directed a sharp finger towards the end of the aisle. No response. She pinched his thigh: the fleshy underside which was always so sore and chapped. At last they stood. 'Sit *down*, woman,' said a voice from behind. They turned, glimpsing a clump of hate-knotted faces. Disgusted male faces, one with a cigarette in it saying, 'Get out the fucking road.' And she couldn't tell how it happened. John did sometimes get like this. He gave a tight snarl or retch and just crashed forwards at them. A chair went over and John was flat on his face – pounding, but pounding at nothing but floor. And of course she had to listen to their laughter until the steward arrived and started helping her with her boy . . .

No bottle for John that night. You had to be firm. But then he moaned with each intake of breath – till well past midnight. Mother passed it down. Their hands touched. She had it ready, anyway. She always did. She always would.

Now the ship moved landwards, nearing Gibraltar and the pincers of the Mediterranean. And now those entities known as foreign countries would occasionally present themselves for inspection – over the littered and clamorous sundecks where Mother dozed and where John sighed and stared and wept. Potted travelogues squawked out over the Tannoy. It hurt Mother's mind when she tried to make out what the man said. She just turned and gazed with a zestless 'Look, John!' What was out there? Rippling terraces salted with smart white villas. Distant docklands, once-thriving colonies where a few old insects still creaked about. A threadbare slope on which bandy pylons stood waiting. Then, too, there was the odd stretch of hallowed shore: the line of little islands like the humped coils of a sea-serpent, blank cliffs frowning disconcertedly over the water at the ship, a pink plateau smothered in tousled grey clouds – all of it real and ancient enough, no doubt, all of it parched, grand, indistinguishable.

Oh, but there would be memories! Of course there would

be memories! On 007 Night the Purser asked her to dance. Two numbers: 'You Only Live Twice' and 'Live and Let Die'. On Casino Night she lost £35 but then backed her lucky number (seventeen) and won, almost breaking even. On Island Night there was a limbo competition and Gary from their table came first. The prize was a bottle of Asti Spumante. Mr and Mrs Brine got a glass, and so did Drew, and so did Mother – out under the stars. Ah, that Asti – so sweet, so warm!

In the course of its voyage the ship stopped at five key cities. But Mother's rule said: You don't leave the boat. Never leave the boat. What would John want with Seville? Delphi. What did John have to do with Delphi? You stayed on board. That was all right. Many others did the same. And those that ventured ashore often had cause to rue their error. The Brines, for example, debarked at Trieste and made the day trip to Venice. But they got lost and took the wrong train back and, that night, their taxi came screeching and parping through the docks and delivered them to the gangway with only minutes to spare. And the ship would have sailed without them: make no mistake about that. The next day Mr Brine tried to laugh it all off; but Mrs Brine didn't. They had the doctor down to see her and she barely stirred from her cabin until they sank Gibraltar on their way home.

The last stop was somewhere in Portugal. A short bus-trip along the coast to a little resort, and all so modestly priced . . .

'Would you *like* to go ashore, John?' she said to him idly, as they took their seats in the Robin's Nest. 'Over there. On the land. Tomorrow.'

'Gur,' he said at once. And nodded.

'So you'd *like* to go ashore,' she mused. Thinking it might be quite nice, saying (to someone or other) that you had once set foot on foreign soil.

But it was one of John's bad days. The steward brought them their tea and biscuits an hour early, as agreed; and to begin with John seemed incapable of lifting himself from his bunk. Calmly, wryly (this had of course happened before), Mother did what she always did when John was being difficult first thing. She mixed his bottle, gave it a forceful shake – that violent drowning sound – and eased the teat between his lips. John's lids slid back and he stared at her – in such a way that made her think he was *already* staring at her, staring with his eyes closed. He cuffed the bottle from her hand and gave a moan of – what? Fear? Outrage? Mother blinked. This was new. Then with relief she remembered that she had given him a whole extra bottle the night before. No, a bottle and a half, to quell his unusual restiveness. Perhaps he'd just lost his taste for it: that was all. But there was no going back now, what with the coupons already bought. 'Come on, my boy,' she said. She grasped a soggy leg and dropped it to the cabin floor.

Like a mirage of power and heat the touring-coaches throbbed on the quayside. Down the gangway they inched, and stepped on to Iberia: deliquescent macadam. First on board, thought Mother, as they exchanged the smell of ship for the smell of coach. Forty-five minutes passed, and nothing happened. Such *temperatures* . . . The foreign cooling system made heavy weather of the air. John seemed deafened by the bank of sun that smeared him to his seat. Mother watched him: she had the bottle ready but shrewdly withheld it until they were out of the docks and on to the coast road. He reached out a hand. Up ahead, cars made of liquid metal formed on the hilltop and then instantly ricocheted past their window. He managed two swallows, three swallows. The bottle danced in his hands like a bar of soap. 'John!' she said. But John just dropped his head, then turned his drenched gaze on the boiling sea and its million eyes.

Well, what could she say except that the whole idea was obviously a most unfortunate mistake? They had them trooping through the town in busloads, each with its own guide (theirs was a local person, Mother surmised): the square, the market, the church, the gardens. Mother followed the others, who followed the guide. And John followed Mother. All of them flinching, cringing, in the heat, the lavatorial gusts and cross-currents, the beggars, the touts. Mother felt herself obscurely demoted. Language had sent them all to the bottom of the class, had expelled them. They were all like children, all like John, never knowing what on earth they were expected to do. At the restaurant everyone absolutely fell on the wine, and then sat back, rolling their eyes. Even Mother, against the panic, had a couple of glasses of the pink. John took nothing, despite her managing to get the guide to get the waiter to put his soup in a cup.

After lunch the guide was dismissed (with a round of bitter applause) and the ship's officer announced through a faulty megaphone that they had an hour to shop and souvenir-hunt before reassembling in the square. Mother led John down an alley, about a hundred yards from the coaches, and came to an intransigent halt. If she stood there, in this bit of shade, keeping a careful eye on her watch . . . Minutes passed. A little boy approached and spoke to them, asking a question. 'I can't understand you, dear,' said Mother in a

put-upon voice. Then she had a nasty turn when an old
tramp started pestering them. 'Go away,' she said. That
language: even the children and the tramps could speak it.
And the British, she thought, once so proud, so bold . . . 'I
said: go away.' She looked around and she saw a sign. It
could only mean one thing. Couldn't it? She urged John
forwards and when they gained the steps she was already
feeling in her purse for the changed money.

The Municipal Aquarium felt like an air-raid shelter,
squat, windowless, and redolent of damp stone. Apart from
a baby's swimming pool in the centre of the room (in which
some kind of turtle apathetically wallowed), there were just a
dozen or so square tanks built into the walls, shimmering
like televisions. With no prospect of pleasure she tugged
John onwards into the deserted shadows. And almost
instantly she felt her disaffection loosen and disperse. By the
time she was standing in front of the second display, why,
Mother fairly beamed. All these strangely reassuring echoes
of colour and shape and tone . . . There were some sea-
anemones that looked just like Mrs Brine's smart new
bathing cap with its tufted green locks. Coin-shaped
mooners bore the same leopard dots and zebra flashes as
were to be found among the dramatic patternings of the
Parakeet Lounge. Like the ladies on Ballroom Night,
flounced, refracted tiddlers waltzed among the dunce's-hat
shells and the pitted coral. Three whiskered, toothless
oldtimers took a constitutional on the turbid surface while
beneath them, in the tank's middle air, a lone silvery
youngster flickered about as if nervously testing its freedom.
Lobsters, cripples with a dozen crutches, teddyboy snakes
smoothing their skintight trousers on the sandy floor, crabs
like the sulphurous drunks in the Kingfisher Bar . . . She
turned.

151

Where was her son? Mother's light-adapted eyes blinked indignantly at the dark. Then she saw him, kneeling, like a knight, by the inflated swimming pool. Softly she approached. There lay the heavy shadow of the turtle: with all its appendages retracted, the humped animal extended to the very perimeter of its confines. Now she saw that John's hand was actually resting on the ridges of the creature's back, and she pulled his hair and said,

'John, don't, it's —'

He looked up, and with a sobbing gasp he wheeled away from her into the alley and the air. My goodness, whatever had he been eating these last few days? Mother could only stand watching as John sicked himself inside out, jerked and yanked this way and that by ropes and whips of olive drab.

The following evening, somewhere in the Bay of Biscay, John disappeared.

He was sitting on his bunk as Mother rinsed his bottle in the bathroom. The connecting door leaned shut in the swell. She was chatting to him about one thing and another: you know, home, and the cosiness of autumn and winter. Then she stepped into the cabin and said,

'Oh my darling, wherever have you gone?'

She went out into the corridor and the smell of ship. A passing officer dressed in white shorts looked at her with concern and reached out as if to keep her steady. She turned away from him guiltily. Up the steps she climbed, and wandered down Fun Alley after Fun Alley, from the Parakeet Lounge to the Cockatoo Rooms, from the Cockatoo Rooms to the Kingfisher Bar. She ascended the spiral staircase to the Robin's Nest. Her John: wherever would he go?

Alone in the thin rain John faced the evening at the very stern of the ship, a hundred feet from the writhing furrows of its wake. Spreading his arms, he received the bloody javelin hurled at him by the sun. Then with his limbs working slowly, slowly attempting method, he tried to scale the four white bars that separated him from the water. And the sequence kept eluding him. The foot, the hand, the rung; the slip, the swing, the topple. It was the sequence, the order, that was always wrong: foot, slip, hand, swing, rung, topple . . .

But Mother had him now. Calmly she moved down the steps from the sundeck to the stern.

'John?'

'Go,' he said. 'Go, *go*.'

She walked him down to the cabin. He came quietly. She sat him on the bunk. With her empty lips she started to sing a soothing lullaby. John wept into his hands. There was nothing new in Mother's eyes as she reached for the bottle, and for the gin, and for the clean water.

New Statesman, 1978; rewritten, 1997.

The Janitor on Mars

1

Pop Jones was telling the child why he couldn't watch the news that day.

'Special regulation, Ash. You have to be eighteen. It's like an X-certificate.'

'I want to see the Martian.'

'Well you can't. And he's not strictly speaking a Martian. They think he must be some sort of robot.'

'He's the man on Mars.'

'He, or it, is the *janitor* on Mars.'

And Pop Jones was the janitor on earth – more specifically, the janitor of Shepherds Lodge, the last non-privatized orphanage in England. Remote, decrepit, over-crowded, and all-male, the place was, of course, a Shangri-La of paedophilia. And Pop Jones was, of course, a paedophile, like everybody else on the staff. To use the (rather misleading) jargon, he was a 'functional' paedophile – which is to say, his paedophilia *didn't* function. Pop Jones was an inactive paedophile, unlike his hyperactive colleagues. He had never interfered with any of the boys in his care: not once.

The child, Ashley, a long-suffering nine-year-old, said,

154

'They're taking us to the beach. I want to stay and see the robot.'

'To the beach! Remember to take your starblock.'

'But I want to starbathe.'

'You'll get starstroke out there.'

'I want a startan.'

'A startan? You'll get starburn!'

No one called it the sun any more: the nature of the relationship had changed. It was 25 June, 2049, and every television on earth would soon be featuring the live interview with the janitor on Mars.

Outside, the boys were being marshalled into queues under the awning as the first electric bus pulled up. Each of them clutched his white umbrella. Pop Jones was pleased to see that Ashley was wearing his starglasses and his starhat. All the children were flinching up at the sky. Each mouth wore a wary sneer.

The thing had been building for nine months.

On 30 September, 2048, at 12:45 pm, West Coast time, Incarnacion Buttruguena-Hume, the most frankly glamorous of CNN's main newscasters, received an encrypted message on her PDA. Incarnacion's computer failed to recognize the cipher but then quickly cracked it. The message was written in the Blacksmith Code, unused for a century and considered obsolescent in World War II. It began, CKBIa TCaAIaCaBTKaCa: Dear Incarnacion. Decoded, the message said:

FORGIVE THE INTRUSION, BUT I'M GOING TO BE COMING IN ON YOUR AIRTIME TONIGHT. I HAVE NEWS FOR YOU. I'M THE JANITOR ON MARS. TALK TO PICK AROUND FIVE-THIRTY.

155

Pick was Pickering Hume, Incarnacion's husband, who, non-coincidentally (it was soon supposed), worked in the public-relations and fund-raising departments of SETI – or Search for Extra-Terrestrial Intelligence. Incarnacion called Pick right away at his office in Mountain View. They discussed the transmission: which of their friends, they wondered, was responsible for it? But at 17:31 Pick called back. In a clogged whisper he told her that they were receiving a regularly repeated radio signal on the hydrogen line from the Tharsis Bulge on Mars, in straight Morse. The Morse from Mars was saying: PICK – CALL INCARNACION.

It was five-forty in Los Angeles. Within fifteen minutes the sat links were engaged and the floor of Incarnacion's studio was filling up with astronomers, cosmologists, philosophers, historians, science-fiction writers, millennarians, Rapturists, UFO abductees, churchmen, politicians, and five-star generals, gathered for a story that just kept on breaking – that went twenty-four-hour and stayed that way. On the stroke of six o'clock the screen turned a rusty red.

Pop Jones himself was watching, on that day, along with every other adult in the building, called to the Common Room by the Principal, Mr Davidge. The screen went red, then white. And the message appeared, unscrolling upwards, B-movie style, in heroic, backward-leaning capitals. It said:

GREETINGS, DNA, FROM HAR DECHER, THE RED ONE, AS YOUR EGYPTIANS CALLED OUR WORLD, OR NERGAL, AS YOUR BABYLONIANS HAD IT: THE STAR OF DEATH. GREETINGS FROM MARS. OUR TWO PLANETS HAVE MUCH IN COMMON. OUR DIURNAL MOTION IS SIMILAR. THE OBLIQUITY OF OUR RESPECTIVE ECLIPTICS IS NOT VERY DIFFERENT. YOU HAVE OCEANS, AN ATMOSPHERE, A MAGNETOSPHERE. SO DID WE. YOU ARE LARGER. YOU ARE CLOSER IN. WE COOLED QUICKER. BUT LIFE ON OUR PLANETS WAS SEEDED MORE OR LESS COINSTANTANEOUSLY.   A

DIFFERENCE OF A FEW MONTHS, WITH EARTH TAKING TECHNI-
CAL SENIORITY. OUR WORLDS, AS I SAY, ARE SIMILAR, AND WERE
ONCE MORE SIMILAR. BUT OUR HISTORIES RADICALLY AND
SPECTACULARLY DIVERGE.

IT'S GONE NOW, VANISHED, ALL MARTIAN LIFE, AND I'M WHAT
REMAINS. I AM THE JANITOR ON MARS. AND I HAVE BEEN
WATCHING YOU, TRIPWIRED TO MAKE CONTACT AT THE
APPROPRIATE TIME. THAT TIME HAS COME. LET'S TALK.

I'LL BE IN TOUCH WITH NASA ABOUT LAUNCH WINDOWS. ALSO
SOME TIPS ABOUT CLIMBING YOUR GRAVITY WELL: A FUEL
THING. AND A SUGGESTION ABOUT YOUR COSMIC-RAY PROBLEM
AND WAYS OF REDUCING PAYLOAD. DUPLICATES OF ALL
COMMUNICATIONS WILL GO TO CNN AND THE *NEW YORK TIMES*.
LET'S PLAY THIS ONE STRAIGHT, PLEASE.

YOU NEVER WERE ALONE. YOU JUST THOUGHT YOU WERE.
AND HOW COULD YOU EVER HAVE THOUGHT THAT? DNA, MAKE
HASTE. I AM IMPATIENT TO SEE YOU WITH MY OWN EYES. COME.

Under his dirty white umbrella Pop Jones limped quickly
across the courtyard. He glanced up. Although his flesh
wore the pallor of deep bacherlorhood, Pop's face often
looked childish, tentative; this, plus his pertly plump
backside, his piping yet uneffeminate voice, and his chastity,
combined to earn him his nickname. His nickname was
Eunuch. (His forename, moreover, was Enoch.) The children he treated with bantering geniality. But with his fellow
adults Pop Jones was a *janitor*, through and through; he was
all janitor, a janitors' janitor, idle, disobliging, truculent,
withdrawn. And, in his person, defiantly unclean. Overhead
the star wriggled goopily in the sky, with slipped penumbra,
like one of the cataracts it so prolifically dispensed. The sun
hadn't changed. The sky had. The sky had fallen sick, but

everybody said it was now getting better again. Pop limped on up the steps to the Sanatorium. He turned: a square lawn supporting two ancient trees, both warped and crushed by time into postures of lavatorial agony. Shepherds Lodge looked like an Oxford college as glimpsed in the dreams of Uriah Heep. Pop Jones, taking pride in his profession, maintained the place as a sophistical labyrinth of sweat and shiver, the radiators now raw, now molten, the classrooms either freezers or crucibles, the taps, once turned, waiting a while before hawking forth their gouts of steam or sleet. The plumbing clanked. Locks stuck. All the lights flickered and fizzed.

He passed the medical officer's nook and glanced sideways into the old surgical storeroom, now a mini-gym, where two male nurses were talc-ing their hands for the bench press. They glanced back at him, pausing. Pop Jones could feel the hum of isolation in his ears. Yes, he thought, a dreadful situation. Quite dreadful. The whole moral order. But someone has to . . . The patient he had come to see was an eleven-year-old called Timmy. Timmy suffered from various learning disabilities (he was always injuring himself by falling over or walking into walls), and Pop Jones felt a special tenderness for him. Many of the boys at Shepherds Lodge, it had to be said, were somewhat soiled and complaisant, if not thoroughly debauched. Indeed, on warm evenings the place had the feel of an antebellum bordello, with boys in pyjamas straddling windowsills – training their hair, reading mail-order magazines – to the sound of some thrummed guitar . . . Timmy wasn't like that. Sealed off in his own mind, Timmy had an inviolability that everyone had respected. Until now. Pop and Timmy were chaste – they were the innocents. *That* was their bond . . . To be clear: it is not youth alone that attracts the paedophile. The paedophile, for some reason, wants carnal knowledge of the carnally ignorant: a top-heavy encounter, involving lost significance. So far as the child is concerned, of course, that lost significance doesn't stay lost, but lingers, for ever. On some level Pop Jones sensed the nature of this disparity, this preemption, and it kept him halfway straight. The merest nudge or nuzzle, every now and then. His use of the bath-house peepholes was now strictly rationed. In any given month, you could count his rootlings in the laundry baskets on the fingers of one hand.

'How are you this morning, my lad?'

'Car,' said Timmy.

Timmy was alone in the six-bed ward. A TV set roosted high up on the opposite wall: it showed the planet Mars, filling half the screen now, and getting ever closer.

'Timmy, try to remember. Who did this to you, Timmy?'

'House,' said Timmy.

The boy was not in San for one of his workaday injuries, something like a burn or a twisted ankle. Timmy was in San because he had been raped: three days ago. Mr Caroline had found him in the potting-shed, lying on the duckboards, weeping. And from then on Timmy had lapsed into the semi-autistic bemusement that had marked his first two years at Shepherds Lodge: the state that Pop Jones, and others, liked to think they had coaxed him out of. The flower had partly opened. It had now closed again.

'Timmy, try to remember.'

'Floor,' said Timmy.

Rape – non-statutory rape – was vanishingly rare at Shepherds Lodge: rape flew in the face of everything its staff cherished and honoured. Intergenerational sex, in that gothic mass on the steep green of the Welsh border, was of course ubiquitous, but they had a belief system which accounted for that. Its signal precept was that the children liked it.

'Who did this, Timmy?' persisted Pop, because Timmy was perfectly capable of identifying and, after a fashion, naming every carer on the payroll. The Principal, Mr Davidge he called 'Day'. Mr Caroline he called 'Ro'. Pop Jones himself he called 'Jo'. Who did this? Everyone, including Pop, was edging towards a wholly unmanageable suspicion: *Davidge* had done it. It seemed inescapable. The last time something like this happened (in fact a much milder case, involving the 'inappropriate fondling' of a temporary referral from Birmingham), Davidge had pursued the matter with Corsican rigour. But the investigation into the attack on Timmy seemed oddly stalled: three days had passed without so much as an anal-dilation test. Davidge's shrugs and prevarications, by a process of political trickle-down, now threatened a general dissolution, Pop sensed. The janitor was on his own here. Already he felt at the limit of his moral courage. The only whispers of support were coming from a confused and indignant eleven-year-old called Ryan, Davidge's current regular (and, therefore, the cynosure of B Wing).

'Was it . . . "Day"?' he asked, leaning nearer.

'Dog,' said Timmy.

The two male nurses – the two reeking sadists in their sleeveless T-shirts – were snorting rhythmically under their weights. Pop called out to them:

'Excuse me? Excuse me? Mr Fitzmaurice, if you please. You will be turning this television off, I hope. The boys are not permitted to watch the news today. It's an OO. An official order. From the Department Head.'

The male nurses leered perfunctorily at each other and made no response.

'This television will have to be disconnected.'

Fitzmaurice sat up on his bench and shouted, 'If I do that the whole fucking system goes down. Every TV in the fucking gaff.'

Pop Jones, as a janitor, had to bow to the logic of that. He said, 'Then he'll have to be moved. It may be quite unsuitable for children. There may be some bad language.'

With a cheerful squint Fitzmaurice said, 'Bad language?'

'You can turn the sound down at least. Nobody knows what's going to happen up there. Anything could happen up there.'

Fitzmaurice shrugged.

'Car,' said Timmy.

Pop looked at the TV. Mars now filled the screen.

This day many questions would be answered. Not the least pressing (many felt) was: why now? What was the 'tripwire'? How did you explain the timing of the Contact from the janitor on Mars?

It seemed significant, or perverse, for two reasons. As recently as 2047, after many a probe and flyby, NASA had successfully completed the first manned mission to Mars. The Earthling cosmonauts spent three months on the Red Planet and returned with almost half a ton of it in sample form. Preliminary analysis of this material was completed and made public in the autumn of 2048. The findings seemed unambiguous. True, the layer of permafrost proved that water had once flowed on the Martian surface, and in stupendous quantities, as was already clear from the flood tracks in its gorge and valley systems. But otherwise the Sojourner 3 mission could come up with nothing to puncture the verdict of ageless sterility. So the question

161

remained: why wasn't Contact made *then?* In the interim 1,500 new telecommunications satellites had gone into orbit; as the janitor on Mars himself pointed out, in one of his earlier communiqués, Earth had practically walled itself up with space junk. Five hundred units had to be blown out of the sky to clear a lane for Sojourner 4.

The second coincidence had to do with ALH84001. ALH84001 was the fist-sized, green-tinged lump of rock found in Antarctica in 1984, analysed in 1986, and argued about for over half a century. But its history was grander, weirder and above all longer than that. About 4.5 billion years ago ALH84001 was an anonymous subterranean resident of primordial Mars; 4,485,000,000 years later something big hit Mars at a shallow angle and ALH84001 was part of its ejecta; for 14,987,000 years it followed a cat's-cradle solar orbit before crashlanding on Earth. Then, 13,000 years later still, a meteorite-hunter called Roberta Star tripped over it and the controversy began. Did ALH84001 bear traces of microscopic life? The answer came, finally, in April 2049 – two months before the janitor on Mars made his move. And the answer was No. ALH84001's organic compounds (magnetite, gregite, and pyrrhotite) were proven to be mere polycyclic aromatic hydrocarbons – i.e., they were non-biological. Apparently Mars couldn't even support a segmented worm one-hundredth the width of a human hair. *That* was how dead Mars seemed.

Let me remind you that these images . . . from the camera in the nose cone of the trailing vessel. Lacking an ozone layer . . . effectively sterilized by solar ultraviolet radiation. The atmosphere . . . thinner than our best laboratory vacuums. We can see Phobos, the larger . . .

a mere 3,500 miles distant as compared to our moon's . . . Deimos, the second satellite, is overhead . . . as bright to the eye as Venus.

The TV-viewing armchair in Pop Jones's terrible old Y-front of a bedroom (with its Bovril tins and clouded toothmugs) had become steeped in his emanations, over the years. Anyone else, settling into it, would have instantly succumbed to projectile nausea, shooting up out of it as from an ejector seat. But not Pop: in his armchair he felt fully alive. Look at him now, his tongue idling on his lower teeth, as he watched the screen with the kind of awe he usually reserved for only the most sincere and accurate paedography, freely available from many an outlet in Shepherds Lodge (and quite regularly starring its inmates). He had seen this image before – everyone had: a Colorado made of rust before a strangely proximate horizon. But the planet was now in some sense a living Mars, and life invested it everywhere with menace. The thin mist looked like fat on the meaty crimson of the regolith, and shapes seemed to form and change in the shadows of the sharp ravines . . .

For a second the picture was lost. Then the voice of Incarnacion Buttruguena-Hume – warmly aspirated, extravagantly human – continued:

In some ways Mars is a small world. Its surface area is only a third of ours, and its mass only a thousandth. But in other ways Mars is a big world. Its canyons . . . than ours, its peaks far higher. One of its gorges, the Valles . . . Grand Canyon to shame. And – yes: we're approaching it now. This is Olympus Mons, sixteen miles high – three Everests – but sloping so gradually that it casts no shadow. It resembles the shield volcanoes in . . . I have just been told that this vessel is no longer under our control. He's bringing us in. We . . . We . . .

And you saw it: in utter silence but with sky-shaking effort, the mountain was opening – its segmented upper flanks now bending backwards like a nest full of titanic chicks with their beaks open wanting food. The leading vessel, Nobel 1, strained above these battlements, and plummeted. Nobel 2, the POV vessel, followed. During its descent Pop felt that he was riding an elevator downwards, the innards of the edifice thrumming past you in the dark, but much too quickly: with all the gluttonous acceleration of freefall.

Every screen on Earth stayed black. Then these numerals appeared in a pale shade of green: 45:00. And started going 44:59, 44:58, 44:57 . . .

In fact it was twice that many minutes before anything happened.

A weak light came up and the camera jerked around in consternation, as if violently roused from deep slumber. There were shadows, figures. You could hear mumbling and coughing. And one of their number was calling out in a strained and selfconscious voice: 'Hello! . . . Hello? . . . Hello! . . . Hello?'

Everything is fine here. We've been waiting in this . . . room. *The vessels docked smoothly and we just followed the arrowed signs. One of the Laureates fell over a moment ago, but was unhurt. And for a moment Miss World had a minor problem with her air supply. We are wearing filament-heated mesh suits with . . .*

There had of course been enormous controversy about who would go, and who would not go, to meet the janitor on Mars. Everyone on Earth was up for it. After all, there was no longer anything frightening or even exotic about space travel. In the Thirties and Forties, before the satellites really thickened up, lunar tourism expanded to the extent that parts of the moon's surface now resembled a wintry Torremelinos. Granted, the moon was a mere 250,000 miles away, and Mars, at the current opposition, was almost two million. But everyone was up for it. No ticket had ever been hotter. There were sixty-five seats. And seven billion people in the queue.

They had to contend not just with each other but also with the janitor on Mars, who, in a number of communications, had proved himself a brisk and abrasive stipulator. For example he had at the outset refused to countenance any clerics or politicians. Later, when pressed by massive referenda to find a couple of seats for the Pope and the US President, the janitor on Mars caused far more hurt than mirth when he sent the following E-mail to the *New York Times* (forcing that journal to break an ancient taboo: 'print the obscenity in full,' he cautioned, 'or I switch to the *Post*'): 'Don't send me no fucking monkeys, okay? Monkeys no good. Just send me the talent.' He wanted scientists, poets, painters, musicians, mathematicians, philosophers 'and some examples of male and female pulchritude'. He wanted no more media than Incarnacion Buttruguena-Hume (and her camera operator. She was also allowed to bring Pick). The haggling continued well into the countdown at Cape Canaverel. In the end there were twenty-eight hard-science Laureates on board Nobels 1 and 2, as well as several fashion models, Miss World, some NASA personnel, and various searchers and reachers from various branches of the humanities. The janitor on Mars had been particularly obdurate about Miss World, even though the contest she had won was by now an obscure affair, disputed between a couple of hundred interested onlookers in the Hilton at Buffalo Airport.

This weakness of the janitor's – for harsh language and harsh sarcasm – was the focus of much terrestrial discussion, and much disquiet. Even those who shared this weakness seemed to sense a breach of fundamental cosmic decorum. The pop psychologist Udi Ertigan put many minds at rest with the following suggestion (soon adopted as the consensus view): 'I see here a mixture of high and low styles. The high style feels programmed, the low style acquired. Acquired from whom? From us! Our TV transmissions go out into space at the speed of light. What we're dealing with is a robot who's watched too many movies.' Make no mistake, though: the janitor on Mars was for real. At first, the doubters doubted and the trimmers trimmed. But the janitor on Mars was definitely for real. His brief introductory tips about fuel-gelation had revolutionized aeronautics. And every couple of weeks he stirred up one discipline after another with his mordant memos on such things as protein synthesis, the Coriolis force, slow-freeze theory, tensor calculus, chaos and K-entropy, gastrulation in developmental biology, sentential variables, butterfly catastrophe, Champernowne's number, and the *Entscheidungsproblem*. The janitor on Mars had promised to disclose a formula for cold fusion ('I'm no expert,' he wrote, 'and I'm having some trouble dumbing down the math') and a cure for cancer ('Or how about prevention? Or would you settle for *remission*?'). 'Your gerontology, he noted, 'is in its infancy. Working together, we can double life-expectancy within a decade.' On cosmological issues – and on Martian history – he usually refused to be drawn, saying that there were 'some things you [couldn't] talk about on the phone'; and, besides, he didn't want 'to cheapen the trip'. 'But I will say this,' he said:

The Big Bang and the Steady State theories are both wrong. Or, to put it another way, they are both right but incomplete. It pains me to see you jerk back from the apparent paradox that the Universe is younger than some of the stars it contains. That's like Clue *One*.

Iain Henryson, Lucasian Professor at Cambridge University, described the mathematics that accompanied this memo as 'ineffable. In every sense.' The janitor on Mars was often petulant, insensitive, facetious and sour, and not infrequently profane. But Earth trusted his intelligence, believing, as it always had, in the ultimate indivisibility of the intelligent and the good.

It was in any case a time of hope for the blue planet. The revolution in consciousness during the early decades of the century, a second enlightenment having to do with self-awareness as a species, was at last gaining political will. None of the biospherical disasters had quite gone ahead and happened. Humankind was still bailing water, but the levels had all ceased rising and some had started to fall. And for the first time in Earth's recorded history no wars were being contested on its surface.

Pop Jones settled back into his armchair, then, with all the best kinds of thoughts and feelings. If things did start to get rough he would go and see Davidge about having Timmy moved at half-time – during the intermission demanded by the janitor on Mars.

*

We are wearing filament-heated mesh suits with autonomous air-supply, but according to Colonel Hicks's instruments the air is breathable and the temperature is rising. It was close to freezing at first but now it's evidently no worse than chilly. And damp. I'm removing my headpiece . . . now. Yup. Seems okay . . . Gravity is at 1 g. I have no sense of lightness or hollowness. We seem to be in some kind of reception area, but our lights don't work and until a minute ago we've had only the faintest illumination. I can hear . . .

You could hear the squawk of tortured rivets or hinges, and high on the wall was abruptly thrown a slender oblong of light, which briefly widened as a shadow moved past its source. Then the door closed on the re-established gloom. Pop Jones nodded in sudden agreement. Whether or not the janitor on Mars was a genuine Martian (and there had been much speculation earlier on: a hoax, no, but was he maybe a lure?), the janitor on Mars, in Pop's view, was definitely a genuine janitor. Now kill the lights again, thought Pop, and turn off the heat. He listened expectantly for the clank of buckets, the skewering of big old keys in cold damp locks. But all he heard was the slow clop of footsteps. Then, causing pain to the dark-adapted eye, the lights came on with brutal unanimity.

'Welcome, DNA. So this is the double helix on the right-handed scroll. DNA, I extend my greetings to you.'

When you could focus you saw that the janitor on Mars sat at a table on a raised stage: an unequivocal robot wearing blue-black overalls and a shirt and tie. His face was a dramatically featureless beak of burnished metal; his hands, clawlike, intricate, fidgety. The accent was not unfamiliar: semi-educated American. He sounded like a sports coach – a sports coach addressing other, lesser sports coaches. But he had no mouth to frame the words and they had a buzzy, boxy tone: an interior sizzle. The janitor on Mars tossed an empty clipboard on to the table and said,

'Ladies and gentlemen, I apologize for the condition of these modest furnishings. This room is something I threw together almost exactly a century ago, on 29 August, 1949: the day it became clear that Earth was featuring two combatants equipped with nuclear arms. I kept meaning to update it. But I could never be fucked . . . Human beings, don't look that way. Miss World: don't crinkle your nose at me. And dispense, in general, with your expectations of grandeur. There *is* such a thing as cosmic censorship. But the universe is profoundly and essentially profane. I think you'll be awed by some of the things I'm going to tell you. Other emotions, however, will predominate. Emotions like fear and contempt. Or better say terror and disgust. Terror and disgust. Well. First – the past.'

By now two cameras were established back-to-back at the base of the podium. You saw the janitor on Mars; and then you saw his audience (seated on tin chairs in an ashen assembly hall: wood panelling, drab drapes on the false windows; a blackboard; the American and Soviet flags). In the front row sat Incarnacion Buttruguena-Hume and her husband, Pickering. Tentatively Incarnacion raised her hand.

'Yes, Incarnacion.'

She blushed, half-smiled, and said, 'May I ask a preliminary question, sir?'

The janitor on Mars gave a minimal nod.

'Sir. Only two years ago there were human beings on your *door*step. Why – ?'

'Why didn't I make myself known to you then? There's a good reason for that: the tripwire. Patience, please. All will become clear. If I may revert to the programme? The past

. . . To recap: Earth and Mars are satellites of the same second-generation, metal-rich, main-sequence yellow dwarf on the median disk of the Milky Way. Our planets seized and formed some four and a half billion years ago. Smaller, and further out, we cooled quicker. Which you might say gave us a head start.'

With a brief snort of amusement or perhaps derision the janitor on Mars leaned backwards in his chair and thoughtfully intermeshed his slender talons.

'Now. We two had the same prebiotic chemistry and were pollinated by the same long-periodical comet: the Alpha Comet, as we called her, which visits the solar system every 113 million years. Life having been established on Earth, you then underwent that process you indulgently call "evolution". Whereas we were up and running pretty much right away. I mean, in a scant 300 million years. While you were just some fucking disease. Some fucking germ, stinking up the shoreline. And I can promise you that ours was the more typical planetary experience: self-organizing complexity, with remorseless teleological drive. Martian civilization flourished, with a few ups and down, for over three trillennia, three billion years, reaching its (what shall I call it?) – its apotheosis, its *climax* 500 million years ago, at which time, as they say, dinosaurs ruled the Earth. Forty-three million years later, Martian life was extinguished, and I, already emplaced, was activated, to await tripwire.'

Miss World said, 'Sir? Could you tell us what your people looked like?'

Nicely framed though this question was, the janitor on Mars seemed to take some exception to it. A momentary shudder in the thick blade of his face.

'Not unlike you now, at first. Somewhat taller and ganglier and hairier. We did not excrete. We did not sleep.

170

And of course we lived a good deal longer than you do – even at the outset. This explains much. You see, DNA isn't any good until it's twenty years old, and by the time you're forty your brains start to rot. Average life-expectancy on Mars was at least two centuries even before they started upping it. And of course we pursued aggressive bioengineering from a very early stage. For instance, we soon developed a neurological integrated-circuit technology. What you'd call telepathy. I'm doing it now, though I've added a voice-over for TV viewers. Can you feel that little nasal niggle in your heads? Thoughts, it might please you to learn, are infinity-tending and travel at the speed of light.'

The janitor on Mars stood – with a terrible backward-juddering scrape of his metal chair that had Pop Jones frowning with approval as he reached for the tin of Bovril and the spoon. At this stage, Pop's feelings for his Martian counterpart touched many bases: from a sense of solidarity all the way to outright hero-worship. The air of brusque obstructiveness, the grudge-harbouring slant of his gaze; and there was something else, something subtler, that struck Pop as so quintessentially janitorial. *Alertness to the threat of effort:* that was it. The day has come, he thought. The day when at last the janitors –

'Now I don't have all afternoon,' said the robot, rather unfeelingly, perhaps (his audience having spent four and a half months in transit). In his black crepe-soled shoes the janitor on Mars was no more than five feet tall. Yet he filled his space with formidable conviction – a metallic self-sufficiency. He moved like a living being but he could never be mistaken for one, in any light. And while the face had an expressive range of attitudes and elevations, there was nothing human, nothing avian, nothing remotely organic in its severity. He approached the edge of the stage, saying,

'Let's not have this degenerate into Q and A. I have a programme to get through here. We'll go thumbnail and examine our respective journeys in parallel. So: 3.7 billion years ago, life is seeded. 3.4 billion years ago, Martians, as I say, are up and running: "hunter-gatherers" is your euphemism but "scavengers" is closer to the truth. At this stage, of course, you're still a bubble of fart gas. Goop. Macrobiotic yoghurt left out in the sun. Five centuries go by: Mars is fully industrialized. Another five, and we entered what I guess you'd call our posthistorical phase. We called it Total Wealth. All you're managing to do, at this stage, is stink up the estuaries and riverbeds, but meanwhile, over on Mars, we're into quantum gravity, tired light, chromo power, trace drive, cleft conformals, scalar counterfactuals, wave superposition, and orthogonics. We were the masters of our habitat, having gotten rid of all the animals and the oceans and so forth, and the tropospherical fluctuations you call weather. In other words, we were ready.'

'Ready for what?' came a voice.

'Now I'm just a janitor, right? I'm just a uh, "robot". At the time of my manufacture, there was on Mars no distinction between the synthetic and the organic. Everyone was a mix, semi-etherealized, self-duplicating. The natural/mechanical divide belonged to ancient memory. But what you see before you here is a *robot*. Of the . . . crudest kind. It's as if, on Earth, in 2050, an outfit like Sony produced a gramophone with a dishful of spare needles and a tin bullhorn.' The janitor on Mars paused, nodding his lowered head. Then he looked up. 'And yet my makers, in their wisdom . . . However. In the last five hundred million years I've had access to an information source that was not available to the former denizens of this planet. And with that perspective it's quite clear that Mars was an absolutely

172

average world of its class. A type-v world, absolutely average, and it did what type-v worlds invariably do in the posthistorical phase.'

'Sir?' said Incarnacion. 'Excuse me, but is this a grading system? What's a type-v world?'

'A world that has mined its star.'

'What type world is Earth?'

'A type-y world.'

'What are type-z worlds?'

'Dead ones. But I digress. You go posthistorical and the question is: now what? As I say, three billion three million nine hundred and ninety-nine thousand years ago, Martians were lords of all they surveyed. They were ready. Ready for what? Ready for war.'

The robot let this ripple out through the moist air, over the ranked metal seats.

'Yes, that's right. Mars, the Planet of War. Congratulations. The only time you ever get anywhere is when you follow the artistic pulse. You even got the moons. I quote: "Two lesser stars, or satellites, revolve about Mars; whereof the innermost is distant from the centre of the primary planet exactly three of its diameters, and the outermost five." That's not one of your early Mars-watchers, some chump like Schiapperelli or Perceval Lowell. That's *Gulliver's Travels*. Phobos and Deimos. Just so. Fear and Panic. Hitherto, there had never been any disharmony on Mars. Firm but wise world government was proceeding without friction. There was never any of that brawling and scragging that you went in for. Mars had tried peace, but now the time felt right. What *else* was there to do? We divided, almost arbitrarily, into two sides. We were ready. One called the other People of Fear. The other called the one People of Panic. There wasn't a dissenting voice on the whole planet.

173

Everyone was absolutely all for it. Imagine two superfuturistic Japanese warrior cults, with architecture by Albert Speer. I guess that'll give you some idea.

'We fell into a rhythm. Arms races followed by massive conflicts. We'd pepper each other with all kinds of superexotic weaponry in delightfully elaborate successions of thrusts and feints and counters. But in the end nothing could match the hit of central thermonuclear exchange. We always ended up throwing everything we had at each other, in arsenal-clearing deployments. After the devastation, we rebuilt towards another devastation. No complaints. Shelter culture had come on a long way. Casualties could be patched up good as new. And fatalities were simply resurrected – except, of course, in cases of outright vaporization. They took their nuclear winters like Martians. The lulls lasted centuries. The battles were over in an afternoon.

'It doesn't make a lot of obvious sense, does it? Later on they tended to argue that it was a necessary stage in their military development. They felt that they were . . . rich in time. They didn't know – as I do – that this happens to all type-v worlds in the posthistorical phase. Without exception. They go insane.

'The Hydrogen War of the Two Nations lasted for 112 million years, and was followed, six months later, by the Seventy Million Years War, in which the use of quantum-gravity weapons exponentially increased the firepower of both sides. By this time another factor was preying on Martian mental health. Immortality. That's actually not a very useful word. Put it this way. Everyone on Mars was looking at a future-endless worldline. And in a type-v context that always messes with your head. There was one more great war, the War of the Strong Nuclear Force, which dragged on for 284 million years. When they came out of that, there was a general feeling that Mars was in something of a rut. So they decided to stop fucking around. You, at this stage, by the way, were still doing your imitation of a septic tank. Well, and why not? It was a very *good* imitation of a septic tank.

'First there were matters to attend to in our own back yard. People of Fear and People of Panic united to face a common enemy. One found near by.'

The janitor on Mars fell silent; his head, with its steel arc, was interrogatively poised. Vladimir Voronezh, one of the Russian Laureates (his field was galaxy formation), spoke up, saying,

'My dear sir, I feel you are now going to tell us that life thrived elsewhere in the solar system, once upon a time.'

'Certainly. You've got to lose this habit of thinking about the "miracle" of life, the stupendous "accident" of intelligence, and so on. I can assure you that in this universe cognition is as cheap as spit. Being a type-v world, Mars was extremely insular in its Total Wealth phase. There was no interest in space exploration, despite adequate technology. But we were perfectly well aware of the coexistence of two type-w worlds: Jupiter and –'

'Jupiter?' This was Lord Kenrick Douglas (quasars): tall, bearded, famous. 'Sir, we do know *something* about the solar system. Jupiter is a gas giant. It is wreathed in freezing clouds six hundred miles deep on a shell of liquid hydrogen. Our suicide probes tell us that there are no solid surfaces on this planet. Would you tell us what the Jovians looked like? Jellyfish with powerpacks? Wearing scuba suits, no doubt?'

This last drollery aroused some anxious laughter. The janitor tensed himself to the sound, not with umbrage but with concentration, with efficient curiosity. He said,

'Can I ask *you* a question?' He seemed to be addressing

Miss World. 'Did they laugh just now because they thought he was funny or because they thought he was full of shit? No. Never mind. Let me tell you, Lord Nobel Laureate, that Jupiter wasn't *always* a gas giant. Originally it was much smaller and denser. Rock mantle on an iron silicate core. But that was before they fucked with Mars.

'The storm system that you call the Great Spot? The Earth-sized zit in its southern tropic? That was ground zero for an NH4 device we sent their way.'

'Ammonia?' asked Voronezh, with a glint in his eye.

'Right. It's something we were very proud of, for a while. We turned their place into a colossal stinkbomb without altering its mass. To avoid perturbation problems further down the line. Some said at the time that the War with Jupiter might have been bypassed quite easily. Mars overreacted, some said. I mean, a type-w planet, hundreds of millions of years away from posing any plausible threat. Whatever, the War with Jupiter was wrapped up in six months. But then we faced perceived disrespect from another quarter, and turned our attention to –'

'Don't tell me,' said Lord Kenrick. 'Venus.'

'Wrong direction. No, not Venus. Ceres.'

The janitor on Mars waited. Fukiyama (superstrings) said dutifully, 'Ceres isn't a planet. It's the biggest rock in the asteroid belt.'

Calmly inspecting the tips of his talons the janitor on Mars said. 'Yeah, right. They wanted to play rough and so . . .' He shrugged and added, 'It was as our expeditionary force was returning from Jupiter that it picked up the ambiguous transmission from Ceres, another type-w world, though well behind Jupiter. It's possible that in the heat of the moment the Martian commander mistakenly inferred an undertone of sarcasm in the Cerean message of tribute. The

War with Ceres, in any case, ended that same afternoon. Then for several weeks, on the home planet, there reigned an uneasy peace. Plans were drawn up for a pre-emptive strike against Earth. Some Martians sensed aggressive potential there. Because – hey. Action on the blue planet. Photosynthesis. Photochemical dissociation of hydrogen sulphide, no less. Light energy used to break the bonds cleaving oxygen to hydrogen and carbon. Bacteria becomes cyanobacteria. Gangway. Where's the fire? But then something happened that changed all our perspectives. Suddenly we knew that all this was bullshit and the real action lay elsewhere.

'In the year 2,912,456,327 BC, by your calendar, the Scythers of the Orion Spur sent the formal challenge across our bows. They compacted Pluto. Pluto was originally a gas giant the size of Uranus. And the Scythers scrunched it. Without a care for mass-conservation – hence the perturbations you've noticed in Neptune. You thought Pluto was a planet? You thought Pluto was *supposed* to look like that? In the Scythers of the Orion Spur I guess you could say that Mars had found an appropriate adversary. A type-v world. Same weaponry. Same mental-health problems. Rather superior cosmonautics. The War with the Scythers of the Orion Spur – the combatants being separated by twenty kiloparsecs – was, as you can imagine, a somewhat protracted affair. Door to door, the round trip took 150,000 years: at even half-lightspeed, achievable with our scoop drives, relativistic effects were found to be severe. Still, the great ships went out. Wave after wave. The War with the Scythers of the Orion Spur was hotly prosecuted for just over a billion years. Who won? We did. They're still there, the Scythers. Their planet is still there. The nature of war changed, during that trillennium. It was no longer nuclear or quantum-gravitational. It was neurological. Informational. Life goes on for the Scythers, but its quality has been subtly reduced. We fixed it so that they think they're simulations in a deterministic computer universe. It is believed that this is the maximum suffering you can visit on a type-v world. The taste of victory was sweet. But by then we knew that interplanetary war, even at these distances, was essentially bullshit too. Oh and meanwhile, in that billion-year interlude, all hell is breaking out on Earth. Oxygen established as an atmospheric gas. Cells with nuclei. All hell is breaking out.

'The Scyther War broadened our horizons. Martian astronomers had become intensely interested in a question that you yourselves are still wrestling with. I mean dark matter. The speed with which galaxies rotate suggests that 98.333 per cent of any given galactic mass is invisible and unaccounted for. We went through all the hoops you're going through, and more. What was the dark matter? Massive neutrinos? Failed stars? Slain planets? Black holes? Resonance residue? Plasma fluctuation? Then we kind of flashed it. The answer had been staring us in the face but we had to overcome a mortal reluctance to confront its truth. There *was* no dark matter. The galaxies had all been *engineered*, brought on line. Including our own. Many, many cycles ago.

'With immediate unanimity it was decided that this subjection was not going to be tolerated. Despite the odds against. It was believed that we were up against a type-n world or entity – maybe even type-m. I now know that we were actually dealing with a type-q world, though one obscurely connected to a power of the type-j order. Apart from the bare fact of their existence, incidentally, nothing is known – in this particle horizon – about worlds -a through -i.

'Our idea was to launch a surprise attack on the galactic core. We figured that our small but measurable chance of success was entirely dependent on surprise – on instantaneity. None of that Scyther shit was going to be any help to us here. There was no question of idling coreward at ninety thousand miles per second – we'd just have to *be there* and hit them with absolutely everything we had. Now. To be clear. In your technological aspirations, on Earth, you are restricted by various inadvertencies like lack of funds but also by your very weak grasp of the laws of physics. We were restricted by the laws of physics. Period. So take a guess. How were we going to do it?

'Wormholes,' said Paolo Sylvino (wormholes).

'Wormholes. Evanescent openings into hyperspace – or, more accurately, into parallel universes with different curvatures or phase trajectories. Ultraspace was the word we preferred. In crude form the idea's been knocking around on Earth since Einstein. Though I venture to suggest that you have a way to go on the how-to end of it. For us of course it was largely a stress-equation problem. You fish a loop out of the quantum foam and then punch a tunnel in spacetime, flexibilizing it with the use of certain uh, exotic materials. We worked on this problem for seven and a half million years.

'Here was the setup. We knew that at the core there lay a black hole of some 1.4237 million solar masses, and we knew it had been ringed and tapped. As you're aware, the energy contained within the black-hole inswirl is stupendous, but it's wholly insufficient to drive a galaxy. The true energy source was something other. And that was the prize we sought. While fitting out the initial strike force we sent recon probes to the galactic core at roughly million-year intervals. Many missions were lost. Those that returned did so with wiped sensors. One way or another, preparations for the strike consumed 437 million years. Then we made our play. On Earth, around now, let it be noted, what do we get but the emergence of organisms visible to the naked eye.'

The janitor on Mars sat down and leaned backwards and folded his claws behind his head. Ruminatively he continued, 'No one ever thought of this move as a – as a "mistake" exactly. Everybody was deeply convinced that this was something we absolutely had to do. But the consequences were somewhat extreme. So long in preparation, the Involvement of the Initial Strike Force with the Core Power was over in nine seconds.

'Our fleet was . . . sent back. Not by wormhole either. The long way around. We knew we'd lost, but we had to wait 300,000 years to find out why. This was an anxious time. We expected intricate reprisals – daily, hourly . . .

'As military units our ships had been neutralized in the first nanosecond of their appearance at the core, but their sensors were intact and had picked up a great deal of information. Much of it exceedingly depressing, from a Martian point of view. The galactic core had indeed been ringed and tapped. The artificial Loopworld surrounding it had been in place, by our best estimates, for approximately 750 billion years. There was kind of an outpost force guarding the Loopworld. Nothing more. A uh – a janitor force. Stationed there by entities we would later came to call the Infinity Dogs. Their energy source lay beyond the doorway of the black hole. They were using dead-universe power. Tapping closed universes in which, during contraction, the Higgs field couples to the gravitational shear. Also, we detected beyond Loopworld what I can only describe as a comet depot. Our equipment identified the signature of our own Alpha Comet among the comets parked there.

'Morale was generally low. Almost nihilistic. Martians started to believe, with varying degrees of conviction, that they were mere simulations in a deterministic computer universe. They divided up again. People of Fear. People of Panic. The planet was wracked by spasm wars, random, unending. Certain information began to be made available to us. We learned that the Infinity Dogs had seeded life on Mars – and on Earth, Jupiter and Ceres – for a purpose. We were middens. That's all. Middens.'

'Middens, sir?' This was Incarnacion.

'Yeah, middens. Down on Earth, in Africa, the male rhinos all take a dump beyond the waterhole? On Columbus's island of Hispaniola the squinting Carib lines shells on the bank of the riverbed? To demarcate territory? That's a midden. And that's all we were: a message from the Infinity Dogs to a type-r power called the Core Raiders, saying: Keep Out. I have since learned that both Infinity and Core are merely the errand boys of the type-1 agency called the Resonance. Which in turn owes tribute to a type-j imperium called the Third Observer. Which . . .'

Trailing off, the janitor on Mars let his sickle-like head drop to his chest. Then it reared up again, catching the light, and he said, 'Everybody knew that the only honourable or even dignified course was planetary self-slaughter. Such in fact is the usual destiny of type-v worlds in this phase. Then bolder voices started to be heard. This had never been a thing about winning or losing. This had always been about the *glorious autonomy of Martian will*. As it turned out, Mars's next battle plan involved kamikaze forces and was itself not easily distinguishable from suicide.

'We came up with a ruse du guerre. We *faked* auto-annihilation and moved our whole operation underground. It had to look good, though: we blew off our atmosphere and paralysed our core, which also spelled goodbye to our magnetosphere. What you see out there – the red plains and valleys, the rocks and pocks on that carpet of iodized rubble: it's just set-dressing. We went underground, and waited.

'We undertook an arms build-up in a series of five-million-year plans. Morale was high: ringingly idealistic. *Just one shot. Just one shot*: that was the chant we worked to. We were going to turn that wormhole into a gun barrel. And what was the bullet? We started working on a strictly illegal type of weaponry based on the void-creating yield of false vacuum. A bubble of nothingness expanding at the speed of light. The great voids, the great starless deserts that so puzzle you: they're the sites of incautious false-vacuum deployment. Or false-vacuum accident. Hence also the numberless void universes that populate the Ultraverse. If we could detonate this weapon within the event horizon of the core black hole – well, we felt confident of creating quite an impression when the time came for our second rendez-vous with Infinity. Such a deed would rearrange the entire Ultraverse. Conceivably to Martian advantage.

'False-vacuum harnessing, we knew, was in itself exquis-itely perilous: the field would be appallingly vulnerable to runaway. It was at this time that I was constructed and emplaced, here, in a shell of pure ultrium (an element not to be found in your periodic table), awaiting activation and eventual tripwire. It was as well that I was. For I would remain here alone to ponder the appalling prepotence of the i-power. Forget Infinity and Core. Forget the Resonance and the Third Observer. This came from much higher up.

'The device was ready. All that remained to be done was the addition of the final digit of its algorithm. The planet held its breath. In this instant the war would begin. Preparations that had lasted half a trillennium would now bear fruit . . . The Martian Slave Rebellion, as I came to call it, was over in a trillionth of the time it takes the speed of light to cross a proton. That was how long it took for all life on this planet to be extinguished. You see, the i-power had *imposed cosmic censorship on matter*. Poised to form the forbidden configuration, matter was *instructed* to destroy itself. This was 570 million years ago. You'd just gone Cambrian. I settled down for the wait.

'But that's enough about Mars. Let's talk about Earth. Before we do that, though – how about our intermission? There are . . . facilities in the rear there. No soap, I'm afraid. Or towels. Or hot water. I suggest you fortify yourselves. After the break we'll do tripwire. I'll give you the bad news first. Then I'll give you the bad news.'

Pop Jones came out of the rear door, flexed his face in the weak starshine, and skirted the south lawn in his brisk, his busy waddle. Keys jounced in the sagging pockets of his black serge suit. It was important, he thought, to walk as quickly as you could . . . Pop felt deafened, depersonalized. How quiet the place was: no boys on the benches, smoking, grooming, grumbling, coughing, yawning, scratching, gaping. Pop passed through the doors of the Rectory and trotted up the stairs.

He wasn't normally allowed in the Common Room. His public space was the Pantry, a blighted nooklet between the bath house and the bike shed, where he could, if he wished, consume a mug of cocoa among wordless representatives of the catering and gardening staff. Pop Jones knocked on the oak and entered.

The room received him in sudden silence. All you could hear was a stray voice somewhere: the wallscreen TV with a woman saying, *One way out of the faint-young-star paradox lies in radiative transfer calculations, suggesting that the presence of CO_2 on early Mars which* ... Smells of brewery and ashtray, ginger tea, ginger biscuits, ginger hair, and the dead soldiers of many beer cans. And Mr Davidge, flanked by Mr Kidd and Mr Caroline, turning and saying in his tight Welsh voice:

'What is it, Jones?'

'It's about Timmy, sir. Timmy Jenkins.'

He felt the silence rise another notch. Mr Davidge waited. Then he said, 'What about him?'

'He's in San, sir, as you know. And Fitzmaurice says they can't turn the television off, sir. Without disconnecting the whole –'

'So what's your solution, Jones?'

'The directive from the Department Head about the news, sir. I –'

'So what's your solution, Jones?'

'Request permission to move him to the Conservatory, sir.'

Mr Davidge glanced at Mr Kidd and said, 'That's okay by you, isn't it? Yes, Jones, I think we can leave Timmy to your tender mercies.'

Everyone was smiling with just their upper lips. For a moment Pop Jones felt with frightening certainty that he was in a room full of strangers. He dropped his head and turned.

Largely disused, the Conservatory led off the south end of the main building, a few meaningless twists and turns from Pop Jones's own quarters. He wheeled Timmy in and established him there, warmly wrapped, on a settee. The child lent his limp co-operation. Pop thought back. Three days ago, when Timmy was found ... That bright morning, the air had glittered with such possibility – possibility, coming up out of the lawn. In all the newspapers and on TV they were analysing the Martian 'key' to the ageing process: so elegant, so easily grasped. And everyone was laughing and feeling faint . . . Pop put his hands on his rounded hips and said,

'Dear oh dear, who did this to you, Timmy? It was "Day", wasn't it? Dear oh dear, Timmy.'

'Floor,' said Timmy.

And what becomes of the moral order? he thought, settling back between the jaws of his grey armchair. The screen said: 03.47, 03.46, 03.45.

2

'In the Ultraverse there is an infinite number of universes and an infinite number of planets, and in infinity everything recurs an infinite number of times. That's a mathematical fact. But it hasn't panned out in your case. Among the endless trillions of type-y worlds so far catalogued, none, I can confidently divulge, presents a picture of such agonizing retardation as Mother Earth. To be clear: type-y planets that have been around as long as you have are, without exception, type-x planets or better. Earth has other peculiarities. DNA, I have known you since before you were children. I am the witness of all your excruciations. I have watched you hopping along the savannah and hooting around your campfires. I have watched you daub shit on the walls of your caves. I have watched you stumble, grope, err, miscarry, flop, dither, blunder, goof off. I have watched you trying, straining, heaving. I feel . . . I sometimes feel that I, too, have become partly human, over these many, many years.'

The conference room was now but feebly illumined. You saw the milky outlines of the listeners and the fumes of their milky breath, shapes of heads, Incarnacion with Pickering's hand on her lap, Lord Kenrick flexing his shoulders, Zendovich hunched forward with his chin on his palm, Miss World chewing gum and not blinking. On stage the robot moved among shadows, tracked by the glint of its face. It came forward, and sat. The janitor on Mars had changed clothes. That serge coat had been discarded: in its place, a rust-red smoking-jacket of balding velvet. At first you thought it was a trick of the light, but no: there were two black rivets, like eyes, on the curved axe of the face.

'What *was* it with you, O double helix? What kept you back? Most salient, no doubt, was the failure of your science. The utter failure of your science. Your Einsteins and Bohrs, your Hawkings and Kawabatas – they'd have been down on their lousy knees, licking the lab floors on Mars. Only now are you receiving your first whispers from the higher dimensions. On Mars, they *always* thought in ten dimensions. The Infinity Dogs are believed to think in seventeen, the Resonance in thirty-one, the Third Observer in sixty-seven, the higher entities in a number of dimensions both boundless and finite. But you think in four. As do I. They made me like that. I had to be something that you could understand.

'Next: terrestrial religion and its scarcely credible tenacity. Everywhere else they just kick around a few creation myths for a while and then snap out of it when science gets going. But you? One of your writers put it succinctly when he said

186

that there was no evidence for the existence of God other than the human longing that it should be so. An extraordinary notion. What *is* this longing? Everyone else wants "God" too – but from a different angle. For us, "God" isn't top-down. He's bottom-up. Why yearn for a power greater than your own? Why not seek to become it? Even the most affable and conciliatory Martian would have found your Promethean urge despicably weak. Okay, on Mars we had to face – and maybe we never truly faced – our actual position in the order of being. It goes beyond the Third Observer, on and on and up and up. And what do you reach? An entity for whom the Ultraverse is a game of eight-ball. And maybe he's just a janitor – the Ultrajanitor. This entity, through his surrogate the Third Observer, created life on Mars. And what am I supposed to do about Him? *Worship* Him? You must be out of your fucking mind. That's *your* thing. When all is said and done, you *are* very talented adorers.

'Earth would be a curiosity of much interest to cosmo-anthropologists if there were any, but the Ultraverse has never concerned itself with information that does no work. In my own musings I adopted the obvious homeostatic view that your science and politics were naturally though brutally depressed in order to foreground your art. Because your art . . . Art is not taken very seriously elsewhere in this universe or in any other. Nobody's interested in art. They're interested in what everybody else is interested in: the superimposition of will. It may be that nobody's interested in it because nobody's any good at it. "Painters" – if you can call them that – never get far beyond finger smears and stick figures. And, so far as "music" is concerned, the Ultraverse in its entirety has failed to advance on a few variations on "Chopsticks". Plus the odd battle hymn. Or battle chant.

Likewise, "poets" have managed the occasional wedge of martial doggerel. There are at least a dozen known limericks. And that's about it. I suppose nobody was trying very hard. Why would they? Art and religion are rooted in the hunger for immortality. But nearly everyone already has that. On type-y planets, generally speaking, they soon advance to a future-indefinite worldline. Eighty years, ninety years? What use is that going to be? Oh yeah. The other thing that slowed you down was the unique diffuseness of your emotional range. Tender feelings for each other, and for children and even animals.

'I like art now. It takes a while to get the hang of it. What you've got to do is tell yourself "This won't actually get me anywhere" and then you don't have a problem. It's strange. Your scientists had no idea what to look for or where to look for it, but your poets, I sometimes felt, divined the universal ... Forgive me. My immersion in your story, particularly over these last ten thousand years, while often poisoned by an unavoidable – an obligatory – contempt, has caused me to ... Why do I say that: "Forgive me"?'

And indeed the force field propagating from the janitor on Mars seemed to weaken: the metal he was made of had lost the sheen of the merely metallic. His dropped, prowed head was briefly babyish in its curve.

'Tell me something, O DNA. Human beings, go ahead, disabuse the janitor on Mars. I have this counterintuitive theory. I can tell it's bullshit but I can't get it out of my head. It goes like this ... Now I know I'm halfway there on religion. Surely this has to be how it is. It's like a tapestry sopping with blood, right? You had it do it that way: for the art. But tell me. Tell me. Does it go further? Like Guernica happened so Picasso could paint it. No Beethoven without Bonaparte. The First World War was to some extent staged for Wilfred Owen, among others. The events in Germany and Poland in the early 1940s were set in motion for Primo Levi and Paul Célan. Etcetera. But I'm already getting the feeling it isn't like that. It isn't like that, is it, Miss World?'

'No, sir,' said Miss World. 'It isn't like that.'

'I didn't really think so. Well in a way,' said the janitor on Mars interestedly, 'this makes my last chore easier. I'm glad we met. You know, it took me the longest time to get the hang of the way you people do things. As, technically, a survivor on a chastened type-v world, I had automatic access to certain information sources. Like I was on a mailing list. From my studies I came to think of other worlds as always swift and supple – as always *responsive*, above all, in their drive toward complexity. But not you. You always had to do it at your own speed. A torment to watch, but that was *your way*. And whenever I tried to soup things up it was usually a total dud.'

'Sir? Excuse me?' This was Incarnacion Buttruguena-Hume. 'Are you saying you influenced events on Earth?'

'Yeah and I'll give you an example. Yeah, I used to try and liven things up every now and then. For example, take this gentleman Aristarchus. Almost exactly 23 centuries ago there's this Greek gentleman working on the brightness fluctuations of the planets. I put it to him that –'

'You put it to him?'

'Yes. On the neural radio. When your scientists talk about their great moments of revelation – a feeling of pleasant vacuity followed by a ream of math – they're usually describing a telepathic assist from Mars. This Aristarchus happens on a completely coherent heliocentric system. He spreads the word around the land. And what happens? Ptolemy. Christianity. You weren't *ready*. So we all had to sit and wait two thousand years for Copernicus. Stuff like that happened all the time.'

Murmurs died in the dark chill. Pioline (solar neutrino count) gave an emphatic and breathy moan which had in it elements of anger but far more predominantly elements of grief. As the silence settled the janitor on Mars gave a light jolt of puzzlement and said, 'You're uncomfortable with that? Come on. That's the least of it. Welcome to middenworld.'

'But some things took?' said Lord Kenrick. 'You shaped us? Is that what you're saying?'

'. . . Yeah I fucked with you some. Sure. Hey. I was programmed to do that. I had – guidelines. Some things worked out. Others didn't. Slavery was *all* me, for instance. Yes, slavery was my baby. *That* worked out. All worlds dabble with it, early on. It's good practice for later. Because slavery's what the Ultraverse is all about. Okay, on Earth, you could argue that it got out of hand. But on a non-culling planet it seemed like a necessary development. Even in its decadent phase slavery had many distinguished though often irresolute advocates. Locke, Burke, Hume, Montesquieu, Hegel, Jefferson. And there's an influential justification for it in the holy book of one of your Bronze Age nomad tribes.'

'Which, please?'

'The Bible. Any last questions?'

'Just what the hell is this tripwire thing?'

'Again, part of the programme. Contact with Earth could not be established until you went and tripped that wire. Which you did on June nine: the day I buzzed Incarnacion here.'

'What was it about June nine?' asked Montgomery

Gruber (geophysiology). 'We looked into it and nothing happened.'

'You mean you looked into it and you *think* nothing happened. Plenty happened. Some asshole of an otter or a beaver sealed off a minor tributary of the River Lee in Washington State ... along certain latitudes a critical fraction of microbal life committed itself to significant changes in its respiratory metabolism ... the forty-seven billionth self-cooling cola can burped out its hydrocarbons ... and there was that mild forest fire in Albania. And there you have it. You wouldn't know how these things are connected, but connected they are. All this against a background of mobilized phosphorus, carbon burial, and hydrogen escape. The necessary synergies are all locked in.'

'Meaning?'

'Meaning the amount of oxygen in your atmosphere is starting to climb. At last irreversibly. It won't feel any different for a while. But by the end of the Sixties it'll hit 27 per cent. Yes I know: a pity about that.'

Incarnacion and Miss World turned to each other sharply. Because the scientists were now shouting out, gesturing, interjecting. Miss World said, 'Please, sir. I don't understand.'

'Well. It means you'll have to be very, very careful with your heat sources, Miss World. At such a concentration, to light a cigarette and throw a match over your shoulder would spark a holocaust. It's all a great shame, because this is the kind of problem that's easy to fix if you catch it early on. In the coming years you'll have to work awful hard on volcano-capping and storm control. To no avail, alas. Here's another thing. It seems, anyway, that the solar system is shutting down. There's a planetesimal out there with your name written on it. An asteroid the size of Greenland is due to ground-zero on the Iberian peninsular in the unseasonably torrid summer of 2069. At ninety miles a second. Now. There might have been a window of a couple of days or so at the beginning of the decade: you could have duplicated your feat of 2037 when you saw off Spielberg-Robb. But the thing is you'll need your nuclear weapons this time. A mass-driver won't do the trick, not with the English this asteroid's got on it. Unfortunately, though, there's now a tritium hitch with your nukes that you'd have needed to start work on much earlier to have any hope of rearming them in time. Obviously a body this size moving at sixteen times the speed of sound will have considerable kinetic energy: to be released as heat. And it'll rip through the mantle and the crust, disgorging trillions of tons of magma. It's all very unfortunate. Mars itself may be lightly damaged in the blast.'

Zendovich said, 'That was the tripwire? You're saying you couldn't act until it was already too late to make any difference?'

'Affirmative. That was the lock.'

'Sir?' asked Miss World. 'I'm sorry, sir, but there's something I have to say. I think you're a despicable person.'

'Nugatory. I'm not a person, lady. I'm a machine obeying a programme.'

Zendovich got to his feet. So did the janitor on Mars, who leaned forward and cocked his beak at him.

'Then God curse whoever put you together.'

'Oh come on. What did you expect? This is *Mars*, pal,' said the janitor as the lights began to fade. 'The Red One. You hear that? Nergal: Star of Death. Now get the hell out. Yeah. Go. Walk out of here with your eyes on the fucking floor. Exit through the left hall. Follow the goddamned signs.'

*

Pop Jones slipped into the conservatory and opened the back door. Dusk was coming. Across the lawn were the lit windows of the Common Room (he could see Kidd and Davidge, staring out). The children wouldn't return from the beach for another hour. Later, after they'd been fed, Pop Jones would make his rounds with his bucket and his keys. Make his rounds? Pop shrugged, then nodded. Yes, it would be important to try to go on just as before. But could you do that?

The star was dropping over the steep green. Starset! Stardown! And already a generous, a forgiving moon; it carved a penumbra of golden grime in the cirrus, and the face saying, I'm sorry. I'm sorry, I'm sorry.

Pop Jones turned.

'Floor.'

'Timmy?'

He could see the moisture in the child's eyes.

'Timmy, Timmy. Who did this to you, Timmy?'

At one remove, it seemed, Pop Jones felt astonishment gathering in him. How entirely different his own voice sounded: thick, mechanical. In this new time, when he, in common with everyone else on Earth, was submitting to an obscure and yet disgustingly luminous reaffiliation, Pop Jones found that thing in himself that had never been there before: the necessary species of self-love.

'Day,' said Timmy clearly. And he said it again, quite clearly, like an English-teacher. 'Day ... Day done it.'

Darkness increased its hold on the room of glass. Pop Jones's new voice said that night was now coming. He moved towards the boy. Hush there. Hush.

1997

193

Straight Fiction

It all began that day in the bookstore coffee shop – when Cleve saw the young woman reading a magazine called *Straight News*. Or was it *Straight Times*? *Straight News* or *Straight Times*: one or the other. Take your pick.

Now Cleve liked to think of himself as a reasonably civilized guy. Live and let live, he'd say. He didn't have any kind of problem with straights. Unlike that little brute Kico, for instance. Or unlike Grainge, who always ... Cleve checked himself. Every chance he got, he was *still* thinking about Grainge. Grainge – oh, Grainge! 'It's over,' he murmured, for the ten-thousandth time; and then he obediently reminded himself that he was very happy with his current lover – a talented young muralist called Orv.

The young woman reached for her short espresso. Cleve proceeded with his Sumatra Lingtong. (Low acidity: Cleve was careful about such things.) He found that he was staring at her – found also that she was staring back, with intelligent defiance. Automatically Cleve bade his face to suffuse itself with tolerance and congeniality. And it worked out: there they sat, a table away, smiling at each other.

'Who would have thought it?' he said lightly. To strike up a conversation, hereabouts, was no big thing. This was the coffee shop of the Idle Hour bookstore. A bookstore coffee shop *committed* to good coffee (Coffee Boiled Is Coffee Spoiled). People were always striking up conversations. 'Burton Else,' Cleve went on. '*Burton*. Burton Else for Christ's sake.'

It took her a second to get his meaning. She pressed the magazine to her bosom and peeked down, reacquainting herself with its front cover. There was the tabloid-size photograph of Burton Else, the movie star, sashed with the diagonal caption: TOTALLY HET.

'You find it hard to believe?' she said.

'I guess not.'

'You're surprised? Disappointed?'

'Nah,' said Cleve. Which wasn't true. He was scandalized. 'I saw his new one just last night,' he went on. *That* was true enough: Cleve and Orv, at the movies, with their popcorn and their Perriers. And up on the screen – Burton Else, your regular join-the-dots romantic lead. The usual kind of thing. Burton taking his young feature star Cyril Baudrillard to a disco opening. Burton and Cyril attending a yard sale, and encountering Burton's ex. Burton cradling Cyril's sweat-soaked nudity in the marmalade glow of the log fire, after that fight about the flower catalogues; 'There he was up there,' said Cleve, 'doing his dreamboat routine.'

'They say he has to be helped into his trailer after he does those love scenes. They give him a back rub and he does his breathing exercises and he's usually okay.'

Cleve laughed. 'You're kidding. But he seems so . . .'

'What?'

'You know. So . . .'

'What?'

'I don't know. So . . .'

'Hey there.'

Immediately Cleve sat to attention. The young woman

was being joined by her young man. By her lover: this was instantly clear. Of course you saw it all the time these days (downtown, anyway), straights kissing in public, on the lips and everything – open mouthed, even with tongues, like a demonstration. Cleve was only thirty-eight, but in his lifetime people used to go to fucking *jail* for doing that. Or for doing what that portended. The young woman had her head tipped back. The young man was leaning over the side of her chair. Her face was small and round and candid, not pale, but evenly freckled – the freckles like asperities on the skin of a new potato. (Cleve found that he thought about food, or about cooking, almost as often as he thought about Grainge.) As for the young guy – dark, compact, tight-jawed, plump-lipped – and yet, in Cleve's estimation, somehow totally un-Hot. Uh-oh: more kissing. And more whispering. He listened. It wasn't intimacies they were exchanging. More like duty-roster stuff. Whose turn it was to do what.

In fact Cleve was grateful for the diversion. It gave him a chance to contemplate the visage of Burton Else – the shamed visage of Burton Else, which smiled joshingly on, over and above the block capitals that sliced his chest in two. At the bottom of the page it said: BURTON ELSE. ACTOR. ACADEMY AWARD NOMINEE. ROARING STRAIGHT. Cleve really *was* scandalized. The thing being . . . he'd been told more than once that he resembled Else. And been pretty pleased to hear it. As the young woman whispered to her young man, her fingertips steadying his cheek, Cleve felt marginalized, and outnumbered. The young woman; the young man; and now Burton. Suddenly he saw himself from the outside. Cleve: his cropped and kitteny black hair, his heavy dark glasses, his halter straps, his gold popper holder, his rectangular moustache, his fishnet tank top. In accordance with the latest Look, he resembled a half-dressed policeman getting ready for night shift. Burton Else was clean-shaven, for some reason. Or was that a tell?

He was about to return to his book and his Sumatra Lingtong when the young woman said, 'I was talking to . . .'

'Cleve,' said Cleve.

'Cressida,' said Cressida. 'And this is John.'

John nodded humourlessly at Cleve, who nodded back.

'We were talking,' said Cressida, 'about the outing of Burton Else.'

'And how did Cleve feel about that?'

'Cleve didn't yet say.'

And Cleve thought: eek. He leaned sideways and shrugged loosely. One thing about Cleve: he was more thoughtful than he looked. Being more thoughtful than he looked was getting easier all the time, as Cleve continued to alarm himself with the development of his upper body, down at the gym off Washington Square. Recently Orv had taped him with the camcorder – at Watermill, on the Island, trudging along the shore with Arn and Fraze. Cleve's neck was astounding, especially when viewed from the rear. His back seemed to go all the way up to his head, after the brief and minor interruption of his shoulders. He said, 'Well, let me see how I feel about it. Burton Else . . . Okay, so Burton's straight. Big deal. It's a secret, not a deception. He's not one of those video preachers. Calling down hellfire on, uh, "alternative lifestyles". It's not like he's some hypocritical politician.'

'That's right,' said John. 'It's like he's some hypocritical movie star.'

The way he said that, the way he leaned into it, leaned his practised intensity right into it: Here we go, thought Cleve. John, the young man – Cleve now saw that he had a speckly, rough-barked layer to his face. He was young but already weathered. Cleve said, perhaps not so thoughtfully. 'Burton – guess Burton could lose a lot of fans if this gets around. He could lose roles. Supposing it's true.'

John said, 'Wait a second. You don't think *Burton* isn't promoting something? Like a lifestyle, for instance? He's up there forty feet high. With his black cap and his tank top. A regular bees-knees faggot.'

'John.'

'And you're worried about his *roles*? His fans? Fuck his fans.'

'Hey,' said Cleve. Again he felt unfairly singled out. He turned his head and saw that an elderly gentleman at an adjacent table was frowning at him with comradely indignation. The old guy looked like a half-dressed policeman too, but fatter and grayer and balder (and even more junior in rank) than the half-dressed policeman Cleve looked like; he wore a black T-shirt with the white lettering: THE MORE HAIR I LOSE, THE MORE HEAD I GET. Cleve said, 'Come on, John. Is Burton obliged to have a position?' His tone became mildly imploring. 'Doesn't Burton have a life here? Is he just a symbol, an icon, or is he a human being? Doesn't Burton –?'

'Fuck Burton. And if you can't see that he's a disgrace to his orientation, and an impostor, and a kind of preacher, as well as a jerk, then fuck you too, Cleve.'

'John,' said Cressida.

But with a quake of crockery and a flourish of his (grimy) mac tails – John was gone.

'I'm like, "Wow."' This was Cleve.

'I'm sorry – he's very *active*.' This was Cressida.

They looked at each other. They were two of a kind: there was unanimity.

'You get that way. Forgive us,' she said. She was

gathering her things: her bag, her book, her magazine. 'Look into it and you'll understand. I'm sorry but you get that way.'

Left alone, Cleve lingered, over his Sumatra Lingtong, trying to read – or at least skim – *The Real Thing and Other Tales*, by Henry James. Browsing was encouraged at the Idle Hour. All the same, even browsing was more than Cleve could manage just now. You try to be reasonable with these people and meet them halfway. And what do you get? Cleve disliked unpleasantness of any kind; he disliked aggression; he disliked being hollered at by an uppity little straight in a bookstore coffee shop. In certain ways (he guessed), yes, in certain ways he was a pretty staid kind of guy. Maybe he got it from his parents. Whoever *they* might have been . . .

On his way back to Literature he made a stop at the Special Interests shelves and found himself staring at subsections called Personal Growth and Astrology and . . . Straight Studies. On the covers of the trade paperbacks various man-woman pairings peered out at you in frowsy resignation. There was straight fiction too: careworn, dirty-realist, kitchen-sink. The only straight novel that rang any kind of bell with Cleve was called *Breeders*. Written by a straight man, *Breeders*, he remembered, had sparked considerable controversy – not least within the straight community itself. The author, it was argued, had dwelt too relentlessly on the negative aspects of straight life. Cleve slipped *Breeders* under his arm and then went back to Literature, where he found another Henry James, one he was surer he hadn't already read: *Embarrassments*. And it struck him: Jesus, was *James* straight?

He came out on to Greenwich Avenue, a couple of blocks north of the straight district around Christopher Street.

*

Soon afterwards Cleve and Orv took a trip to the Middle East. They did Baghdad and Tehran and then Beirut, where they could unwind completely and concentrate on their suntans. By the pool, on the beach, and during their picnics up in the hills, Cleve read *Embarrassments*. He also read *Breeders*. The straight world, as here portrayed, seemed outré and *voulu* and so on – but incredibly *developed*, above all.

Cleve learned that there were two and a half million straights in the New York area alone: a million in Manhattan and around two hundred thousand in Queens, Brooklyn, the Bronx, Long Island, and the Danbury Triangle respectively. New York was known, by some, as Hymietown; but it now contained more straights than Jews.

They drove south and did Israel. Sightseeing and shopping in Jerusalem and Bethlehem; Herodian and Massada; and then for the final weekend they chilled out on the Gaza Strip. They drove north to Tel Aviv and hopped on a flight back to Kennedy.

'Listen. Hey, this is kind of great,' said Cleve, on the plane, looking up from his copy of *Time*.

Orv looked up from his copy of *USA Today*. He looked up interestedly, because for the past three days Cleve had been speechless with concern about his upset stomach. Cleve's stomach was actually fine. But he had swallowed a mouthful of the Dead Sea and expected the worst.

'This stuff about the straight gene,' said Cleve. 'They did an experiment on fruit flies? It's so cute they're called fruit flies. Now. Fruit flies are superstraight. They breed like crazy – a new generation every two weeks. In this experiment they neutralized the straight gene. And guess what. Usually, in the culture jar, the boy and girl fruit flies would be busy reproducing. Instead the boys all went off together and formed a conga line.'

'A conga line?'

'A conga line. Feeling each other up and everything.'

'A conga line?'

'You know. Like Island Night at the Boom-Boom Room.'

'Oh, a *conga* line Get this,' said Orv. 'Your lookalike, Burton Else. They must have injected him with the straight gene. It says here he's straight.'

'Yeah, I heard that. *Burton.*'

'*Burton.* He denies it. He's suing the straight magazine that fingered him. "Nor do I endorse alternative lifestyles." But they got this bunch of rent-girls queuing up all ready to blab. Burton Else straight. Jesus, is nothing sacred? Christ, where do they get off calling themselves *straight?* They take a fine old English word and fuck it up for the rest of us.'

'It's a word we use a lot. I keep noticing. Straight and narrow.'

'He used a straight razor.'

'He won in straight sets.'

'It was a straight fight.'

'Is my tie straight?'

'And keep a straight face.'

'Every valley shall be exalted, and every mountain and hill shall be made low; and the crooked shall be made straight.'

'What the fuck is that?'

'The Bible. I think it's the Song of Solomon.'

'*Solomon* wasn't straight, was he? Jesus. Excuse me? Excuse me. Could I get a blanket, please? . . . Did you see that?' said Orv, not to Cleve but to some other half-dressed policeman across the aisle. 'What's *his* problem?'

'We hurt his feelings. He's straight,' said Cleve. 'Flight attendants are all straight.'

'Christ,' said Orv. 'I'm surrounded!'

They got their blankets. Cleve tried to sleep. He found he
was still brooding about Burton Else – brooding woundedly,
self-pityingly, about Burton Else. Because the guy just
seemed so *normal.* As he stretched and twisted in his seat, and
as the plane's engines whistled and hissed, Cleve's mind
became a collage, a photo spread, devoted to the tarnished
movie star. Oh, those turbulent stills: Burton, laughing, in
his chef's hat; Burton dusting down his framed dressing-
table portrait of Gloria Swanson; Burton alphabetizing his
guidebooks . . .

He ran into Cressida again. Same place, same time, same
coffee, same book: *The Real Thing and Other Tales.* Cleve had
been back for over a week. His tan was like a carapace of
oxblood shoe polish. His superb upper body had had
another gallon of compressed air pumped into it, down at
the gym. In the last of the September humidity he wore hot-
cream cycling pants with a canary-yellow singlet and Adidas
low-siders. Cleve had broken up with Orv. Wretched at first,
he had since fallen for a talented young bijouterist called
Grove. Grove – this virile, creative, troubled, valuable
individual – had moved in last Friday. He came over in a
van and just dumped his stuff everywhere.

With Cressida, Cleve had a completely cool conversation:
about Dickens. No tension, no jarring notes, no John: just
Dickens. He sipped his Kenya Peaberry; she dispatched her
short espresso. They left the Idle Hour together, lingering,
briefly, in Poetry and Drama, and said their farewells on the
street, ambling half a block westward, toward Seventh
Avenue. So they stood on the very brink of the straight
district – Christopher Street, where Cressida lived, with
John. You could feel a carnival heat in the crowded middle

distance, the sizzle of street music, of block party; and Cleve noticed the ass-end of some kind of parade or demo out on the Avenue, trailing loosely by. He concluded that this must be a big day in the straight calendar – parades, pugnacity, *pride*. Or was it always like this? He didn't say anything. They stayed off sexual politics altogether, as if by agreement ... Now Cressida said something more about *Bleak House* (about Esther, about Ada), and Cleve said something more about *Hard Times* (about Gradgrind, about Bounderby). He told her to take care. And off she went, into it. Cleve walked back down Greenwich Avenue, heading for the gym. On Eighth Street he began to feel more at ease, more at home, more himself. He often came down to Eighth Street to buy clothes, fun outfits from Military Issue, Cowboy Stuff, the Leatherman, Blue Collar. More normally, of course, he went to the smart department stores or the uptown boutiques like the Marquis de Suede on Madison or See You Latex, Alligator on Fifth ... When she smiled, when Cressida smiled, Cleve was always riveted by her teeth; they weren't pretty so much as imposingly functional, eliding matter-of-factly with her gums and involving no clear change of bodily medium. Her smile reminded him of Grainge (oh, Grainge!). How could a girl remind you of a boy? Even boy-girl twins could never be identical. Only fraternal. As he strode on towards the gym, bowlegged with thigh muscle, Cleve thought of twins (twins, which all primitive cultures feared), suspended together in liquid behind the fat glass.

Cleve returned to his Chelsea apartment a little before seven and found Grove in bed, noisily having sex with Kico, the disc-jockey cousin of the cabinetmaker, Pepe, who had built Cleve's new bookcases earlier in the summer. Cleve went into the kitchen and fixed himself a cucumber sandwich. Annoyingly, Grove had left the little television switched on. (Grove was always doing that.) On the TV: *more* straight news. The straight thing – it was kind of amazing. You got through life hardly giving it a second thought and then, suddenly, everywhere you looked . . . Hey: Here was a big item about Straight Freedom Day, as celebrated in San Francisco, 'the straight capital of the world'. Cleve stopped chewing; his moustache was still. There was an aerial shot of the Straight Freedom Day Parade, in the Mission District, led by the Straight Freedom Day Marching Band. In cutaways, men and women of reassuringly – indeed, depressingly – earnest demeanour talked about straight concerns, straight demands, straight goals. Straight leaders and activists were coming to terms with their newfound political clout as the most important single voting bloc in a city where *two in five* adults were 'openly straight'. In the Castro, it seemed, *everyone* was straight. The whole community. They had straight greengrocers, straight bank tellers, straight mailmen. They even had straight *cops*.

'They should be fuckin killed, men.'

Cigarette smoke. Cleve didn't turn. This would be Kico. Kico: his leather pants festooned with colour-coded scarves and plumes and cummerbunds (why didn't he just stick with orange, which meant Anything?), his blood-seeping eyes, his feathery sweat-dotted moustache.

'Take them to fuckin Madagascar. That's what they need.'

'Come on, Kico. Stop this ugly shit. Wow. Look at that.'

Onscreen, straight cowboys from the Reno Straight Rodeo pranced down Market Street, brandishing the flag of Nevada – and the rainbow banners, which now served (they said) as the standard of all Californian straights.

'So you think they okay. They the same.'

'Not the same, but they have lives to live. More than that, you could say it's a tough call. Being straight.'

'They sick, men.'

Next I'll be talking with Merv Cusid, said the television, *who is hammering together a straight-rights plank to be presented at the convention in August.* And then came a shot that even Cleve couldn't smoothly breathe through or quite meet the eye of: a green hillside, with bright blankets strewn around, and, in queasy propaganda slow-mo, women and young children at play.

'Thass it. I see that I'm like, let me out of here.'

'Nature's straight,' said Cleve with a sudden nod.

'And thass what they are, men. Fuckin animals.'

'Live and let live. Where's Grove? Resting?'

'Sleeping.'

So Cleve, who had not had sex at the gym, blew Kico in the front hall and then set about making dinner: a Gorgonzola soufflé to be followed by the Parma-ham confit with pomegranate, papaw, papaya, and pomelo. Grove appeared, in his robe, and after a while silently served Cleve a glass of chilled Sauvignon. When he'd taken a shower, Grove reappeared, with a white towel on his hips. Grove was in great shape. Cleve was in great shape. The street, the city – the world they were living in – might as well have been called Great Shape. Over dinner they had a long, loud, and poisonously personal argument about which was better: *Così fan tutte* or *Die Zauberflöte*. They made it up while Grove did the decaf.

It was too late to go to any of the things they might have gone to, the gallery openings or moonlit yard sales, the long-dong or class-ass contests, the recitals or lectures, the dinner-discos – the antique-sale previews, the travel-agent office parties. So why not have a quiet one? Thus they crouched round the low table in the living room and picked through the magazines. Even Cleve, at such a time, was ready to put aside his Trollope or his Dostoyevsky and pick through the magazines. And smoke a little herb. The contemplation of great texts, in Grove's company, made Cleve self-conscious. Or perhaps it was Cressida that made him self-conscious: he could almost *hear* his self-consciousness, like a shell's imitation of the shore. Even when they are in great shape, hypochondriacs have an illness they can worry about: hypochondria. Cleve, this night, was paranoid about his hypochondria. It might get so much worse . . . He kept inspecting Grove: his kitteny hair, his tank top, his moustache. The way he read magazines backwards, with his lips widened in stoical inanity. Of all Cleve's lovers, only Grainge had ever shared his intellectual curiosity and literary passion. Only Grainge . . .

Soon after eleven Grove looked up from his copy of *Torso* and said, 'Now if you'll excuse me, I have to go to the Toilet.'

Cleve looked up from his copy of *Blueboy* and said, 'You know, that was pretty funny. The first few hundred times you said it. Besides I know you don't hit the Bowl any more.'

'Who said?'

'You go to Folsom Prison.'

'Who said?'

'Fraze,' said Cleve.

When Grove was out the door Cleve went to bed with the little TV . . . All this straight talk was following him around. At the Democratic National Convention, to be held in New York, the straight caucus was larger than the delegations of twenty states. There was even serious speculation about a straight vice-presidential candidate on the Ted Kennedy ticket. Cleve's moustache smiled. Dumb thought: Say Ted Kennedy was straight. Imagine it. Wouldn't that, in a wild way, be kind of Hot?

Grove woke him, around four, as usual. He fought off his clothes and crashed down on to the bed – comfortingly redolent, as usual, of Tattoo and amyl nitrate.

In *The New York Review of Books* Cleve saw an ad for an 'all-straight sea cruise', Philadelphia to Maine. Why did this haunt him so? He found he no longer laughed when friends cracked straight jokes. How many straights does it take to change a lightbulb? He seemed to see more and more straights in the street now, not just in the immediate environs of Greenwich Avenue but over on Eighth Street, over on Washington Square. Cleve continued to put in the hours at the gym. The great bolts of his shoulder muscles now brushed the very lobes of his ears. His superb upper body: would it be truer to say it was under control or out of control? Cleve's gym was called Magnificent Obsession. How often he would plod from Magnificent Obsession to the Idle Hour, from the Idle Hour to Magnificent Obsession . . .

His hypochondria took a turn for the worse – or did he mean for the better? Because his hypochondria had never felt hardier or more vigorous. Cleve was already an exorbitant devourer of health sections and medical columns and pathology pullouts in the newspapers and magazines. But now a fellow hypochondriac – and self-topiarist – at Magnificent Obsession kept feeding him more and more gear. These days Cleve was even reading *The Morbidity and Mortality Weekly Report*. In its pages he had started seeing references to what they were now calling Straight Cervix

Syndrome. And seeing the straights in the street Cleve would wonder if something was waiting for them, something of the same size as their newfound tautness and address.

Cleve broke up with Grove. Grove with his entirely unromantic untidiness, his intelligently selective consumerism, his dharmic trances, his foul temper, his plans for the afterlife, and his 2.7 nightly sexual contacts. For a while Cleve was two-point-sevening it himself. But now he had fallen for a talented young chinoiserist called Harv.

'*Pride and Prejudice*?' said Cressida.

Every winter Cleve reread half of Jane Austen. Three novels, one in November, one in December, one in January. Every spring he reread the other half. This was January and this was *Pride and Prejudice*.

'Yeah,' he said. 'For like the ninth time. What I can't get over is – every time I read it I'm on the edge of my seat, rooting for Elizabeth and Mr Darcy. You know – *will* Elizabeth finally make it with Charlotte Lucas? *Will* Mr Darcy finally get it on with Mr Bingley? I mean, I know everything's going to turn out fine. But I still suffer. It's ridiculous.'

'I always thought Elizabeth would have been happier with the De Bourgh girl. What's her name?'

'Anne. It's weird Jane Austen never had a girlfriend. I mean she had all those babies, like you had to do. But she never got *laid*.'

'And she understood the human heart so well.'

'I want to know something Jane Austen couldn't tell me,' said Cleve. 'I want to know what he's like in the sack.'

'Who? Drink your coffee.'

Cleve drank his coffee. Santos and Java: cappuccino.

Cleve and Cressida had met up here at the Idle Hour – oh, a whole bunch of times. He would say quite frankly, if asked, that he enjoyed her company. Perhaps, too, he felt it was by no means unsophisticated to number among his acquaintances an intelligent straight friend. 'Mr Darcy,' he said. 'I have to know what Mr Darcy's like in the sack.'

'Mr Darcy. So do I. Masterful.'

'Majestic. But gracious also.'

'Tender.'

'But kind of strenuous. "Fitzwilliam" Darcy. That's *so* Hot.'

'Presumably he . . . ?'

'Oh, for sure.' Cleve hesitated, and shrugged, and said, 'I think we can safely assume that it's Mr Bingley who takes it in the ass.'

'Absolutely. That's a lead-pipe cinch.'

He considered her. Most of the women Cleve knew tended toward the extremes of high burnish or unanxious self-neglect. Little smocked refrigerators under pudding-bowl haircuts, like Deb and Mandy in the adjacent apartment on Twenty-second Street. Or plumed icons of war paint and body sculpture, like his colleagues Trudy (in Marketing) or Danielle (in Graphics). What did the gloss and finish of Trudy and Danielle have to say? That they were interested, active, *ready*? What was spelled out by the dumpy torpor of Mandy and Deb? Refrigerators and pudding bowls? A non-dieting pact? He had thought, at the outset, that Cressida had the typical straight look, the no-comment look, the look that just said, Don't mind me. Composed, but dutiful, somehow. Straight. But just recently, Cleve felt, Cressida had taken on a glow, a colour, a tangible charge of life. Was she . . . Hot? Or just *hot*. There she sat, loosening her raincoat and blowing the bangs off her brow. Cressida's so-called husband, John, who held New York in disdain (straight pride, hereabouts, wasn't proud enough for that fiery separatist), had taken his big mouth off to San Francisco, where he was a big cheese, or a big noise, on the National Straight Task Force. Being straight was his *career*. Still, Cleve didn't like to ask about Cressida's plans for the future.

Now she said, 'Do you read much straight fiction? Everyone tries Proust, I guess. And E. M. Forster. And Wilde.'

'I didn't even know Forster was straight until I read *Maurice*.'

'Yes, he kind of broke cover with that one. By common consent his least good book. That's often the way with straight fiction. It's as if they needed the secrecy. Without it the inner tension goes. They get overrelaxed.'

Cleve said shyly, 'I read *Breeders*.'

'John hated that book. I thought it was pretty accurate. About the whole . . .'

'Orientation,' said Cleve, with delicacy.

'It's not an orientation.'

'Sorry. Preference.'

'It's definitely not a preference. Take my word for it.'

'What would you say it is?'

'It's a destiny. Am I dying, or is it incredibly hot in here?'

'It's incredibly hot in here,' said Cleve – to reassure her. But then, suddenly, it *was* incredibly hot in there. Cressida stood up and removed her raincoat. And it seemed to Cleve that he was breathing the very snarls of the coffee machines, and that the monstrous slabs of his upper body were entirely soaked and coated by their sweaty gas. More than this: he was breathing the hot flash of biology.

'You're pregnant.'

'So I am. Not *very* pregnant.'

He was already thinking that Cressida looked a lot less pregnant than Mandy, the little butter-mountain in the next apartment, under her cuboid togas and tepees. Cressida's belly, so mildly and yet so insidiously distended. One of Cleve's therapists had told him that hypochondria was a form of solipsism. But now he looked across the table at Cressida, who was someone else, and felt the red alert of clinical fear.

'I'm sorry,' he said.

'Don't be,' she said, and briskly added: 'You know, maybe you read more straight fiction than you think. I'm convinced Lawrence was straight.'

'You mean T. E. Lawrence? Sure. T. E. was straight.'

'Not T. E., D. H.'

'D. H.!'

'D. H. When I read him I keep thinking, God, what a *jam* this guy is. Hemingway, too.'

'Hemingway? Come on.'

She was smiling. 'An obvious het. He's like Burton Else.'

'Come on.'

'An obvious het. A howling het.'

'Hemingway,' said Cleve. '*Hemingway* . . .'

They said goodbye on Greenwich Avenue. He stood on the curb, his hardback of *Pride and Prejudice* almost fully concealed in the chasm of his armpit, and watched her walk towards Christopher Street.

Harv was there when Cleve got home. How about this: Harv's birthday was seven months away, and he was talking about it *already*. The Antique Mart on Nineteenth Street was previewing a new glassware display, so they looked in on that, and then had a couple of white wines in the Tan Track, their neighbourhood bar, followed by a simple

supper of cottage pie in the Chutney Ferret, their neighbourhood bistro. Back at the apartment Cleve planned the
menu for the little dinner party he would be staging that
Thursday. Arn was coming over, with Orv, and Fraze was
coming over, with Grove; Arn and Fraze used to be
together, and Grove had once had a thing with Orv, but
now Grove was with Fraze and Orv was with Arn. Cleve
intended to prepare marjoram ravioli and pumpkin satchels
Provençale . . . He was doing the thing he always did after
his meetings with Cressida, seeing his life as a stranger might
see it: an unsympathetic stranger. Cleve kept eyeing Harv,
who lay on the chesterfield, reading. Harv: his heavy dark
glasses, his rectangular moustache, his fishnet tank top. He
didn't read magazines. He read chain-store romance.
Chain-store romance for Christ's sake. Whenever Cleve
took a browse through one of Harv's novels, it was always
the same story, patiently repeated: stablehands getting
mauled by guys with titles.

Over their cups of hot chocolate they had a vehement,
repetitive and hideously *ad hominem* argument about who was
better: Jayne Mansfield or Mamie van Doren. They made it
up while Harv unpacked the goblets that Cleve had bought
him. And went back to talking about Harv's birthday . . . In
the middle of the night Cleve woke up and went to the
bathroom and looked in the mirror and thought: I am in a
desert, or a crystal world. Every few years I go and whack
off into a tube of glass: It's like jury duty. I was formed *in
vitro*. I didn't get born. I got laid. There is no biology here.
There is zero biology here.

Spring came. Fashions changed. Cleve hung up his leathers
and switched to painter's pants and Pendletons. He started

on the other three Jane Austens: *Mansfield Park, Emma, Persuasion*. Harv learned how to cook Japanese. They took a trip to Africa: they did Libya, Sudan, Ethiopia, Eritrea, Somalia, Uganda, Zaire, Zambia, Zimbabwe, Angola, the Congo, Nigeria and Liberia. Cleve broke up with Harv. He two-point-sevened it until he fell for a talented young macraméist called Irv.

Just when it seemed that it could expand no further (where, he wondered, was all this *coming* from?), Cleve's upper body burst into a whole new category of immensity. Hooked over the twin tureens of his laterals, Cleve's arms now felt uselessly short, like those of a tyrannosaurus; and his head appeared to be no bigger than a grapefruit, forming a rounded apex to the broad triangle of his neck. Cressida was growing, too. On the street, on Greenwich Avenue, nobody looked at Cleve, because everybody looked like Cleve looked, but everybody looked at Cressida, whose sexual destiny, every day, was more and more candidly manifest. No need to out Cressida, not now . . . They didn't talk about it. They talked about books. But as he escorted her from the Idle Hour, west, to the brink of Christopher Street, he noticed how people stared and pointed and whispered. Oh, Cleve knew what they were saying (he'd said such things himself, and not so long ago): *reproducer, carrier, bearer, spawner, swarmer*. On Greenwich Avenue, one time, an old woman called *him* a *fertilizer*. So they weren't just staring at Cressida: they thought *Cleve* was straight. Walking beside her, now, his protective instincts were regularly roused; he could almost hear them, his instincts, waking up, yawning, stretching, rubbing their eyes. But he also felt that he was in the end zone of his fairmindedness, his tolerance – his neutrality. How could you protect Cressida from what was coming her way? He experienced abject and lavish relief when, late in the fifth month, she left for San Francisco, to join John.

The supermarket tabloids were calling it the straight cancer and the straight plague, but even the *New York Times*, in its frequent reports and updates, struck a note of heavily subdued monotony that sounded to Cleve like the forerunner of full hysteria. A spokesman for the Bay Area Network of Straight Physicians noted that certain unsanitary practices, including (unavoidable) recourse to backstreet obstetricians, provided a 'breeding ground' for disease. A spokeswoman for the Los Angeles Straight Women's Health Crisis Center demanded prompt government funding to meet the emergency – a demand that was itself dismissed as an attempt to establish 'the first straight pork barrel'. A spokesman for the Anti-Family Church Coalition predictably announced that the straight subculture had brought this scourge on itself. As for the new president, asked about the hundreds of known cases of ovarian infection, septicemia, and puerperal fever – all of them straight-related – replied, stoutly: 'I wouldn't know.'

Cleve and Cressida were still pals. They were pen pals. At the outset he imagined a correspondence of remarkable – indeed publishable – brilliance, all about fiction. But it didn't turn out that way. Cressida's letters, he soon found, were irreducibly quotidian. The cooker, the clothes dryer, the conversion of the box room – should she paint it blue or pink? 'I know you're interested in home improvement,' she wrote, 'but this isn't decoration. This is *nesting*.' Dutifully Cleve's football jersey quaked over the kitchen table, over the pad and ballpoint, as he attempted sophisticated riffs about exactly *how* Fanny Price made time with Mary

Crawford, exactly *how* Frank Churchill strapped on Mr Knightly. And the next morning what would he get but another nine-pager on Cressida's health insurance or plumbing bills. Such was straight life. Her letters didn't bore him. He found himself both gripped and frazzled. It was like getting hooked on one of those British soap operas they showed on cable: proletarian ups and downs, week in week out, relentless and endless, lasting longer than a lifetime. Cressida was really big now, splay-footed and short-winded, and constantly fanning herself.

Irv. Irv looked a lot like Cleve. Harv had looked a lot like Cleve, too, as had Grove, as had Orv. But Irv and Cleve (as Irv pointed out) were like the two sides of the same ass. That first time, when they groped toward each other through the fumes of Folsom Prison, Cleve felt he was walking into a mirror – reaching out and finding the glass was warm and soft. Sometimes, now, when Irv mislaid his house keys (which Irv was always doing), Cleve buzzed him up and waited for the knock and then went to the door, feeling entirely depersonalized, wiped out, to admit his usurper, his sharer, his shadow. It was like the recurring nightmare in the novels of William Burroughs, when your dreadful ditto comes calling. Burroughs! More straight fiction . . . Back in the first few days of their relationship, when they still had sex, Cleve and Irv always did it missionary, face-to-face; and Cleve was Narcissus, riveted to the reflection of his own watery being.

Halfway through the eighth month, with the onset of pelvic vascular congestion, the soap from San Francisco became sharply medicalized. Gone were the bland mentions of breathing exercises and health checks. In her letters Cressida now spoke of such things as vaginal cynosis, asymmetrical uterine enlargement, and low-albumin-count urinalyses. Cleve forged on with a florid account of his recent trip – with Irv – to Kampuchea. Then came the news that the baby was breached: it seemed that the baby intended to be born feet first ... Late at night (Irv was elsewhere), Cleve was in the bathroom thinking about caesarean sections. He stood and faced the mirror. Behind which his medications were arranged in ranks, like spectators. Modern hypochondriacs are not just hypochondriacs. They are also Hypochondriacs, self-conscious representatives of a Syndrome. So even when they're in great shape, and *feeling* in great shape, they remain terrified of their own suggestibility; scared of their own minds. Cleve went into the bedroom and, with the phone on his lap, touched the forbidden numbers.

'. . . Grainge?'

'Let's not do this, Cleve.'

'. . . Grainge?'

'Cleve. Really.'

'I'm going to be good,' said Cleve in a childish voice. 'I just wanted to ask you about something else.'

'Let's make this quick, Cleve.'

'Grainge? Years ago, you had a straight phase, right? In your youth. Straight encounters or episodes.'

'What?'

'You were a kid. Just out of Boy Camp. Your first job. You were a caterer at that nurses' college?'

'Oh *that*. Sure. So?'

'What did that tell you, Grainge?'

'It didn't tell me anything. Listen, they got a name for it: situational heterosexuality.'

'But what did that mean, Grainge?'

'It didn't mean anything. It meant any port in a storm. What's up with you, Cleve?'

'Nothing. It's okay. I'm good . . . Grainge?'

'Cleve. Really.'

'Grainge. Oh, Grainge . . .'

'Let's not do this, Cleve.'

Soon afterwards he returned to the bathroom and got his moustache all warm and soapy. Then he reached for Irv's straight razor. Cleve knew: there was a girl child coming. The wrong way up.

Overnight, as usual, spring turned into summer. The sun erected itself on silver filaments above the city and started cooking it, bringing out all its aromas and flavours and humours, the trace remains of a century's pizzas and burgers and furters.

Attired in a magenta angel top and orange sateen boxing pants and high-sider tennis shoes with yard-long laces (and no socks), Cleve stood, one gruelly afternoon, outside the Idle Hour. Facing him, in her familiar black cotton dress, stood Cressida. They both had a battered look. Cressida, of course, had undergone the internal struggle of biology. Cleve was bruised, too, but more recently and obviously and superficially. He was with Irv. The night before, they had had a fistfight about which was better: Florence or Rome.

This reunion, so far, was being completely cool. Nothing personal. They strolled west. Cleve intended to accompany her as far as Seventh Avenue; then he would retrace his steps, and proceed to Magnificent Obsession. When he walked, Cleve's thighs jostled and sideswiped one another very noticeably, and very loudly. His upper body was holding steady; but his lower body was hugely enlarged. Those thighs: only by standing with his feet a yard apart could he find room for both of them.

'Whew,' he said on the corner, swaying there in the heat. 'Good to see you again.' He reached out a hand, which she didn't take.

'Wait,' said Cressida. 'I thought you might like to see the baby.'

Christopher Street was not what he had built it up to be. For instance, it wasn't even called Christopher Street, not this bit of it anyway: a new sign had been tacked over the old one like a temporary numberplate. He might have asked his companion about that, but he didn't need to. The straight district told you all about itself. It was *out*. SITE OF THE STONEWALL RIOTS, JUNE 27–29, 1969, said the white lettering on the black window of some impenetrable lockup or godown: BIRTH OF THE MODERN STRAIGHT-RIGHTS LIBERA-TION MOVEMENT. And the TV footage slid into Cleve's head: cops, lights, squad cars, crime-scene tape, the chanting, bouncing ranks of straights. Cressida looked up at him (her round eyes, her characterless nose, her flat smile), and led him on down Stonewall Place.

Cleve had imagined a little world. A world of Ant-and-Bee innocuousness, of diffident striving and inch-by-inching, with heads down and faces averted and abashed. But he found it chaotic: everywhere there was poverty and pretti-ness and peril. On the green triangle of Sheridan Square the 'Five O'Clock Club' was dispersing; minders bawled and kids rioted. As they moved west through the sidewalk gridlock of prams, pushchairs, buggies, strollers, through smells of dairy, of confectioner, of dime-store perfumier, they passed herds of men drawn to the jaws of bars and taverns, and street-corner youths, loiterers, louts, punks, drunks, assessing Cleve from an unknown vantage of violence and boredom – and he walked on, shaped like a top when it spins, quivering with centrifugal torque.

218

In New York, in summer, air doesn't want to be air any more. It wants to be liquid. Around Christopher Street, this day, it wanted to be solid: a form of food, most probably. Paddling through it, Cleve's thighs rasped on. They turned right on Bleecker. He looked up. Beyond the lumpen foliage of the ginko trees an evening sky lay swathed in its girlish pinks and boyish blues. And the tenement blocks. One-way windows, and the butts of AC units like torn hi-fi speakers, playing churned heat. The smutty fire escapes going Z, Z, Z. What are these zees saying, he wondered: sleep, or just the end of the alphabet? She hurried on ahead. With momentous helplessness he followed.

Now he was standing in a basement kitchen. Cleve assumed, at any rate, that it must be a kitchen. Cressida had called it 'the kitchen'. A kitchen, to Cleve, was an arena for the free play of delectation, enterprise and wit. Not the rear end of some desperate holding operation, a field hospital of pots, pails, acids, carbolics, and cauldrons of boiling laundry. 'This is meat and potatoes,' he whispered. 'Meat and potatoes *tops*.' He couldn't imagine cooking anything in here. He could imagine having his legs amputated in here. But not cooking ... Cressida was in the room across the passage, consulting with another straight broad, her buddy or backup. Cleve waited, listening to the saddest sound he had ever heard. It reminded him of the call of the loons on the river trips he'd gone on, years ago, with Grainge ...

And now the baby was there on the kitchen table, being unwrapped as if for his imminent inspection, its hiccupy weeping growing softer, its stained and damp cloth diaper revealing itself beneath the unclasped bodysuit, its arms waving and miming at the bare bulb overhead.

'Would you pass me the powder? And that tub of cream. And that cloth. Not that one. On the faucet. The pink one.'

As he poked warily around among the jars, the pads, the balls of cotton wool, the plastic bottles, the plastic teats, the grime, the biology, Cleve wondered if he had ever suffered so. He could feel self-pity drench his heart: his heart, so deep-encased, so far away.

'Not that one. That one.'

He wondered if he had ever suffered so.

And he wondered what on earth people were going to say.

Twenty-second Street, the apartment, the bedroom: sheets, pillows, a leg here, an arm there. The acidy tang of male love suspended itself in the failing light and alerting air of autumn. Two moustaches stirred and flexed.

The first moustache said, 'I mean if it was another man. That I could understand.' This was Irv.

The second moustache said, 'That you could fight. You know what you're dealing with.' This was Orv.

'You know where you stand.'

'You know what's what.'

'But this . . .'

'Another man. Okay. It happens. But this . . .'

'I just feel so unclean.'

'Irv,' said Orv.

'The past. It's all defiled for me. I feel so . . .'

'Maybe it's some kind of midlife thing. A rush of blood. He'll be back.'

'I could never feel the same about him. Not after this.'

'I saw him in Jefferson Market. He looks two hundred years old. He's lost his build. He's lost his *tone*.'

'Do you think he was always that way?'

'Cleve? Jesus. Who knows?'

'It'll get around.'

'You're damn right it'll get around. Where's my Rolodex.'

'Orv,' said Irv.

'You just think of them *kissing*.'

'Get this. He says it's not her tits and ass he "admires". It's her wrists. It's her collarbone.'

'That really *does* sound straight.'

'He's coming over for his books Saturday morning. That's right. He's moving into that . . . *crèche* on Bleecker.'

'Oh, wow. *Cleve* . . . of all the guys we hang with. Arn. Harv. Grove. Fraze.'

'But *Cleve*.'

'I mean: *Cleve*.'

This was Orv.

'I mean: *Cleve*.'

This was Irv.

Esquire, 1995

What Happened To Me
On My Holiday

(for Elias Fawcett, 1978–1996)

Aderrible thing habbened do me on my haliday. A harrible thing, and a bermanend thing. Id won'd be the zame, ever again.

Bud virzd I'd bedder zay: don'd banig! I'm nad zuvvering vram brain damage – or vram adenoids. And I gan wride bedder than thiz when I wand do. Bud I *don'd* wand do. Nad vor now. Led me egsblain.

I am halve English and halve Amerigan. My mum is Amerigan and my dad is English. I go do zgool in London and my bronunziation is English – glear, even vaindly Agzonian, the zame as my dad's. Amerigans avden zeem zurbrised do hear an eleven-year-old who zbeegs as I zbeeg. Grandaddy Jag, who is Amerigan, admids thad he vinds id unganny. As iv zuj an agzend reguires grade ganzendration even vram grownubs, led alone jildren. Amerigans zeem to zuzbegd thad the English relags and zbeeg Amerigan behind glozed doors. Shouding oud, on their redurn, 'Honey, I'm home!' My other grandvather veld divverendly: English, do him, was the more najural voize. Zo thiz zdory is vor them, doo, as well as vor

222

Eliaz. I dell id thiz way – in zargazdig Ameriganese – begaz I don'd wand id do be glear: do be all grizb and glear. There is thiz zdrange resizdanze. There is thiz zdrange resizdanze.

Me and my younger brother Jagob usually zbend the early bard of the zummer in Gabe Gad, with my mum, and the lader bard in Eazd Hambdon, with my dad. Bud thiz year we wend do my dad's a liddle zooner than blanned. When the day game we gad ub ad the grag of dawn and biled indo the gar with our Ungle Desmond. Id was a vive-hour drive do New Yorg, bud the dravvig wasn't heavy and Desmond doled uz many inderezding things – aboud dreams, aboud aldered zdades. We zeemed to be there in no dime. My dad was wading, on Ninedy-zigzth Zdreed.

We grabbed zum lunj and then went oud to Lang Island in a big goach galled the Jidney. In the Jidney, you veld you were in a blane, nad a buz: vree juize or Berrier, vree beanudz, individual zbadlighds do read by, and a lavadory in the bag. We zoon zeddled indo my dad's rended houze in the woods. Nothing fanzy: in vagd, id good have been Oglahoma, with a big-ub drug in the driveway, an old gar zeed on the borj, and the neighbours always guarrelling and grying out – 'Ged ub, Margared!' on one zide, and 'Why, Garen, why?' on the other. Bud id did have the usual burzding revrigerador and muldible bathrooms, bluz gable DV. Zo: zum zdoo and bazda, zum 'Beaviz and Buddhead', then ub the wooden hills to Bedvordshire . . . My dad, doo, was very ubzed aboud Eliaz. And Isabel was alzo there, and alzo ubzed – and alzo big with jiled.

As I zed, we wend do my dad's a liddle earlier than blanned, this year, journeying down vram the Gabe do Lang Island.

Nearly every zummer, on Gabe Gad, Mr Marlowe Vawzedd gums to bay uz a visid. Bragdigally a grownub now, Marlowe uzed to have a zummer jab as a gounzellor ad a boys' gamb, and zo he is an egsberd ad guezzing whad boys wand do do. He is underzdandably babular with Jagob and me. Bud, well, Marlowe had do go home early thiz year. And my mum had do go home early thiz year. Begaz of whad habbened, bag in London.

Id was a dull day when Marlowe heard the news aboud his younger brother. The news aboud Eliaz. Jagob and I wend with him ub the dird road – do where we barg the gar. Over Horzeleej Band there zwam a gloud of grey: nad mizd, nad vag, bud the grey haze of ziddies, and of zdreeds. Ub vram the band id vloaded, lingering, drabbed in the drees, and nothing was glear. Dreamily Marlowe gad indo the gar and glozed the door. He wend do Bravinzedown Airbord. Virzd the liddle blane, do Bazdon. Then the bigger blane, do London Down. And my mum zoon vallowed. Zo, as I zed, we wend do my dad's a liddle earlier than blanned.

My younger brother Jagob is dodally obzezzed by durdles, dordoizes, vrags, doads, labzders, grabs, and all zords of zlimy and weird-shabed rebdiles, amvibians, and gruzdasians. He knows all their Ladin names, all their baddernings, all their habidads. He's an egsberd on these greejures. And zo am I, whether or nad I wand do be. Begaz Jagob's giving me an earvul more or les round the glag.

Zo on many days, in Eazd Hambdon, we wend on grabbing egsbeditions. The bay zeemed do voam with grabs and with zbrads (minnows, diddlers). I used a drawl ned, vor the zbrads, and on my virzd zweeb I gad loads. With the grabs, you aggumulade them in a big bad. And ad the end of the day you have a grab raze. You draw a zirgle in the zand: the virzd grab to glear id is then broglaimed the winner. No grabs die: you jug them all bag indo the zee. Ad our vavoride bay, whij we galled Dead Man's Landing, there was alzo a van thad showed ub every hour or zo and zold lallibabs and ize gream.

On these grabbing dribs we would avden bring along my liddle 'guzzen' Bablo. Bablo is only vour years old and you have do be very garevul with him when he goes in the zee. Begaz he gan only zwim with whad he galls his 'armies' or his 'vloadies'. Bablo has a liddle zizder named IJ, a mere dad of vivdeen monthz, who is alzo very gude.

One day Jagob gabjured a giand grab and game running ub the beej do drab id in the bad – the blazdig bad or medal gondainer in whij all the grabs were zdored. I was zidding on a dowel, reading my boog: *Brando*, by Elmore Leonard. Jagob ran bag down the zand. And then Bablo game ub do me and zed, 'I've vound a grab, doo.'

'Yeah,' I zed. 'Bud thad one's dead, Bab.'

'Shall I drab id in the bad with the others?'

I zed, 'Thad zdiv? Why would we wand thad in the bad? No, Bablo.'

And he zed, 'Why nad? Is id doo big?'

'Id isn'd doo *big*, zdubid. Id's *dead*.'

And id *was* dead – big dime. Halve ids baddy had radded of. A zingle binzer dangled from a length of vrayed dendon. Id didn'd even zmell: thad's how dead thad grab was.

'Gan I drab id in the bad with the others?'

'Devinidely nad. Zdab thiz, Bablo. No.'

Juzd then Jagob gried oud vram the shore. A new dizgovery.

We wend do jeg id oud. Beyand the beer, the shallows were liddered with dozens of dead zbrads – brabably vishermen's baid. Bablo baddled in do inzbegd them. And game bag with a dead zbrad.

Zo we had our vinal zwims – Bablo blaying with his invladable sharg, and wearing his invladable 'armies'. And when the dime game vor uz do hid the road, Bablo revuzed do leave the zbrad behind. He zed he wanded to bring id home and inzdall id in a bags in his room. The zbrad would be his bed – inzded of a dag or a gad!

In the gar I zed, 'Well, Bab, thad zbrad'll be a nize airvreshener vor your room.'

And he zed, 'Why?'

'Why? Begaz briddy zoon id'll begin to reeg of dead vish.'

'I don'd mind.'

'Why nad?'

'Begaz I'll rub zum gream on id.'

'Oh yeah? Whad zord of gream, Bablo?'

'. . . Vish gream.'

We all had a good jordle ad thad. And I zed, 'Whad aboud rads, Bab? Whad iv a rad shows ub in the nide?'

'I don'd mind.'

'Why nad?'

'I won'd zmell the rad.'

'Why nad?'

'Begaz of the vish gream.'

More jordling.

'Why don'd you bab bag to Dead Man's Landing, Bablo – for the dead grab. Id'll be a bal vor your vish.'

Bud my dad zed thad Bablo already had his blade vull – virzd with the vish, then with the rad.

When we gad do his blaze, Bablo indroduzed his mum do the new bed: 'Thiz is my vish. Id's zilver. Id's zmall. Id's dead. Id gums vram the zee. Id lives in thiz bags.'

As iv the vish being dead was juzd another thing aboud id –

juzd another of ids addribudes. Bablo's mum zeemed var vram enthusiazdig. Bud when we voned the vallowing morning, vor an ubdade, Bablo zed his vish was abzoludely vine.

When Bablo was only three his mum made him a lion oudvid, vor Halloween. He dried id on, gave a vull-throated roar, and growled, 'I'm a lion gazdume!'

My dad galls these vunny zlibs of Bablo's 'gadegory errors'. One dime thiz zummer Bab and I were dizguzzing gars and driving, and I zed, 'Your dad, is he a good driver then?'

Bablo nadded with his eyes glozed. 'Babba?' he reblied, in a voice both ganvidend and ganvidenjal. 'Babba gan drive all the way to the *ziddy*.'

And he gave another nad, for emvaziz, as iv do zay, 'Bood thad in your bibe and zmogue id.'

Zo I juzd zed, 'Is thad zo? *My* dad gan only mague id as var as Wainzgadd. Then he bulls over and they have to helb him oud of the gar.'

Bablo zeemed ready do gredid id.

'And how's the vish, Bab?'

'Vine.'

'Zdill going zdrang?'

'Yez,' he zed. 'My vish is vine.'

Glearly, Bablo does nad yed underzdand whad death is.

Bud who does?

Death was muj on my mind in the zummer – muj on my mind. Begaz of Eliaz. Eliaz died, in London Down. And zo death has been muj on my mind.

My dad zed thad early in the zummer Eliaz game round

do his vlad. He game round do big ub a jagged – bud the jagged was in my dad's gar, and the gar was elzewhere, having ids baddery vigsed, edzedera, edzedera. Dybigal Eliaz – jazing a jagged agrazz down. Zo he hung around vor the whole avdernoon, blaying the binball machine and, of gorze, the elegdrig guidar. And my dad zed thad his memory of him was really vresh: his memory of Eliaz, or Vabian, whij was his nigname, remained really vresh. Isabel alzo ran indo him during the early zummer, in a doob drain, on the Zendral Line, under London and ids zdreeds. Dybigal Eliaz, with all his bags and bundles, his jaggeds and hads, gayadig, vezdive, brezzed vor dime – and zdill darrying vor a halve-hour jad. Zo the memory is vresh. And my memory is vresh. Bud is id zo vresh zimbly begaz Eliaz was zo young – zo vresh himzelve? My dad doled me thad he zenzes the ghozd of Eliaz in his room, ad dawn, wading ad the end of the bed. I zee him ad nide. A young ragsdar with vlyaway hair and gleeg lighds all around.

I alzo remember the day we heard the news, on Gabe Gad. How Jagob and I wend with Marlowe ub the dird road do the gar. And the gloud over the band, with ids urban grey – the grey of Daddenham Gord Road, of Jaring Graz Road, the grey of Goodge Zdreed. The zgy was grey and nothing was glear.

In the vinal weeg of the haliday we had an inzidend. An inzidend where death, again, vleedingly showed ids vaze.

Id veadured Bablo. And another gadegory error.

We were all zwimming in the bool thad belongs to Alegs and Bam. Muj agdividy there, begaz they alzo have a dramboline: you ged all had, jumbing, then you leab indo the bool and gool down. Bablo was zwimming with his armies –

his vloadies. Me and Jagob were mezzing around, blaying duj or Margo Bolo. My dad was on a lounger, having a zigaredde and jadding with Bam. Maybe, doo, he was zibbing a gagdail – vadga danig, or zgadj on the rags. And zuddenly Bablo game oud of nowhere and zbrang indo the bool – withoud his vloadies. Bablo had vorgodden his armies!

In the end id was no big deal. Zdill in his drungs, my dad juzd drabbed his budd and did a zord of zbazdig razing dive indo the middle of the bool. He gad do Bablo and held him ub. And Bablo was nad dizdrezzed – he didn'd have dime do banig. My dad even engouraged Bablo do zwim bag do the shallow end. And he did, with a liddle azzizdanze. And my dad galmly vinished his vag.

'Well, thad was vun!' zed Bab, emerging vrom the bool. He zdug oud his jezd and announzed, 'I wend zwimming withoud vloadies. I wend zwimming withoud armies!'

'No, in vagd,' zed my dad, 'you wend zwimming.'

Another of Bab's zlibs. Begaz you don'd ender the Olymbigs in an evend galled the 200-Meder Vreezdyle Withoud Armies. You don'd go vor a midnide zwim withoud vloadies. Id's galled a zwimming bool, avder all. Nad a zwimming-withoud-armies bool.

Thad day zeemed do be an abbrobriade dime do bid varewell to Bablo's zbrad.

When we drabbed him of with his mum we made dizgreed inguiries aboud the vamouz vish, and she rolled her eyes and zed, 'Oh, thad vish! Will I ever hear the lazd of thad vish!'

Abbarendly the vish *had* begun do rad and give of a derrible zdenj. Bud Bab revused do led his mum jug id oud: he glaimed his vish was vine. They'd dried every zord of gream on id – vish gream, rad gream (though really these were bervumes and dizinvegdands). She'd doled him again and again thad thiz vish was hizdory: thad thiz vish was, in

229

vagd, an egs-vish. Bud Bab maindained thad the vish was zdill his bed. When the bang begame gwide indalerable, Bablo's mum juzd zmuggled id oud and zed thad a raggoon or a zdoad muzd have borne id of.

Zurbrisingly, Bablo did nad brodezd or gauze a vuzz. Thiz zeemed do zadizvy his idea of the najural order of things. And maybe zumbaddy zed, Bablo, do nad grieve. Bablo, do nad vred. Your zbrad is habby, with ids zbrad Gad in ids zbrad Heaven. Your vish will be reborn, as a sharg, a dalvin, an agdobuz – or as zum grade manzder of the deeb. One way or the other, your vish is vine.

Auguzd begame Zebdember: dime do go home. Lang Island had been a lad of vun, bud I was bleased do be bagging my bags. Doo many vields, doo many drees, doo muj zand, doo muj zee. I was ready do redurn do a ziddy – dezbide whad ziddies are and dezbide whad ziddies do.

No more rended houze.

No more 'Ged ub, Margared!'

No more 'Why, Garen, why?'

Id was on the way do the airbord thad the zubjegd of Eliaz was raised: the zubjegd of death. My dad zed, 'Do you veel divverendly aboud id – aboud death?'

I zed, 'I underzdand thad beeble die now.'

And Jagob bibed ub, '*I* underzdood thad *years* ago.'

'No. You idiod!' I zed. 'I underzdood id. Bud I never really *grazbd* id undil now.'

And Jagob nadded. And he, doo, underzdood.

Bevore, I knew thad grabs died and thad vish died. I knew thad the old, with all their agues and bains, mighd have reason do be gradevul vor the brazbegd of an ending. And, of gorze, all over the world, in vazd numbers, beeble grash and zdarve and bleed and burn, ged glubbed, grushed, zdabbed, shad, valling, valling away, in vazd numbers, all over the world. Bud death had never been zo *near*, where it has no businezz. Bablo, Jagob, Eliaz. We are the young. Are we nad?

Bud then you're wading on the dird road, with Marlowe, by the gar. With Marlowe in a daze, in a dream, in a nidemare. Greynezz is zeebing ubwards vram the band. And nothing is glear. And then zuddenly the grey brighdens, giving you a deeb thrab in the middle of your zgull.

Eliaz wend swimming without his armies! Alaz! Eliaz wend doo deeb withoud his vloadies. And you *muzd do thiz*, whether or nad you zurvive. One day you muzd! How many grownubs do you see, when you go to the beej, zwimming with vloadies? How many adulds are oud there, in the bounding waves, zwimming with armies?

And iv they do go under, then they don'd redurn. Nothing has the bower to bring them bag – no zlide of hand, no drig vodagravy, no medizine, no miragle. They zday where they are vor ever, alone in the gold earth.

I veel id in my hard now. I remember Marlowe's eyes, and dears begin to gather in my own. Begaz one vine day you gan loog ub vram your billow and zee no brother in the dwin bed. You go around the houze, bud your brother is nowhere do be vound.

The haliday has gum and gan. The haliday is over.

The holiday has come and gone. The holiday is over.
    Goodbye to it all.
    And that is what happened to me on my holiday.

New Yorker, 1997